THE SOPHOMORE

BY BARRY SPACKS

Prentice-Hall, Inc., *Englewood Cliffs, N.J.*

The Sophomore
by Barry Spacks

© 1968 by Barry Spacks

Copyright under International and Pan American
Copyright Conventions

Library of Congress Catalog Card Number: 68-11274

Printed in the United States of America

T

Prentice-Hall International, Inc., London
Prentice-Hall of Australia, Pty. Ltd., Sydney
Prentice-Hall of Canada, Ltd., Toronto
Prentice-Hall of India Private Ltd., New Delhi
Prentice-Hall of Japan, Inc., Tokyo

FOR PATSY AND JUDITH

This Harry ran straight up a wall,
But found he wasn't there at all,
And so he had a horrid fall.
— Alas, alack for Harry!

THEODORE ROETHKE

ONE

Muse, sweetheart, let's not be too hard on Harry Zissel, let's save the judgments and the morals and so on till later, the symbolic significance and the redemptive advice, because if Zissel's life to date reveals nothing so much as a persistent and painful tendency toward the inconclusive, who are we to throw stones or refuse to take him seriously or look down our noses? He's twenty-two years old and still a sophomore, his love life is all loused up, he's back at school but that isn't working out, it's as if his experience were being managed by a Metaphysical Force with a weakness for farce or pathos but lacking a middle range. What he needs is some quiet understanding, so for the moment let's merely observe, leaping in at the middle, or rather going back about a month when the weather was just turning warm, and Harry and Miriam—she'd been living with him for only a few weeks at the time—had managed to borrow a lakeside cabin some six miles out of town for the weekend, very quiet, the cabin set toward the top of a sloping meadow with rocky pinewoods rising behind. There were still traces of snow among the trees and a rotting rowboat turned keelside up on the pier and across the lake a white house with several outbuildings and a formal garden.

Harry had let Miriam sleep late that Sunday; it was past ten when the sunlight on her face drew her up from sleep like a cup filled to brimming. She'd begun to smile in the last slow moments of her dream; her father was with her there, the smoke from his cigarette drifting mildly; in the dream it was dawn, she and her father were in lawn chairs, reclining, looking up at a pale sky; they were on a terrace of old brick, she knew that coffee stood on a table between them, he had built the house, he had built everything, he was saying "No need to hurry. Do whatever you want." She had savored the peacefulness of that last moment of dreaming with her whole body as she came awake.

The cottage had been very still; Miriam was conscious of bird-sound, nothing more, and then she heard a chair creak in the other room, a chair or a table, and realized that Harry was up, heard the sound of his pen scratching; she could imagine him there at the pine table under the windows, wearing khakis and a white shirt, bent to his writing. Still lying warm in bed, she'd felt completely happy; she hunched her shoulders against the lumpy mattress and turned to thrust her face into his pillow, because she had made it happen, he was working, they would never leave, they would have their food delivered and stay on in the cabin like children in a cave.

Later she brought him coffee, they settled side by side in the wide, stepless front doorway, wearing sweaters, their legs dangling, reading old advertisement-throwaways addressed to *Occupant*. "How come you're all dressed?" he asked. "You off somewhere?"

"Sure, I've got another man for the weekends, over there, in that long white shed. He's a gamekeeper."

"Does he give green stamps?" Harry moved his big toe along the instep of her foot.

"Plaid."

"Nice clean habits and all?"

"Shut up," she said, mock-swinging at him. "He's *clean,* all right, not a slob like you."

2

"He's a dear," Harry said, "but I'm your friend." He was still in his pajamas under the sweater; unshaven. "You were working," she said.

He laughed. "Oh sure."

"Weren't you? You were, come on!"

"I wrote three speeches. Count 'em—three."

"Well? That's great! What do you expect?"

"And they've gone to their just reward."

"You tore them up?"

"Flushed them down. That's what I call a morning's work." He put his arm around her and she leaned against him. They sat in the doorway. An Irish setter came sniffing through the long grass near the lake; Harry whistled and the dog paused, head turned, then ran back the way he'd come.

"The beasts of the field," he said.

And it had all become sad, just like that. Before them the winter-ruined meadow sloped down toward the water. Near the far shore the lake glittered, the March morning was bright, a boy in a riding habit came along a path of the estate on the other side and disappeared behind the white shed, which might have been a boathouse, emerging beyond the farther edge mounted on a brown horse, transformed from walker to rider as if in a circus joke, looking too small for the size of the horse; when he began to trot they lost him among the trees.

"Don't be discouraged," Miriam said. "It's such a nice day."

"You know, Kafka could never finish anything either."

"Then you're in good company."

"Oh, sure. I've always got lots of company when I'm writing, there's a whole grand jury up there in my head. They sit in those steep rows like people watching an operation."

"Who? Who are they?"

"Oh, there's one section reserved for everybody I've ever known, relatives and teachers and so on. Friends. They're mostly asleep. Then there're all the critics, they throw things, or else they twirl their noisemakers. And then there's the central section full of writers packed in there. Dickens and Homer and Scott

3

Fitzgerald. Old Ibsen, and Hemingway, and Ezra Pound—all those guys."

"What do they do?"

"The writers? They become violently ill. Or stand aghast. What do you suppose that means, 'stand aghast'? Sounds great, doesn't it?" Miriam shrugged. "Sometimes," Harry said, "when the critics go to sleep, the writers twirl the noisemakers or say *cheap, cheap* like a stack of birds. Or sometimes the relatives wake up and start going *best-seller, best-seller, best-seller!* And then sometimes one of the writers stands over my shoulder and I write a sentence and look up at him and he shrugs. It's usually Aeschylus, he has a very expressive way of shrugging, so I cross out the sentence and then the whole audience goes crazy shouting at me."

"Shouting what?"

"Chicken!"

"Really?"

"No. Of course not. You know *why* Kafka couldn't finish those novels? Because that's the point, it was what he was writing about—nothing makes any sense, so how can you have a conclusion? For conclusions you have to have logic, isn't that right?"

"Poor baby."

"Listen, Mir, there's no need for you to keep on at the shop, I can always get a job and let you go back to school."

"I know. Don't get started now."

"Shit," he said, "it's hopeless." He cursed himself. "Why do I have to be so completely hung up? In everything I do? Everything!"

She took a cigarette from the pack in his sweater pocket, her first in a long while. The initial drag made her light-headed. "I was working for Johnny before you ever came in for a bed lamp, remember?" They had gone over this ground before; she tried to keep it light, but the edge of impatience showed through. "I'm not doing anything for *you*," she told him. "You're always saying everyone should feel free. So . . ." she

4

faltered. "Sometimes I think you'd *rather* have to work. I mean at a regular job, like if you had a big family or something."

He gazed out at the lake. He needed a haircut, the hair feathered out around his ears. She burrowed into his neck: he smelled like sunshine. Closing her eyes, with a humorous feeling, she touched her tongue to his ear. He lay back against her. She ran her lips dryly along his nose, and he groaned and pulled her to him. They kissed, and in the kitchen of the cabin the old refrigerator began a rhythmic buzzing like a dentist's drill, which made them laugh. She'd whispered, "You're my horny friend." They eased down from the doorway, fell together in the matted grass and he was above her.

"Baby, my skirt . . ."

The ground was painfully cold, it seemed to be cutting into her, but his legs covered her and she felt hidden beneath him and gradually it was as if her body drank. His mouth was open against her ear. He pressed into her one last time and for her it was pain and the smell of wool and then she came, like stone melting into a river of silk, of sun, and at that moment she was certain a child had come alive inside her. Later, after she'd changed her clothes, she became frightened, and immediately angry at herself for that. She thought she would have his child. It was all right. An exaltation followed her fear. He was showered and dressed, cleanly shaven, looking years younger. He sat in the main room, reading in front of the fire. He had gone away from her.

She'd felt proud. At her very core, she'd felt a strange warmth and pressure and in her pride she had wanted to talk of it, wanted to make a joke, say it, so that they could be together with what they had done. She was about to speak when he glanced up from his book and his eyes were harsh. He'd looked then like a frightened boy, this man of hers who had given her a child.

"That wasn't so smart," he said.

"No."

"What time of month is it?"

"The wrong time."

5

"Naturally."

She could taste his bitterness, his sense of betrayal, as if he had passed it like a wafer from his tongue to hers.

Tears had come to her eyes. It had never been so good for her before, but she didn't tell him that. Always before whatever pleasure she had taken from sex had been what she imagined it was supposed to be, what a woman was apt to feel. She only wanted him not to destroy it, their one good time.

"I thought you still had your thing in," he said. "Didn't they say you were supposed to leave it in for twenty-four hours?" He looked at her and stopped.

"Shit," he said. "What are you so sad about? *What?*"

"Just shut up," she told him, "can you? Do you know how to do that?"

He slammed down his book and locked his hands behind his head. She went to the bedroom and when she returned he was lying on the floor, smoking pot, his head propped up on the book he'd been reading. The sweet odor of marijuana hung in the air.

"You want?" he asked, holding out the flimsy cigarette. She said nothing. "Say, where you going? Miriam? Listen, look at the wall. No, look there, at the wall, there's three, there's four ants walking up, all coupled together like a . . . coal train."

"Don't take too much," she said. "Don't make yourself sick again."

"Oh boy, it's starting to hit me. Oh man, that's lovely stuff. Hey, Mir? Come'ere, baby. Where you going?" He reached behind him for matches. There was an ant on the cover of an old copy of *Life* magazine on the floor. She saw the ant rear up and move its antennae. It was a big one, shiny beads. The ant moved across the lips of the sad, bearded, boy-like face of Ernest Hemingway on the slick-paper cover of the magazine.

6

daughter, she lived in a housing development south of Hartford, he could think of few people whose condition in life interested him less. "Ah," said Flora, "she got herself pregnant again."

"You didn't tell me," said Harry's mother.

"Who can tell *you* anything? She stuck her thumbnail through her diaphragm, that's what she gets with those fancy fingernails." A sound like a death rattle came from the closet, hangers clashing, what was Miriam doing in there? "It's nothing," Harry said, "it's the wind—shouldn't we go? Uncle Raymond's probably starving in the car."

"They're not speaking," Flora said. She sat on the plush chair, openly watching the closet. "I'll tell you, Harry, your mother, even if it has to be her own sister that says so, is one extremely touchy individual."

"You're not telling me anything," he said. "Let's go eat, okay?"

"We've been here a half a minute," his mother said, "what's the big rush? What's the mystery? For one thing, I'm going to straighten up in here." She popped to her feet, but he gripped her by the shoulders. "Momma, don't be ridiculous. Come on, it's depressing, let's go out to Hulbert's."

She picked up a decaying liverwurst sandwich from the ironing board beside the table in the kitchenette, and then didn't seem to know what to do with it. She sat down again. "So if it's depressing why can't you come home sometimes? Even Gordon in Los Angeles I see more than you. Am I a widow whose sons move out on me or is that a lie? At least at home you'd have hot meals, a warm, human atmosphere—"

They were settling in for the afternoon, their eyes riveted on the closet door. Miriam would smother in there in another minute. He played with various possibilities. *I want you to meet Miriam Hippolyto, she sublets the closet. This is my friend Miriam, she just stopped in to develop some photographs.*

"Sonny," his mother said with a sorrowful look, "just offer me an explanation. There's your lovely room at home, you got a desk, a book case, nobody would bother you—"

"Five times a year we have the same argument, Momma."

"So explain it to me, that's all I ask. You couldn't transfer to Adelphi? What's the attraction here, the dirt?"

"And who'd accept my freshman credits? I've told you, I'm working, I'm trying to get the scholarship back. We don't even speak the same language."

"I don't speak English?"

"Look, please, can't we go eat?"

"I don't read? I didn't join the book club? I'm not a widow whose sons walk out on her? Listen, when your Cousin Stanley, a Ph.D. in public relations already, says it's a pleasure to come into my house for a meal—"

"Momma, am I trying to change your life? Am I? You've got your card game, your color television . . . what do you want?"

"It's a sin to look at color television? Let me tell you, you're the crazy one. You. In the insane asylum all the crazys think everybody else is crazy, did you realize?"

And then a really major noise took place in the closet. "It's nothing," he said, shrugging. "The wind." The two sisters looked at each other with pronounced frowns; Hannah Zissel rose and began to walk casually across the room.

"Oh, it must be my rat," Harry said.

His mother came to a halt and turned to him.

"Don't bother him, Momma, it's his lunchtime, he'll come jumping out."

"You've got a rat in there?"

"Certainly. It's a sin to keep a rat? I've started to teach him how to talk."

"Harry, you're crazy." She looked at Flora, as if for confirmation. Flora shrugged.

"There's a part in my play for a talking rat. Can I help it? I'm writing a play for my creative writing course and there's a part—"

"He's teasing you, Hannah," Flora said. "It's a joke."

"Some joke. That's a nice way to joke to your mother? A rat in the closet? You've got a *girl* in there!"

12

crummy closet . . ." "Shut up," he hissed and ran on tiptoe through the debris on the floor trying to look as if he'd just awakened. His mother and his aunt were dressed in identical powder-blue suits, both wearing pillbox hats and silver-fox collars. "Well look who's here!" he cried. "For goodness sakes!"

"We're not supposed to come in? You're busy or something?"

He embraced them, filling the doorway. "Wonderful," he shouted. "Why didn't you phone? It's a mess in here, just wait on the landing, I'll be out in a flash."

"Don't be ridiculous, Harry." They pushed past him with a gust of perfume, small, plump-faced women, their pillbox hats riding level. "Something unkosher going on," his mother said. "What's all this junk on the floor? Something fishy, there's something fishy here, Flora, something's—"

"I was sleeping, didn't you hear the alarm?"

"Sleeping? It's lunchtime, how could you be sleeping?"

"Huh? Is anything wrong at home?"

Aunt Flora told him that while the store was being renovated they were taking a little vacation to Canada. "Sleeping?" his mother said, "in this kind of mess?"

"Quit it," Flora told her sister, "give the boy a chance to catch his breath."

Boy—he'd always be a boy to Aunt Flora; his heart went out to her. "Harry,"—she reached up to kiss him on the cheek— "how are you, honey? How come you're undressed? Uncle Raymond's waiting in the car, he and your mother aren't speaking already, can you imagine? It's an argument about your father's tombstone."

"Wonderful," he said, darting off at top speed to the bedroom. "Have a seat, have a seat, I'll be ready in a second, we'll go out for lunch."

"Here, I brought you lunch," his mother called. He ran back for the tiny paper bag she held out to him. "Look at this place, it's like a maelstrom in here!" Across the room the closet door moved minutely ajar; Harry saw Miriam's eye at the crack. Maneuvering over he leaned back languidly until he heard the

9

latch click. "Some living conditions you got," his mother said. "This is *sickening,* I'm not kidding. Why are you living here instead of the dorms?"

"Have a seat, Momma. Relax, will you?" He raced down the hall and threw on a pair of pants and some shoes, but his mother's voice followed him: "A seat? Where? Where's there to sit with all this junk?" Returning, pulling a fresh shirt over his head and emerging from the other end, he saw the apartment for an instant through her eyes, through the eyes of a floor-waxer, an ashtray emptier. She was inching across the room toward the closet door. "Ready!" he cried. "Let's go!"

"Ready for what? Comb your hair, Harry. Open the bag, eat, it's a lox and cream cheese sandwich." She screwed up her features as if she were contemplating an unpleasant smell. "Tell me, is somebody else here?"

His face made an effort to express incomprehension. "Of course not."

"You sure? In that door there?"

"That's the closet, Momma, how could anyone live in a closet?" But she was on the scent, it made him terribly nervous, he could see poor Miriam in among the stored winter coats and things, her head ducked under the shelf, sweating away in the terrycloth robe, all self-pity and suffocation. She might just come walking out, she was opposed to relatives, opposed on principle. "What's so important in the closet you can't come home for a weekend? You got to stay right here even on Easter vacation?" His mother sat abruptly on the couch, which was riding a little high with the clothing he'd stuffed under the cushions. "This is some comfortable couch," she said. "Like a camel."

"We thought we'd take you over to Sheila's with us," Aunt Flora told him. "Uncle Raymond can drive you back after supper. Otherwise we won't get a chance even to see you, we'll be on the road to Canada by eight in the morning."

"Wonderful," he said, but then Aunt Flora sat down too. "How *is* Sheila these days?" he asked, standing for an instant hip-shot and casual. Sheila was his cousin, Aunt Flora's married

"A rat! A rat! His name's Polonius." A rapid rattle of coat hangers; that crazy Miriam! "See, he heard his name. Do you want me to bring him out on the leash? Hey, Polonius, recite something."

"I'll have a heart attack," said Hannah Zissel levelly as a rhythmic squeaking sound came from the closet. "Flora, let's get out of here—maybe he'll be saner in the fresh air. You can come out of the closet now," she sang. "We're just leaving."

"The wind goes in there through a hole in the wall," Harry explained to his aunt. "It's always rattling the coat hangers or something."

"We're just leaving," sang Hannah. "All the stuff in this place! A junk shop he's running! Rats! Be careful where you walk, Flora, you could break a leg in here. What's *this* junk-heap?" She stopped before Harry's construction.

"An art work," he said, "it's not finished—it's for my studio lab. I'm a Renaissance Man, I'm trying everything these days, I mean someday I may figure out—"

"—an art work? What do you mean an art work?" She walked gingerly around the construction, toward the closet side. "Look," she said, "on the top he's got a skull with a zipper and buttons stuck on. You can come out now," she crooned to the closet door. "We're going to lunch."

And Miriam rattled the coat hangers once again—he had to remove his mother's hand from the closet doorknob finger by clenched finger. "Quit it," he kept saying, "haven't you ever heard of human rights?"

"I won't hurt her," said his mother. "I just want to *see*."

After he'd got them out at last and they'd all ordered cheese-burgers and coffee at Hulbert's he excused himself, said he'd better grab a coat if he was going over to Sheila's with them, and raced back to the apartment to make sure Miriam was okay. What a rush of pure admiration he'd felt the last time she'd rattled the coat hangers! What a gutsy woman she was! What a gumdrop! As he ran down Beachum Street he recalled the time she'd bought the haddock: a weekend ad for the Double-D Food Jamboree revealed that haddock was going at a fantastic price, and with him trying to keep up she'd raced to the store, banging into a smallish clerk with a black plastic bowtie as she went up the aisle to fill their cart with fifty frozen sticks of fish, zooming right through the check-out, eleven cents a pound, because once an impulse took Miriam there was no hope, the clerk at the Double-D was lucky she hadn't been mounted on a motorcycle, she would have come right out of the closet in another minute, aunts and mothers or no aunts and mothers. She was great, a great woman all right, even if they had been eating haddock for a month. But she was gone. Impossible, but she'd somehow gotten out of the apartment already—he couldn't find her in the living room, the bedroom, the bath. He opened the closet to get his raincoat and there she was: he laughed, crowded in after her, tried to bite her at the smooth curve of the neck and shoulder. "Don't. I hid out. I thought it was all of you coming back for some more conversation."

"Polonius the Rat," Harry said, gripping her by the bony shoulders. He gave her the little bag his mother had brought. "Lox and cream cheese on a bagel! Save me a bite, okay? I've got to get going, I said I'd go to Sheila's with them, I just wanted to see—" He saw Miriam's brassiere, snuggled cozily between two of the couch cushions like a snake in a nest. "In plain sight, no wonder they were all that suspicious." He held the bra like a fish by the tail. The label read *Gevner's* ARMORED CLOUD. He handed it to Miriam who proceeded to hitch it on, gazing right at him, frowning, her hair still mussed, her face grim. "Why are you going to Sheila's?"

"I don't know. They want me to go so I'll go. What am I supposed to do, spit in my mother's face?"

"Oh no. Think of your mother, by all means. At all times," she said fixing the tie of her blouse. And then: "Why did I have to hide in the goddam closet? Haven't you told them about me at all?"

"Tell them? My mother would tear you to pieces! Look, I may not be home till late, Mir, it's an hour's drive."

14

"Are you ashamed of me or something?"

"Don't be crazy. Listen, I'd better run--"

And that was the moment she'd picked to give him the news. Twelve days overdue. And she was as regular as the tides. He sat down and held his head and rocked like a mourner.

"Are you sure?"

She pursed her lips. She was sure.

"Was it last month, out at the cabin? Jesus, Miriam!"

"Take it easy," she said, "don't get hysterical." She smiled, mimicking his fake-Yiddish accent: "You've got something against children?"

"Don't joke," he said, "God almighty."

He smoked two cigarettes while she put on lipstick, combed her bangs with her fingers, stepped into her shoes, and made herself a cup of tea.

"We'll have to get an abortion," he said. "It must have been that time—"

"—Oh God," said Miriam, "just go away, will you? Dissolve, please. I made it all up, forget about it."

He asked if there wasn't some sort of test, so that they could be sure, and she threw up her eyes and frowned, sitting at the table with her tea, biting into the lox and cream cheese sandwich. "Maybe it's just a rat in the closet," she said. "The wind." She was sorry she'd said a word, but she was enjoying his reaction. She chewed, then grinned, cream cheese on her lips, and his heart went as cold as a rock at the bottom of the sea.

At Hulbert's his cheeseburger had waited, dying a natural death, the edges of the cheese like old parchment. The family stared back at him as he came through the door with his black raincoat over his arm, all three of them at the big table in the rear chewing grindingly away. His heart worked to the same rhythm, chewing, grinding his insides.

"Well," he laughed, "tell me something. What's happening with the store, Uncle Raymond?"

"Expanding," Raymond said. "Growing larger."

"Being fruitful and multiplying," Harry said.

"Why not?" said his uncle with a laugh. "After all, it's a fruit

15

store, no?" He nudged his wife: "Get it? Fruitful? fruit store?"

"Very good," said Flora, "I never said you weren't gifted, Ray."

"What took you so long to get a raincoat?" Hannah inquired. "You couldn't find it in the closet? Things were too crowded in there?" Harry said nothing. They ate. "Listen," his mother said, swallowing, "do you happen to be married?"

He went pale at the word.

"You know what I mean, Sonny."

"Oh," he said, "the *brassiere!* I'm just"—he laughed dryly—"a clothes fetishist, that's all."

"A *what?*"

"Nothing, nothing, forget it."

"A clothes-what?"

"Nothing, Momma. It's a joke."

"My son's living with a girl up in his apartment," Hannah Zissel commented to the waitress, who grinned politely. "Twenty-three years old and he's still a sophomore."

"Twenty-two," Harry said.

"Listen," said Flora, "that's how they are now. I was saying to Penny on Parent's Day, all I said was her skirt could be a little bit longer so she wouldn't catch pneumonia in the private parts, and you should have heard her, just like him, we don't talk the same language, there's the new morality, on and on."

"What's the new-morality?"

Flora shrugged. "Sex," she said. "Drugs. What else?"

"Orgies," said Uncle Raymond. "Incest."

"I wouldn't mind," said Hannah, "if he had some common sense. He got kicked out of college once already using bad language on the radio. What if something happens? Some husband he'd make!"

"Why don't you ask Raymond to have a little talk with him?"

"Raymond and I are not speaking."

"Ray, she wants you to have a little talk with Harry."

"About what?"

16

"Sex and so on."

"Sure," said his uncle, "fine. You know about rubbers?"

"Harry will be careful," Flora said. "Won't you, Sonny? The two of you are *living* together in that place? Her parents allow her to do that?"

"Who are you talking about?" Harry inquired with a certain degree of cool. But a sickly smile kept nudging itself into his face.

"These things are all part of an education today," said Flora.

"I bet he's living off her."

"Who?"

"The girl in the closet. I bet he's living off her."

"No he's not. Are you, Harry?"

But his aunt had to repeat herself, he was a little distracted; his attention wasn't exactly riveted to the conversation. Twelve days overdue. But that didn't prove anything, there were women who did that all the time. False pregnancy.

Not Miriam, his voice whispered to him. *Miriam's as regular as the tides.*

So we'll get married, he told the voice. What's wrong with marriage?

Ha!

Which was true enough.

You're not the type, the voice informed him, *you don't have the discipline. Better join a monastery. Or take a part-time job, save up a little money and get yourself a fast abortion, what do you say?*

Would Miriam go through with a thing like that? An abortion?

Wouldn't she?

He decided she wouldn't, it would be bad form, she'd simply have the baby, Happy Mother's Day; one morning he was going to wake up and there'd be a baby in his bed and she'd go off to work and the baby would start crying and then what?

You'd have to feed it. Change its diapers or something. How should I know what to do with a baby?

17

With such thoughts he sat in the back of Raymond's Olds-mobile with his mother, hearing how Aunt Berthe looked since her operation (terrible), picking up the latest from his brother Gordon in L.A., who according to Hannah was doing chiroprac-tic on all the big movie stars now. They were expanding the store, incorporating the Quality Drug, putting up a new facade and new fixtures; it would be double in size, be a regular super-market by the end of the month, and meanwhile a vacation in Canada, which would be one jolly trip, since everything his mother had to say went first through Aunt Flora.

"Tell him why is he driving so fast? What's the rush?"

"Ray, she wants you to slow down."

"Ray-she-wants-you-to-slow-down! Let *her* drive! All I hear is criticisms!"

Twelve days overdue. And cousin Sheila's pregnancy was a grim reminder; she'd married a fat accountant named Sheldon Suberstein and they were always busy making more Substeins. How many did they have? Two sons, the infant girl, this other one on the way, and Sheila barely twenty-four—if she kept at it she'd break the inter-suburban record. Children! No wonder they called these clumps of houses *developments:* they were local population explosions, that's what they were. What did people see in children? Children and money, that was all his family could ever get really interested in, which made him wonder how much it might cost for an abortion; he doubted they would even look at him if he listened to the voice and applied at a monastery.

When Sheila's two younger ones were in bed at last they sat down to supper, and all through the meal Aunt Flora kept tell-ing Derek, the five-year-old, to finish his carrots. "Don't you want to see in the dark?" she would ask pleasantly, and the fat little kid, all smeared with grease and a mangled chicken leg in his fist, said, "Feh, who want gooky old carrots?"

Children.

"I *despise* gooky old carrots!" shouted Derek Suberstein, and his father shouted back: "Derek! Shut your mouth and eat the goddam carrots! Look at his face! Somebody wipe off his mouth, for chrissakes! One of these days I'm going to give him such a clop he won't be *able* to eat, he won't have no teeth!"

Head down Derek muttered, "I'll clop *you,* buddy," and the adults smiled.

"I'll clop him and clop him," Derek said. "Clop! Double clop!"

On Harry's left Uncle Raymond belched and rose from the table. On his right his mother took out her knitting. In the living room the television played without sound: the screen showed a woman opening and closing a refrigerator door. This seemed to give the woman great pleasure, so she did it again. Maybe he should have hidden Miriam in the refrigerator. The face of the woman on the television screen came up large with some mute, earnest talk. Wink. Dissolve to refrigerator spinning off into the distance like a dancer.

All was silent at the dining table. Harry, Sheila, Hannah gazed transfixed at the disappearing refrigerator. "What's on?" said Derek, twisting in his chair.

"Drink your milk to the bottom," Sheila told him as she left the room, "and you can watch *Great Fortunes* with the big people."

Flora came up and whispered, "Hannah, join us, Sheila's getting nervous. Come on, be a pal."

"I'll ride with him in the car," Hannah said, "for your sake. But that's all." She attended to her knitting, her lips tight.

"Honestly, this is ridiculous. Izzy, may he rest in peace, he has a stone over his head, doesn't he? The man's not exactly lying in an unmarked grave."

"Sure he has a stone. A beauty. And I have a bill for three hundred dollars."

Her knitting progressed as if it had a life of its own as she gazed at the television screen. Her husband had died the year before, and as far as she was concerned it was the store that had killed him, as sure as if the roof had fallen in on his head. For twenty years he had worked there like a ditch-digger, like a working-machine, with never a complaint, and after his first coronary how long was he at home? Three weeks exactly, because if Raymond stayed alone in the store they'd all be in the poorhouse.

"Come sit in a comfortable chair, Aunt Hannah," Sheila called.

"I'm knitting, it's all right."

"Knit in here, you'll miss *Great Fortunes*. It's John D. Rockefeller."

"I can see, darling, don't worry."

"She likes to be a hermit," Flora said.

For the store, he died for the store . . . so who should buy the headstone? Her insurance money? Raymond should have the nerve to tell her the store doesn't owe the man a stone for his grave? It can kill him, but it can't afford a stone?

"Oh Hannah, what are we going to do with you?" said Flora. "You act like you're simple-minded."

"Fine. So don't talk to me. Thank God I've got a son to knit a sweater for, even if he is a madman. And if Sheila's nervous I'm sorry, I should have stayed at a motel."

"Now it's *Sheila's* fault?"

"I didn't say that."

"Hannah, you're a compulsive complainer."

"The store killed my husband. Is that a lie?"

"His *heart* killed him! His *life* killed him! What's wrong with you?"

On the television screen the others watched a youthful J. D. Rockefeller passing out dimes to a crowd of orphans at Christmastime, "The First Noël" swelling up over the argument at the dining table.

"He's gone," Flora said. "Whatever took him, not paying for a tombstone won't bring him back."

Hannah reached for a handkerchief.

"Darling, come talk to Raymond. Come on. It's uncomfortable traveling this way."

20

She shook her head, tears in her eyes. "I want three hundred dollars," she said.

"Hannah . . ."

"I want . . . three hundred dollars . . . from that store . . ."

THREE

"God, it sounds *dread*ful," Miriam said. "Why did you stay so late?"

"I don't know. I sort of go all limp. I just sit till they're finished with me, it's always like that."

"Dreadful," Miriam said. "Families are dreadful." She was sitting up in the middle of her bed in the position of royal ease, her yoga book open on her knee. "There should be State nurseries. Which reminds me: when are you going to do your Plato and Aristotle paper?"

"They don't mean any harm, they just don't know what I'm for. It's like I'm sort of a gadget you can't figure out what it's supposed to do but you keep it around and every once in a while you fiddle with it. People are always trying to *use* you somehow."

"Did you have a talk with your cousin?"

"Oh God no, she's so fakey. Did I ever tell you what she did to me when we were kids? This is Sheila, all right. You know how kids are so interested in anatomy? So we agreed to let each other have a look, I pulled down my pants, she looked, all right, did she ever look, but then she wouldn't pull her pants down, can you imagine? She chickened out."

22

"Are *you* feeling all right? You look like you might have a fever or something." She got up and put her hand to his brow. "Cool as an iceberg. It's funny, I was reading this thing on the identity crisis—"

"—I always get sick when I'm with my family."

"Poor baby. Do you have a headache?"

He nodded.

"Should I get you an aspirin?"

"If it wouldn't be too much trouble."

"Poor Puss," she said, "you look dreadful. Didn't *anything* nice happen at your cousin's?"

"I took the dog for a walk." But he didn't tell her about that, it was too depressing. Astronaut, the Substeins' Irish setter, had swished his tail and jumped around when he was being put on the leash, and then he had pulled like a ski-lift, Harry leaning back until it seemed that either his arm or the leash or the dog's neck would break, and then they were running, trotting past lawn after lawn, dog and man. Every three hundred feet stood a lamppost designed in gaslight-era style. The houses were islands in ponds of clipped grass, all alight behind their picture windows. Even the ones where people were away had automatic devices for turning on the lights to keep out the burglars. One place was dark and had its blinds shut. Who lived there? The burglars?

Split-level. Ranch. Split-level. Ranch. Family tableaus revealed themselves like picture postcards. The television screens were distantly blue. At the speed they were going he could follow several programs at once, but then the dog stopped to use a tagged white stake as tall as the tree it supported. Cherry. All the little trees were tagged, there were no tall ones. In the distance he could see the lights on the hills of Hartford, but around him nothing but the star-filled sky was more than four years old—the developers had leveled the earth and started all over again, country clubs and churches and shopping centers and split levels and ranches, each house with a front door in one of six colors, he had counted. The dog tracked a lawn where the

"Poor baby."

"Boy, you should see where they live. You'd have to be out of your mind to live in a development, you'd spend your whole life just mowing the lawn. Listen, they have one peach tree, one pear tree, all the people have ten fingers and ten toes and once a year I bet they take inventory! One sexual organ, three TV's—you know what I mean? And my mother, God Almighty! And Uncle Raymond fell asleep in a chair, so I took the dog for a walk. Depressing. Boy! You know how it feels to be with my family? It's like sitting in a huge room where you're trying to read and the light is just a little tiny yellow bulb way up in the ceiling."

"Poor Harry. I wouldn't have a thing to do with them, that's the reason I send a letter to my mother once in a while, just to keep her at bay."

"How are *you* feeling, Mir?"

"Me?" She gave him her crazy-clown look, head bird-cocked toward the shoulder. "Fine," she said. "Just fine."

"Lonesome?"

"No. I played the banjo a little. Then I was reading, you know. The boss phoned."

"Johnny? What did he want?"

"Nothing. He wants us to come over Friday, he's giving a party."

"Is he after you again?"

"No, he's been perfectly sweet since you threatened him. I think it's you he's really after."

"Well, let's both keep alert, never turn your back while he's in range."

"You know something? You've got a mind like a running sore."

"Thank you."

"I mean he doesn't mean a thing, he does that with every girl in the shop."

"It's just a friendly gesture."

"Sure."

"He does it with the stock-boys too."

"Exactly."

"It's just that he likes *people*. He's friendly. I wonder how he feels about dogs? Antelopes?"

Silence.

"You're feeling okay?"

Shrug.

"Nothing . . . new?"

She shook her head, returning to her book. "How come you never mentioned me to your mother?"

"Listen," he said, "what should we do?" His heart shifted weightily in him like a lump of dough. "We've got to talk about it, Miriam. Do you think we'd better get married?"

"Why? Why ever get married?"

"I don't know. Children, I suppose." He shivered.

"Do you need a license to bring up children? No, I'm serious, it's insulting. You're about the most bourgeoisified person I know, do you realize? There was this girl they used to talk about in high school, she had a baby senior year from a sailor or something and she just took the baby with her to class."

"I bet."

"Well, she did. And she graduated. She's at Mount Holyoke, she's going to be a psychiatrist. Maybe she didn't bring the baby right into class, but they said you used to see her between classes out on a bench, nursing it, just as happy, she didn't care, she was glad to have a baby, it didn't slow her down at all."

"What happened to the sailor?"

"Who knows? Drowned, I hope. I mean, my mother and father are married—is that a recommendation? That's why there's all this god-awful family stuff, because of marriage. Have you ever known anybody who was married who had a single good word to say for it? No, listen, when I was fifteen my father actually told me it was *my* fault that he'd had such a miserable life, because if it wasn't for me he would have divorced my mother years ago. I mean, they haven't slept together for a century—what he does is play handball or something to work it off.

24

I told him I never asked him to do me any favors. But can yo[u] imagine? Isn't that a shitty thing to say to a fifteen-year-o[ld] girl?"

"I know."

"So then after they did finally get *separated,* what does he d[o?] He hangs around weekends with this sad-cheerful look, telli[ng] my mother she should have been the president of the world, s[he] was organized like a major corporation, what was she trying [to] do, raise me to be the first female five-star general?—on and [on] like that."

"You told me. Maybe we should get to sleep—I'm exhauste[d.]"

"No, listen, he just wanted to work off his guilt at getting [out] of the house and laying all the girls at the office. Only I did[n't] know that, I didn't know anything, I thought he was great, [he] was always slipping me ten bucks on the sly. So my moth[er] ask me to straighten up my room and if he was there he'd [say] why not let Miriam do it when *she* wants to do it, and [my] mother'd say 'Nothing good can happen till you straighten [up]' and he'd say you couldn't straighten up till something g[ood] happened. Things like that. I thought he was so *witty!* [No] wonder I'm nervous. You know what my mother told me? [She] said if I never forgot that men were children I wouldn't win[d up] with children to raise all by myself like she did. Which I sup[pose] is true enough."

Long silence.

"About what I said, about being overdue—forget it, let's [just] wait a while, maybe it's something I ate. I can never remem[ber] what time of month it is anyway." She'd begun to feel sorr[y for] him again.

"Isn't it supposed to kick you," he asked, "if it's in th[ere?] That's later, eh?"

She threw up her hands. "Forget it. I made it up to see [what] you'd do, honestly."

"Now you're mad at me."

"No I'm not. I'm mad at myself. Listen, Harry—"

"Yes you are mad, and all I was trying to do was find o[ut]

25

driveway held three Oldsmobiles. Then he began to pull and they were running again, going uphill, putting on a final burst toward the top. Below was a deserted shopping section, every window lit. The long parking plaza held a single car. Above each store sign gleamed: GIRTA's MATERNITY. SHOPPERAMA. KIDDIEKRAFT KOLLEGE. Diagonal parking lines stretched in double rows out to infinity, like the treadmarks of a giant's tractor. He had stood there looking down, with a thought like a headline, like a neon shopsign: TWELVE DAYS OVERDUE. And as if the dog had done his work, had led him to his destination, he began to pull Harry back to the Substeins. The quaint gaslights along the curving, deserted streets glowed, glowed, and they were running again, Harry and Astronaut, the dog anxious to settle for the night in his basket by the fireplace where a stack of three electrically-illumined logs would spread their neon comfort through the dark as the dog sighed, shifting about, dreaming of ancestral days, of bonfires in the forest, of the smell of lake water, the rousing of the hunt. But first Astronaut stopped again in the driveway holding the three Oldsmobiles, and methodically, like a craftsman, pissed on the right rear tire of each car, while Harry kept saying "Good *boy*. Good dog!"

Miriam handed him a glass of water and the bottle of aspirin. She didn't seem at all anxious to get married. Maybe she *wasn't* pregnant! But why the shadow of worry on her usually bland face? He knew there was something about pregnancy that made females very conservative, revolutionary principles or no revolutionary principles; and since his return from Sheila's he'd several times caught an expression on Miriam as of someone naked in the storm, peering around for an old shirt or some straw to crawl into. She must have been suffering from her unmarried state, and since he actually felt like an old shirt a good part of the time, naturally Harry thought she had him in mind.

"When are you going to work on your Aristotle?" she asked conversationally when they'd settled to go to sleep. But he told her not to nag. And then he inquired if she'd like to take another shot at *The Kama Sutra*, but she said she'd tried it once

27

and didn't like it. "Listen," she told him, "will you remember to get bread when you go out in the morning?"

"Our daily bread. Levy's Jewish Rye?"

"Why not? 'You don't have to be Jewish to enjoy it.' "

"But it helps, by God!"

"You're funny," she said. "In a way. I suppose I'll try to put up with you a little longer." Raised on his elbow he studied her, sixteen inches away in the other bed: wasn't she already a little swollen about the middle? Impossible. Too early. She didn't seem to expect a thing of him—how could that be? He sensed ultimate danger: the next time he really tried to get into her bed she'd whip out a marriage contract and a fountain pen from under her pillow, he could just see it. But maybe that was unfair. As his old roommate Arthur Thompson from his pre-army days always used to tell him, you could get too categorical about women, forget they were people, too. So maybe they didn't all want to get married and bake bread and become five-star suburban generals?

Ha, said his voice, *what does Thompson know?*

Plenty, Harry replied. Thompson had been a veteran already when they'd teamed up in Harry's abortive freshman year—a senior, three years in the navy behind him, huge wads of experience.

Sure. And where did it get him?

Which was true: the last Harry had heard from Thompson he was taking a Ph.D. in Humanities at Stanford, which was bad enough, but at least he wasn't married. Or maybe he was—what was wrong with marriage? What? Why was he feeling so self-protective, so scared out of his mind, so anxious to be off for South America down the Wilbur Cross Parkway? Because, he told himself, because you have a nasty, morbid, suspicious nature. Because you believe in your heart of hearts that women were put here on this earth to make a man eat apples, that they were secret castraters every one of them, all dedicated to the sweat of the brow and the watering of houseplants, he knew that. So how could a man get any living done with a woman around? It

28

wasn't that he didn't approve of women; for one thing they were very sexy. It was just that he'd seen, heard about too many *couples:* they rusted away like links from a broken chain. And he was too young for that! He was only a sophomore! He laughed to himself, turned over, grabbed his pillow, and the dying words of Archimedes suddenly came to his mind. He had the back of one of his desk drawers filled with the final statements of famous men, some on index cards, some on notebook paper. *Let me finish my problem,* Archimedes was supposed to have said. First-class dying words: let me finish my problem.

And what did that have to do with Miriam, sleeping not more than a body's width away? Sick, he was sick, he'd always been, he'd been sick in the womb, maybe he should see an analyst. Dying words. People saved stamps, coins . . . he saved dying words. He raised his head and looked again at Miriam. She switched on her bedlight and began reading about the identity crisis, propping her reading glasses low on her nose; she didn't mean any harm, she was just pregnant and trying to be cool and not able to sleep and wanting to be a little funny about it. If he could only join up, buckle down, build a nest! Maybe what he *needed* was some family life. John Adams, he thought: *Independence forever!* B-plus dying words. John Keats: *I feel the flowers growing over me.* David Garrick: *Oh dear.*

He was dozing, running again with Astronaut the Dog, passing ranches and split-levels, all dark, snuffed out, the quaint gaslamps glowing eerily along the curving, deserted streets. He opened his eyes: she was still reading, sucking a lollypop. "Any hope?" he said. "For the identity crisis?"

"Not according to this fellow."

"No cheer? No uplift? What's he writing about?"

"Pre-frontal lobotomies." She gave him a wide grin and resettled the lollypop. He slammed his fist into his pillow, then gave it another hug. And what if she did want an abortion in the long run, how would they pay for it? He wasn't hip enough to steal, so he'd have to work: one more part-time job: soda-jerk, salesman, paperboy—unthinkable. At the very notion his stom-

29

ach sank. Abortions. Archimedes. It was enough to make a man contemplate suicide.

Say, what about that? his voice threw in.

"Listen," he said to Miriam, talking into the pillow, "don't get mad. I'm just thinking out loud. You remember that doctor Nardiman and Gloria were going to use?"

"Yes?" she said, stiff as steel. He took a peek from behind his pillow: she was gazing straight ahead, the book face down on her stomach.

"Well, see, I was just thinking, you know, like maybe I should look for a job and start—"

"What?"

"Start saving for an abortion."

"Sure," she said. "As long as you're happy."

"Let's be serious, okay?"

"Okay. Fuck you, Harry. Seriously."

"Did you really miss your period?" he asked, suddenly sitting up.

"Did I?" She'd gone back to her book.

"Say, what's that in my typewriter?"

"A note. I left you a note. I wasn't sure when you'd get back. *If* you would. It doesn't—"

"No, let me see, I never get any mail."

The note read:

> See you after work, if you didn't go off and join the Foreign Legion. Say, do they still have the Foreign Legion? Follow the clues and you will find a much more interesting communication in the front-room closet.

The note on the floor of the closet, in capital letters decorated with flowery curlicues, read simply:

IF READ AFTER MIDNIGHT:

THIRTEEN DAYS OVERDUE.

It was after midnight. He stood in the closet with the note in his hand.

FOUR

So now it's Wednesday morning, April 14th, bright as a bell jar; at the Substeins' outside of Hartford the aunts and mothers and uncles are getting ready to face the northbound traffic and a day of three-cornered chat about tombstones, while Sheila is already cleaning up behind them, screaming children clinging to her every limb, and Astronaut sits in front of the television set, waiting for someone to tune up the sound. On Beachum Street Harry is awake, though he doesn't realize it yet. Awake and still brooding. He's not heartless, he feels considerable affection for Miriam, it's just that he's a kind of moral mongoloid, over-sexed, under-motivated, which may be what America is all about. In any case he doesn't know what to do with himself. It should be clear by now that he has a curious attitude toward marriage, marriage strikes him as a way of joining the human race with a lifetime contract, and he's not sure he has a vocation for that sort of thing. This morning he woke with a vision: he saw himself as a homeless goldfish considering a bowl, wary and yet tempted— terrified of being locked in but with his nose pressed up against the glass in envy of the others flipping around in there in the shallow, warm communal waters. He doesn't know what right he has not to wish to be domesticated—who was *he,* anyway, to expect special treatment?

Less than nine months ago he'd emerged from the U.S. Army with a sense that maybe he could claim what they call a "service-connected disability," in his case incoherence of the lifeline, a massive confusion as to goals, yardage, and the very nature of the game, if it was a game. His experience ever since, barring the brief period when he and Miriam had something really good going, represented one continual rehumanization trauma. He wasn't making it, that was clear, so maybe he *should* get married? Was that the thing to do? *He* didn't know. And what was he going to say at the end of the vacation when he had to commit himself to an academic major, the choice being completely arbitrary and Miriam with her famous sense of humor pushing for City Management? Meanwhile there were hundreds of books to read and papers to write and nothing seemed to get done, he was smoking too much pot, there was a period of two weeks there when he literally couldn't get to a class before four in the afternoon, sophomore sleeping sickness, and all the while he figured that the reason Miriam had been getting increasingly impossible to live with or get any sex out of was that she'd started to pay the rent and so must have been expecting him to win the Nobel Prize any minute. In the army he'd decided that it didn't make any sense to be anything but an artist—at that point he was mainly interested in music and painting—but what happens to a prospective artist who can't seem to produce a single, durable word or note or stroke of *art*? And what was he doing back at the very college that had booted him out into the army in the first place, twenty-two now and still a sophomore? They had kicked him out for "trafficking in scatological, obscene, and irresponsible language over campus radio"—perhaps if he really offended the sensibilities of the campus once again they might just kick him out with no reprieve this time and he could work at something pleasant like being a beachcomber. Or maybe he should major in Animal Husbandry? Or become a spy? You probably had a lot of free time as a spy, you could write or sculpt or make films on the side.

But he couldn't think straight, not with Miriam acting so

strangely. If she was pregnant, then what happened next? She had him completely off-balance, but for years he'd been following reports in the newspapers on what happened next. The wedding march. Marriage. Brooks Brothers suits. Buttondown collars, buttoned-down opinions, a lot of handball or squash or something on the side. Marriage—it was supposed to be better than to burn, but there were those who reported they found the situation curiously unsatisfying. *Man and Wife* was one thing, it had a large, biblical sound to it. But what about *Oak and Mistletoe,* or *Dog and Leash?* He could just see himself attached to a lawnmower, selling encyclopedias, bouncing little Zissels on his knee, telling them to eat their carrots. Insane, and in any case what can we do, he's looking ahead a few pages, Marriage-and-the-Family seems to be looming up like an armored cloud out of the mist and he feels a strong temptation to wander off, to disappear, never mind where, to throw it all up. It strikes him that he just doesn't have the stuff to be a college student, or the proper working conditions or the right friends or something. He feels an urge: to become a cowboy, a taxi driver, a monk. He senses a huge brush hanging over his head which is about to fall and paint the remainder of his life one uniform, connubial gray. And of course his instincts are right, it's true we're going to have to knock him around quite a bit from here on out, there's more at stake than his personal comfort, there are institutions to be defended, the survival of the species—but for the moment it is only Wednesday morning, Harry is pulling on his khakis, brushing his teeth, thinking back to yesterday before Miriam's revelation, thinking back to the time when he still vaguely figured everything would somehow work out for him if he just remained cheerful, unanxious, though his sole accomplishment since the beginning of Easter vacation has been to add a few odds and ends to the construction in the living room: a dog collar, an automobile fender, a small framed sepia print of Strindberg with a crack running diagonally down the glass. Other items for the construction are everywhere about the apartment, mainly on the stained green living room rug; there one could

33

find without too much trouble a plaster bust of Leopardi, a large collection of magnets and worn automobile valves, a fishbowl full of black buttons, a collection of fragments of colored glass in an El Producto cigar box, a NO PARKING sign (7:30 to 9 A.M., 4 to 6 P.M.) picked up late one night in February on Eastern Avenue, and a green felt hat with a dejected peacock feather. There were days recently when Harry would fish out a button, cheerfully dab it with Elmer's Glue, and then wander around and around the construction, seeking the inevitable spot for that particular button, keeping in mind the exquisite articulation of parts which an artwork demands, until the glue had dried and he decided to toss the button back in the fishbowl with its friends, not forcing the issue.

Miriam is still asleep. It is only eight-fifteen. In just a while Harry will be going out for the morning bread, but for the moment it is important to record how much he admires Miriam's back. Among other things, he's spent a significant amount of time since they first began to live together merely rubbing her back for her, or scratching it, since she goes in for that sort of thing. Now he gazes sadly at Miriam as she lies in bed, broods upon her, his self-made college dropout, his dark-haired, erratic girl. Since the apartment is perversely still being heated, overheated, she wears nothing by morning but the bottoms of her cotton pajamas, printed all over with tiny purple hearts. The little hollow of her back, just above the buttocks with their covering of purple hearts, can sometimes move him to tears. He's much too easily moved to tears, as we will have the opportunity to observe, but in fact Miriam has a slim, handsome body, she's a touching girl, her back looks particularly warm, and up toward the shoulders very brave and solid. The hollow, however, is Harry's favorite spot; everything vulnerable about her is centered there. So he settled in to gaze at the hollow, but instead he found himself rather furtively making up his bed, which wasn't the sort of thing he'd normally do. Their bedroom is narrow; the beds practically touch. Harry leans over from the window side and grabs the mattress corner to shove the sheets

34

under. He inches back out, his eyes on Miriam. The room, though long, is not really intended for two beds plus book cases and Harry's desk at the far end, plus a shoulder-high pile of cardboard cartons in the corner holding most of his worldly possessions, and in addition a debris of shoes and discarded clothing, a kind of domestic battle scene in the no man's land of open floor space between beds and desk. He had wanted to switch to a double bed when Miriam moved in, but her strongest intellectual line was the separation of the species—she knew certain key passages in the works of D. H. Lawrence by heart. Besides, she'd been able to pick up a floor-sample single bed at half price from the shop where she worked, a chi-chi furniture store called Beds-'n-Things.

Harry settled in at his desk and sharpened a pencil by rubbing the point on the underside. She would sleep, unless he woke her, till ten or eleven. He took up the first paragraph of his Plato-Aristotle paper. In progressively more of a scrawl this read: "Aristotle claimed that he loved Plato, but loved truth more. Is this really true? And *loved* in what sense? Can we tell, at this late date? And how did these two venerable Greeks come to differ on the Mind-Body Problem in the first place? It's a question, all right. I feel the flowers growing over me."

That was as far as he'd gone. He set down these sentences and took up instead a page of manuscript from a shallow pile, the lower portion of the top sheet marred by coffee stains which had aged to the brownness of dried blood. His play. For his creative-writing course. Some play. It was practically all stage directions and a two-page list of characters. Maybe he should turn it into a film? Instead he swiveled around and looked down the room at the bottom of Miriam's feet. She had callousses. He rolled the desk chair slowly toward the beds, considering her back, the lobe of her ear, the swelling edge of her left breast against the sheet. Marriage. Maybe it *was* time for him to get married, what else did he plan to do with his life? At which point Miriam moved with a pleasurable groan; a rose-brown nipple appeared and disappeared like a jack-in-the-box; at her neck a tendril of hair

35

curled like an upside-down question mark. He knew that if he touched her she would stretch and wake, she might even feel playful, and he gave some thought to that. But then he set the page of manuscript neatly on top of the pile, took up his sneakers, had one long thoughtful look at Miriam, and moved down the hall through the larger front room. He pulled the door shut behind him and went slowly down the four flights of stairs.

Outside he sat on the top step and pulled on his sneakers. Off to get the daily bread. He felt strange in a familiar way, like an amputated limb. It always took him a long time to get started in the mornings. He had no special plans for the day: maybe he'd smoke a little pot, take a walk, study the leaves on the maples around the square, just coming forth like unwarned virgins.

Ah well, he thought. The important thing was not to panic. Calm, due calm, that was the ticket; disengagement; cunning. Exile. He thought of James Joyce, which made him think of his own four unfinished novels—unfinished? unstarted!—which got him going picking among the prospects for his dying-words. A new possibility presented itself: *I should have majored in Animal Husbandry*. He tried it out in an inward whisper, punctuated by a pitiful cough; in this version—he was enjoying himself now—it would be lung cancer that carried him off, so he'd reach for a last cigarette, the death-bed watchers gasping, he wetting his lips : "I should have [cough] majored in [cough] Animal Husbandry."

It was going to be a lovely morning.

He sat on the steps, tying his laces, and when he looked up the street cleaner was coming along the curb on the other side with his pushcart, a crunched together little blue-eyed man like a gnome who'd pushed his way into the world through a manhole cover. The street cleaner nodded. Harry had known him since freshman days, admired him: he followed a useful profession. "Nothing like weather, eh?" the street cleaner said, shifting in his tiny mouth an unlit black cheroot. "How you been? Haven't seen you for a while."

Harry told him he'd been so-so.

36

"That right? Listen, the Sox dropped two—hopeless, eh? My wife's brother come to live with us. Yankee fan, no imagination."

"Tell me," said Harry, "are you happy in your work?"

The street cleaner shrugged. He scooped up three beer cans from the gutter on the end of his shovel, squinted into each, then released them clattering into his cart. "The shame of the cities," he said. He looked at Harry, the street between them. "You got troubles? Listen, my wife says what it is about men, they don't understand women. Now my brother-in-law run off from his old lady, who blames him? So my wife says to him, all a wife wants is for a man to go out to work and for that he gets laid, the rest is talk, culture, you follow me? She says men want to climb up Everest."

"Do you want to climb up Everest?"

"Sure," said the street cleaner, "why not? Naa," he added, trundling off, "what I'd do, I'd stay at the bottom and clean up the pieces when they drop off. Woman's work." He waved to Harry. Harry waved back, then stood watching him clatter all the way down Beachum and out of sight.

At Hulbert's the waitress who had served his family yesterday was just opening up. The bread lay in the entryway; she carried the baskets in, put a loaf of Levy's in a thin white bag for him, six Danish in another, a brown bag. "How's your missus?" she asked. She mimicked his mother: "My son the sophomore. He's living with a girl up there, living off her." Harry lifted his brow, but shrugged. He looks his most boyishly appealing in the mornings, before he's combed his hair. The waitress, a tough character, laughed with affection. She had terrible teeth. He'd heard she'd do sex stunts for five dollars. How's your missus? So how's your prostate, he should have said.

Outside he dropped a dime in the box and took out a newspaper. The usual: wars, rapes, sporting news. One excellent headline: BEAUTY MANHANDLED IN BOSTON? He thought he saw the word OVERDUE, but it was an optical illusion, the column was headed

TRANSIT IMPROVEMENT DUE

37

Down Eastern Avenue he could see to the Square and the rusty rise of the Dunnbar Street bridge. He loved the neighborhood in the early mornings, the spires and greenery of the university at the horizon like Birnam Wood on the way to Dunsinane. That was an echo of his play, where Macbeth complains to Mrs. Macbeth that there's no future anymore in being a tragic hero; that in the old days all you *needed* was a character flaw and everything followed, people got killed, Birnam Wood came to Dunsinane, there was some system. If you wanted action nowadays, you had to get up and carry Dunsinane all the way to Birnam Wood, Macbeth said, and who had the energy? "Excuses," Lady Macbeth replied. "That's all I ever get from you, excuses."

Some play.

Harry stood in front of Hulbert's, watching a trolley-bus glide to a stop at the far end of the Square. In furnished rooms above the dreary shops along Eastern Avenue, the derelicts, the painters, the perpetual students, he imagined them all snug in their dreams: the Bohemians, the shopkeepers, the virtuous poor. His friends. His colleagues. After he'd failed to survive in this town the first time, why did he return to the scene of the crime? He nibbled at one of his pastries. The sunlight seemed mild and well-meaning. In the window of the Double-D Food Jamboree he saw they had a special on Easter Lilies; the lilies drooped, a bit wan. Across the street a tall elegant boy, a painter he knew slightly, in bedroom slippers and a black sweater and yellow pants, waited while his dog did its business against an innocent mailbox. Harry waved to the painter. The dog was a large poodle, artistically trimmed, looking like chocolate farmlands seen from the air, a patch of fur here, another there. Harry used to feel sorry for such poodles in their indignity, to have their fur mauled that way. He thought of Astronaut, the Substeins' setter—now *there* was a dog, a no-nonsense dog, a model of greatness. Why didn't poodles bite? They had good teeth, their teeth hadn't yet been half pulled-out to make a pattern, so why did they submit? Astronaut would never put up with it, he'd piss all over the

Oldsmobiles. At which point Harry lost respect for poodles, having seen through to their inadequacy, that they were followers, sycophants, that they couldn't stand up for themselves like an Irish setter. You didn't see Irish setters walking around all chopped up like a Mondrian design.

He paused at the corner, gripped his Danish in his mouth, and unfolded to the Woman's Page, because the letters on the Woman's Page were the only reason for buying the otherwise worthless newspaper. Sometimes the ladies who wrote in over pen-names went on and on for months giving each other advice and warnings and encouragements, back and forth, comical stuff. So he stood reading in the quiet of Wednesday morning at the corner of Eastern and Beachum, somehow loath to return to the apartment. There was a letter from TIGHTWAD again, she was known on the Woman's Page for feeding her family of eight within a strict limit of ten dollars a week. This time she offered a recipe for sow's belly and canned tomato soup."Get the butcher to save the sow's belly for you," TIGHTWAD advised with her thin-lipped, old-craftsman's air. He could just see the TIGHTWAD children, like figures carved out of matchsticks. Still, ten dollars a week, it added a sporting element to their lives, and if TIGHTWAD kept the children alive for a few years on ten a week it would give her a sense of accomplishment that would maybe solve her woman-problem.

He stood reading, trying not to think about Miriam. There was a letter from a certain TELEPHONE GIRL, very involved, she seemed to be asking for information about erogenous zones. And then there was the sort of thing he always looked for, though this time somehow he failed to be amused. A challenge to HAPPY WIFE, signed HAPPIER WIFE. HAPPIER WIFE said HAPPY WIFE certainly had a mature and over-average husband, but he was nothing compared to her own. HAPPIER WIFE said her husband had passed away recently, and the insurance didn't amount to much, but in twenty-eight years of marriage he'd not only worked five days a week selling encyclopedias, he'd also had a job on Saturdays, mowing lawns or shoveling snow, "according

39

to the season." Also he was never short-tempered, he was always marvelous with the nine children, and he did the vacuuming and otherwise made himself useful about the house in the evenings and on Sundays. She said she couldn't have been happier, while it lasted.

There was also a note from GRANDMOTHER FERNANDO. She passed on some advice her mother had given her as a girl: never learn to clean fish, iron shirts, or pluck chickens.

Harry tucked the paper under his arm and started slowly back down Beachum. He had finished the piece of pastry, cherry, his favorite. He ran his tongue over his teeth. For a moment he paused; he groaned; he turned to gaze at the unawakened shopfronts along Eastern Avenue, where a few morning cars went whizzing through the intersection toward the Parkway. And then he found that he was returning to the corner. What does he think he's doing? He straightens up. *He raises his thumb!* Harry, who do you think you are, Percy Shelley? But he doesn't hear, he juts out his thumb, a little Fiat gliding through the blinker at the intersection halts, toots its horn, and he's running, running across Beachum, he's dropped the white bag of bread and soon he'll see the last of it in the Fiat's rearview mirror and later the blue-eyed street cleaner may pick it up and squint at it or some kids may use it as a football, or a passing poodle may take it home between his teeth to his master. Harry's not even encumbered by a toothbrush. His hair remains uncombed. And back in the apartment Miriam is still settled asleep on her stomach with no one to appreciate her back, lying sprawled out, one foot hanging in the gap between the beds, deserted though she doesn't know it. The other, Harry's bed, is approximately ten inches away from her squarish-nailed big toe. His bed, of course, is empty, neatly made, as if its blank surface intends to serve for the note he really should have left her, though when he walked out fifteen minutes ago he didn't consciously intend to go anywhere except to Hulbert's for the paper and a loaf of bread.

Oh, is Miriam going to be angry and disgusted and disillusioned with Harry when she wakes up and finds him gone. But now she smiles in her sleep, she's easy-hearted, and meanwhile Harry is being sped by the Fiat down the tree-lined, four-lane highway, reading official signs that advise the motorists not to kill one another, discussing Dante with the Fiat driver, a former seminarian now traveling in Bibles and rosaries, a black-suited, middle-aged party who looks like a defrocked baseball umpire or a cut-rate dentist, his overexcited glance leaping at Harry through spectacles that glint like switch-blades. "What about that part where they push the boulders at each other—great? Isn't that great stuff?" "Terrific," says Harry. "And when Beatrice really bawls him out for being such a slob—God Almighty!" Dante. What does Harry know about Dante? Has he put Miriam out of his mind and life already? On the other hand, Dante and Virgil are two of the chief characters in his play, so a certain connection obtains. What a wonderful list of characters in that play: Jesus; Samuel Gompers; Thomas Mann! Some of them turned up also in a short story he completed four pages of back in the freshman year; that time he'd made the mistake of asking his apartment-mate Thompson for a critical reading. Poor Harry, he always has trouble finishing a piece of literary work, because once he gets the characters going and reasonably confused and pounding with despair, then what can you do with them, what can you say, *they all lived unhappily ever after?* Or drop the atomic bomb for a smashup ending, noting that the action had in fact been taking place all along in Hiroshima toward the end of World War II? It was a problem. But why should he worry about endings, he had enough troubles trying for a running start. He will fetch up by the end of the afternoon in New Jersey; with mindless enthusiasm he will see his former apartment-mate Arthur Thompson again; but for the moment he's on the move, we can only observe, following in a helicopter for a God's-eye view. It's a wonderful springish day, he's beginning to feel great, and back in the apartment on Beachum Street in the university and skid-row section of the fair-sized Connecticut city which has not been named here for fear of reprisals, back in Fear of Reprisals, Connecticut, Miriam Hippolyto, nineteen-year-old neurotic female, tosses and mumbles and changes positions, a committed sleeper, totally unpregnant, smiling as she dreams.

FIVE

On this same Wednesday morning, at the very instant that Harry chooses to take off hitchhiking into parts unknown, Arthur Thompson lies rigidly abed on the outskirts of Cordelia, New Jersey, listening to sounds from the kitchen below where his wife Doris is preparing to bring him breakfast in bed. The toaster pops, and Arthur responds with an inward twitch. Doris is humming; in the background he hears the idiotic burbling of the coffee pot. He feels as if he is about to explode, but he fails to move in the slightest, he keeps his eyes trained on the map of Greenland that the ceiling cracks have sketched out above his head. That's where he would like to be, in Greenland, and he finds it impossible even to swing his long legs over the edge of the bed. He's had a hard night, an even harder year. Harry would hardly recognize him if he saw him, his old friend Thompson, a ghost strung out on quivering wires. Not that Arthur was exactly carefree in the old days when his ad in *The Daily Student* had fetched Harry to share his living quarters; no, he had always been a thin, slow-moving, haunted-looking man. But recently Thompson's pale, greenish eyes had begun to act as if they were unfairly imprisoned in their sockets; his lean cheek occasionally twitched toward the jaw as if he guessed that his fly

43

was surely open but didn't dare risk his dignity to check. Ever since he'd married and left Stanford for a job at Cordelia College, Thompson had begun to feel very old, as if anxiety had gone to work on him like acid on a copper plate. Just the other morning he'd caught a glimpse of himself in the toaster: hair thinning, nose sharp, the rest of him long and insubstantial as a reed. He'd even taken to mumbling to himself in the john. Centuries ago he had come out of a farm in Wisconsin, had gone into the navy with no premonition of his future calling. And then he'd begun to read; that was his tragic mistake. For a while he'd acted like any other sailor, rolling drunks in Honolulu, spending long weekends in the flimsy whorehouse hotels of Sassibo or Yokahama. But his heart wasn't in it. What he really wanted was to sit and study, contemplate, write a book and change the world. The time came when he'd just about exhausted the shipboard library of the carrier *Wasp*—by then he'd taken to carrying his duffle bag half-filled with paperbacks. Off-duty, he'd settle out on the fantail of D deck and toss the pages, ripped out as he finished them, into the sea. To this day the floor of the Pacific is littered with the remains of Arthur Thompson's youthful education. In fact, at one spot off the Philippines, two hundred and eighty-three miles northwest of the Mindanao Deep, there is a page by John Barth from one voyage neatly resting on a page by Karl Barth from the voyage before—a coincidence so curious that it is not likely to occur again throughout all recorded literary history.

So Thompson went to college, and by the time Harry knew him he was a senior, already something of a snob, with a working knowledge of six languages, a growing suspicion of anything published in English after 1616, an important, paying job on the campus radio station, and a nice fellowship already fixed up for graduate work in the Humanities Program at Stanford. Arthur and Harry had played chess, talked books, argued into the night on such topics as sex, drugs, the meaning of existence, the costs of civilization, and whether anything really was worth reading after 1616. But what first made Thompson important to Harry

44

was his long socks. Harry claimed that he learned more from contemplating Thompson's elegant hose than in any of his freshman classes. His apartment-mate would sit reading, legs languidly crossed, and there would be the socks, mounting endlessly. This made Harry ashamed of his own sagging ankle-length cotton argyles; it was his first pure taste of culture, and he was grateful for it. He also found Thompson's limp and hopeless manner immensely seductive. They would walk over to the Student Union, pausing to watch as one of the big elms outside the Chemistry Building was brought down by the busy crew from Buildings and Grounds. "On this campus," Arthur would say, "even the trees are sick." But then, despite his cynicism, without knowing why, he would find himself caught up in one or another of Harry's enthusiasms. For a time he was waking at five-thirty in the morning to handle the controls at the campus station while Harry tried out a disk-jockey program, *The Morning Watch*. He read Harry's manuscripts, commented on them as if they could in any way be taken seriously. He was always trying to do some work of his own, but it was hopeless; with Harry around, he found himself focusing eventually, exclusively, on Harry's affairs. If Arthur had known that his old friend was already on the move in his direction, he might have had himself committed to the nearest convenient psychiatric nursing home and called it a day. As it was, he lay counting the slams of the refrigerator door while more than two hundred miles away, Harry, bursting with the joy of sudden freedom, energetically goosed the air with his thumb as the semi-trailers and the station wagons and the Oldsmobiles went zizzing by.

Arthur had contracted for his job at Cordelia College for Women mainly because the college had been willing to let Doris teach too, giving her one course in the department of domestic management and another in preschool education. But why had he married Doris in the first place? He couldn't remember. It had seemed the natural thing to do out at Stanford where the air was clear. Why, for that matter, couldn't he get himself up out of bed? Why was he wasting the Easter vacation, why couldn't

45

he get going on his thesis? Because it seemed less of a compromise to lie still as the refrigerator thumped. He had passed a very hard night, and wondered whether he might not in fact be going slowly out of his mind.

Meanwhile, outdoors, on the inlet side of the town of Cordelia, the day is doing beautifully. Seagulls and sand grass; low tide on the ocean inlet; gulls cawing, sailing through a sky pale with the early hour, bland with distance. And the air, the salt air, clean, unused, gives off a hint of weathered wood, of pitch and seaweed. A lovely day, temperature 72, though it will rise into the low eighties before nightfall. Below the house appear the remains of one of the concrete shore emplacements that protected New Jersey from amphibious landings twenty-some years ago. Cables and hunks of rusted metal stick up out of the sand.

The Thompsons' house is all alone above a narrow stretch of inlet shoreline; it had once belonged to the family of a man who ran a boat-repair shed at the top of the inlet, but now it is owned by Cordelia College and rented out to academic families. "That's what I am now," Arthur thinks, "an academic family." And on the ground floor Doris moves about the kitchen. She is twenty-three, with small, brilliant teeth, intense blue eyes, a square-bottomed chin, and a master's degree in Education from Santa Clara. Her reddish hair starts in a fringe not too far down across her brow and rides up to a kind of natural pompadour, curving in again at the ears. Her hair is luxuriant, rich as a rain forest; if she were a circus performer she would let it grow until it could be woven into a rope reaching to her waist, by which she would hang from the top of the circus tent, spinning colored loops on her wrists and ankles, juggling oranges, flashing her narrow grin. She has arranged Arthur's breakfast nicely on a tray and has managed to get through the door into the back hall by balancing the tray on her raised thigh. Now she is climbing the stairs, and she is vaguely pleased; something has begun to stir again in Arthur, last night he showed some small degree of warmth. When they'd first arrived at Cordelia in September he'd been reasonably lively; lively for Arthur, anyway. He'd even

46

begun a clever little lecture at the first faculty meeting on how things were done in the Humanities Program on the coast, before he was shouted down by the older members. Oh, he'd tried to help everyone, explain to them; once he argued with the head of the Pure Science Department for an hour until this lady asked how *he* would arrange the science major, and when he told her in endless, excited detail she replied simply, "I couldn't disagree with you more." The college just wasn't up to him. Doris was perfectly happy herself—or would have been if Arthur would make love to her once in a while—but it seemed he couldn't stand the place. She remembered several times when she'd seen his brightness dim right before her eyes, like a pair of glasses when someone breathes on one lens and then the other. He wasn't appreciated in the Humanities Department, she always told him that. Once they were having a Coke between classes when the humanities chairman came up to the machine. "I understand you were in Russia over the summer, Dr. Stock," Arthur said, as friendly as could be, though he immediately began to display the tic he had developed at the jaw. "That's right," said the chairman, his expression sobering. "I imagine it was very . . . very nice?" Arthur said. "Didn't go for pleasure, " said Stock, bending to take his Coke from the slot. "Church trip." His jowls sagged. "Did Moscow, naturally," he said. "We did that. *Swan Lake* was on."

"How did you—?"

"Very enjoyable. Ballet is essentially simpleminded, seems to me, but very enjoyable. We came in, me and Mrs. Stock, and it was full up. They sit on benches, you know. Well, they saw we were Americans—they can tell, somehow—and one of them led us down to the front row, you see, and made 'em shift over."

"My!"

"Polite? The politest people in Europe, the Russians are. No doubt about it."

"Really?" Arthur said, "I didn't know that. Did you get any idea——"

"Politest people in Europe," said Stock grimly. "Course,

47

they're forced to be that way. Forced. How's your work, Mr. Thompson? How's it coming along?"

Arthur had shrugged. At the time he'd been trying to finish his doctoral thesis on *The Lay of Hildebrand* and get out of Cordelia immediately, but nothing much had come of it. He was a perfectionist. He would spend two days worrying a single footnote into shape and then drop it out again. He couldn't bear *The Lay of Hildebrand,* but that made him feel all the more obligated.

"Get it done," Stock had said. "Waste of time in any case, but don't let it drag on, that's my advice. Say, how come you two Thompsons are so interested in the Russians? Some of your colleagues around here to whom I wouldn't mention that fact."

When he was out of earshot, Arthur had said, "Stupidest man in New Jersey. Forced to be that way." But there was no heart in it. He seemed stricken. Doris laughed, but his eyes had dimmed. "Forced to be that way," he said.

And then it had been a mistake for Doris to urge that they take Inlet House when it became vacant at mid-semester. Arthur was less unhappy in the tiny apartment on campus. She had only wanted to take better care of him, he'd seemed so sad by then, so worn by Cordelia and his responsibilities—but he'd drawn back from the house and from her; he seemed confused, burdened. She knew it made him attractive in a new, soulful way, and yet she missed the old Arthur, the one who talked, the one who had once said he expected to become a great scholar. When she saw him emerge from the car, tall, bony, gray-faced after the day's teaching, she would rush to make him a drink, which he'd more than likely refuse, saying he had to grade papers. She was sure he was ill. He was trying to accomplish too much at once, trying to keep the house from falling in on them, trying to fight off his colleagues, trying to actually *teach* the Cordelia girls. There were so many things she could do for him if he'd only let her help, but in some strange way he seemed actually afraid of her. Their sex life had just about come to a halt; she noticed the way his eyes shifted after a brief glance at her, as if taking an appreciative look at your own wife were a criminal offense. But then she couldn't blame him for being woman-shy, the way the whole first semester had been clouded by the Miss Visniac affair.

Miss Visniac wasn't a regular student of Arthur's—she was the roommate of a certain Miss Hendries, the real cause of the trouble. As far as Doris could make out, the thing with Miss Hendries started as a perfectly ordinary college-girl crush. Doris herself had also had Miss Hendries as a student, in Preschool 102; an unsmiling, emaciated creature with a bang of black hair which seemed to be made of patent leather cutting across her bony brow. The humanities papers she wrote for Arthur were terribly confused, full of poetic apostrophes to the trees and the sea and walking barefoot through the long quiet grass and the soul's quest for its lover, deeply chained in the bowels of this finky world. As Miss Hendries put it, she had psyched-out of better schools than Cordelia. That information came in a letter, ten pages long and on Plaza Hotel stationery, which Arthur had shown to Doris midway through the first semester. The letter announced Miss Hendries' understanding of his problems, her contempt for the other girls in the class who made fun of him in the dorm, her lack of concern for the D-minus he'd given her on the Plato and Aristotle paper; she went on to an expression of her enjoyment at his teaching technique, his gestures, the way he was always stumbling over the wastebasket or flinging out his arms or standing there listening to a student, straight as a pencil, with that tortured expression on his face. She knew he had scorn for her work, scorn for the girls at Cordelia in general, and she admired him immensely for it. At this point in the letter there were extensive excerpts from what Arthur told Doris must have been Miss Hendries' Keats notes. She ended by wondering if Arthur was happy with his work. Did he have enough stimulation in his life?

"The letter's better than any of her papers, anyway," Arthur had said. Doris urged him to recommend Miss Hendries to the school psychiatrist at that point, but the psychiatrist was a dodo and badly overworked and nothing came of it. Then, after it

49

became clear that he wasn't going to react to the letter, Miss Hendries started showing up at his classes with a tiny tape recorder. And then somebody new was sitting beside her. This was the roommate, Miss Visniac. They both wanted to talk to him. They were having extrasensory perceptions about his emotional state. Miss Visniac was actually a more healthy-looking girl, very large, her clothes fitting like cylinders without much indication of where you would look if you were trying to find her waist, but with freckles and reddish hair; she wore skirts, as far as Doris could remember, usually beige or green, and printed blouses.

The two girls were having a strange experience. They'd felt themselves *drawn* to Arthur's office at certain moments, as if he needed help. He reassured them and told Miss Visniac it was probably all right if she sat in on the class, and made a few skeptical comments about ESP and LSD and told Miss Hendries that her last paper might have been a C-minus if she'd followed a single line of argument, and then he sent them away, and for a while nothing further happened. Miss Visniac attended the humanities class, following his every gesture with her mouth slightly open, and Miss Hendries finally had to be asked to please stop bringing her tape recorder, which put him off his stride. But there was a lull for several weeks before he received a phone call rather late one night from a colleague, Joe Milgrass. Milgrass was very mysterious. He wanted to know if Arthur felt all right, and was he sure, and had he been terribly depressed lately? It turned out that Miss Hendries and Miss Visniac had phoned and told him that Arthur was about to commit suicide in despair over the world situation, and would he please get in touch and not say where he'd learned about the matter. They even told Joe Milgrass how Arthur was going to do it: by eating lilies of the valley. Miss Visniac had learned from a lecture given by the Applied Science Department that lilies of the valley were fatally poisonous when eaten.

Arthur had had another talk with the two girls then and according to what he told Doris, he was cruel. He'd asked them to lay off, he had enough troubles being a college teacher without even thinking about the world situation. He told them it wasn't proper to trifle with other people's lives that way, and he strongly recommended a visit to the dodo psychiatrist. This interview was held on a bench on campus; Arthur had got wrought up, making a number of gestures which the girls seemed to enjoy until he realized that there were tears in their eyes.

But after this encounter, Doris thought he'd heard the last of it. Miss Visniac deserted his class, and Miss Hendries seemed chastened. She dropped her eyes when there was any danger of their meeting his in the classroom. It was when they started sawing down the trees next to Stimson Hall to build the new parking lot that the climax arrived. First Arthur had to see Dr. Stock, and then the Dean, and finally, outrageously, he had to have an interview with the analyst, who got him off the hook. Many a night thereafter they would talk it over, Arthur and Doris, trying to work out the logic of the last development. Doris finally made him understand how Miss Visniac might have gotten to the point of accusing him of sexual advances—that could be explained as a matter of hurt pride, though God knows what might have been going on in Miss Hendries' head when she threw in the bit about his having tried to give her a spanking with her notebook. What neither Arthur nor Doris could understand was the girls' claim that he had tried to get them to consort with him, both at once, *in his stall shower,* an item that had thrown the Dean and Dr. Stock and delighted the psychiatrist. Arthur didn't even have a stall shower, it was just an old tub with a curtain. Had he done something to provoke Miss Hendries in the first place? She had the decency to transfer to another humanities section after the sex in the shower charge failed to hold. But did he provoke her? He decided that giving low grades at a woman's college was the single most dangerous thing a male teacher could do. It was the power of disdain, which worked on females like an aphrodisiac.

All in all, it had been an exhausting semester for Arthur,

Doris knew that. And things had gotten worse when they moved to Inlet House. The college had been willing to rent them the place, even though they were both new on the faculty, simply because it was the least desirable, the most distant from the campus, of all Cordelia's faculty dwellings. It wasn't a particularly pleasant house, a large frame box of no nameable style, the nearest neighbor being the former boat-repair shed, currently a bicycle shop. Trolley tracks ran three blocks away along Gorman Avenue, but there weren't any trolleys anymore. At night, across the neck of the inlet, Arthur and Doris would look out their screened bedroom window at seven storage tanks of the Mobilgas Corporation, like canned goods in a huge, dark cupboard. A lonely situation. At first Arthur had agreed that it would be a good idea to get a little distance between him and the campus, for the sake of the work on his dissertation. But he was uneasy. The house disturbed him. When he and Doris spent all of a Saturday painting his study only to find the surface blistered the next day, he said he should have known. The driveway was a rutted sandy track where various mushrooms would appear, called by the first dew and discovered with a sinking heart when he rushed off at seven-forty for his eight o'clock class. Tiny umbrella mushrooms among the blades of saw-grass; furry shingles at the base of the one old pine on the property; and a peculiar, loathsome black fungus like small lumps of bituminous coal clustered in front of the garage. "It must be built on an old graveyard," he'd said, but Doris thought it was only the fertility of the subsoil.

She would ask other college people to dinner when he was willing to have them, studying him while he wasn't looking with the intensity of a fox at the edge of a clearing. She was getting terribly horny, but he didn't seem to notice. Or maybe he did, maybe that was the trouble. She was sure he was the most brilliant man in the world, but they hadn't made love for a month. Did he think she was another Miss Hendries? In any case, before last night she'd felt at a dead end with her marriage. If she were to strip naked and sneak upstairs to the study and sit gently on his lap while he was working and stick her tongue in his ear, he would most likely arch his long neck, rest his chin on her bare shoulder, and continue mournfully typing on *The Lay of Hildebrand* without realizing she was there.

But last night, thank God, a little something had happened. Last night he'd agreed to cook out for the first time since the weather had turned warmer, just the two of them, sitting on the rocks above the inlet. When it was fully dark they went in, but it was a windy night; she climbed upstairs where he was working and said she was frightened, the house was groaning so. He came down. They sat together in the dark and the wind howled. It might have been an accident, but his lips brushed her hair. And then, just as he'd done that, at that very moment, came a thump.

A thump. A single, giant heartbeat. To Arthur it had sounded as if the last judgment were being announced. He sat rigid. After a moment it came again, a dull sound, like a padded hammer striking an empty tank; a strange assertive resonance among the Lilliputian agonies of disgruntled pipes and floorboards. "Where are you going?" Doris whispered. "Arthur, please, if it's a burglar you're supposed to leave him be, it says so in the college housing regulations!" But Arthur gave a grunt and darted into the next room. She followed, clutching her polka-dot wrapper at the neck. She'd noticed the thump at intervals before, it was something in the basement, a pipe or a loose board that the wind manipulated—she'd never given it any thought. But now he had made it seem frightening. In the dark he bumped his shin against the dining table and jumped on one foot, trying not to cry out. "What *is* it?" she whispered. "What are you *doing*?"

The thump. Like a muffled gong. All Arthur could think of was how bad the news had been in the paper that morning. And in two days the income tax was due. He found a flashlight and they inched through the kitchen, the beam of light dipping into the shelves of the cupboard, moving across the refrigerator, the electric range, the pegboard phalanx of pots and pans. Outside it had begun to rain, and the sound of the April wind had lessened. Within, all was still. Arthur opened the door to the narrow basement staircase. "I'll be damned if I'll go down there," he whispered. She stood behind him as the flashlight fingered the stairway reaching below. It had been a full minute since they'd heard the thump. "Why are we whispering?" she said. "Why are we standing here in the dark?"

"Sssh," said Arthur, "I'm waiting for it."

But she went quickly through the sparsely furnished rooms turning on lamps and ceiling lights. Arthur sat at the kitchen table. The tic was going at his jaw. "Arthur," she said, "you can turn off the flashlight. Look, it's raining. Should we have something to eat?"

"Did it stop thumping as soon as the rain started?"

"I didn't notice. Want some scuttled eggs?"

"I think that's when it stopped, just as the rain started."

"And it started just when there was a gust of wind. It was the wind! Come on, Arthur, don't be so nervous, really. Are you distressed about old Hildebrand again? You've been looking a little . . ."

"No," he said.

"Is it something you want to talk about?"

"No. I mean, of course. Sure, it's my thesis. It's everything. But it's not that."

"Then come toast some bread for me," she said. "This is just a spooky old place, that's all. It may be mice. Don't they bang into things? A couple of times I was down there getting something out of the locker and I found those little pellety things."

"Droppings?"

"Yes. The mice could be thumping into the water tank."

"Taking flying leaps?"

"Why not? Maybe that's what they do for exercise."

Doris stirred eggs in a pan. "It was the Organization," Arthur said.

"Or Miss Visniac! Come on, Arthur, don't be so morbid." She couldn't stand it when he got started on his *Organization* tack. There was a pregnant pause. "What you need is some family

54

indecent gestures when Arthur prowled the blackboard
his back to the audience. And then the buzz-saws had
d. They were tearing down the trees to make an asphalt
ng space for student automobiles, nothing could be heard in
assroom but the roaring vibration of the machines and
girlish laughter as Arthur stared threateningly at the
ws, grinned at the students, tried to carry on, gave a long-
shrug at last and dismissed them, leaning against the
oard to get out of the way as they rushed out to watch the
ome down, with his young wife alone at the back of the
staring wordlessly at him across the expanse of empty

ten," said Arthur, "I revised sixty pages of my thesis last
and they disappeared. No, that's all right, I found them.
here? Where do you think I found them? In the john. In
n wastebasket. I swear to God!"

ll, sometimes a person just absent-mindedly—"
d those noises last night. Why did the thump stop just
he rain began? It's not funny, it really isn't. You think
zy, I can tell."

illed his coffee cup. "I think you need to have a long talk
ur loving wife," she said. "Tell me about the Organiza-
hat's it trying to accomplish?"

e in silence. They could hear the lapping of waves on the
It's not that I really think there is an Organization,
you know it's a joke. A metaphysical joke. But the
t things do happen to me. Everybody hates me at the
why is that? And we . . . we haven't . . ."
just don't appreciate you. None of them."

think so?"

odded briskly. "And you're just trying too hard, Arthur
andards are too high, you've got to relax, you take lif
was just a continuing disaster. And another thing, yo
any exercise. You should do some sit-ups and so o
orning like I do. Some push-ups."

ou're interested in physical education."

life," she announced firmly. "Would you please stop holding
that bread and put it in the toaster?"

Later it stopped raining. Arthur was settling down to sleep; an
airliner passed above the house on its way to a safe landing at
Shannon, Ireland, and as the hum of the plane dimmed, as he
switched off his reading light at last, rolled over, grasped his
pillow, he seemed to hear the distant, tinkling music of the
spheres. Doris had told him she was going to bring him breakfast in bed. There had been sighs and kisses after the scuttled
eggs. His head hummed. The world refused to be logical, that
was the trouble. People were so incalculable. And he was practically thirty years old. The whole setup was crazy, you started
off wanting to do good and you wound up just nursing your
wounds. Maybe he didn't have enough stimulation in his life. He
felt the slow vibration of Wagnerian chords bearing him off
toward sleep. It was the Wedding March from *Lohengrin*. It
seemed to be coming from below, a notch louder now, as if
someone had touched the volume knob with a cautious finger.

Had she left the radio on?

He nudged her. "Did you leave the radio on?" And as if in
answer the sound of the music seemed to rise in a quavering
vibrato, and then voices joined in, dimly, with excruciating
slowness, a quartet, a chorus . . .

"Are you doing that?" he shouted. She came awake with a
start.

"Doing what? Are you going out of your mind? Doing what,
Arthur?"

"Don't you hear anything?"

"What?"

"Music. The Wedding March."

"Go to sleep, baby. It must be somebody's hi-fi."

"Yes." He felt immediately easier. Then he was up, sitting in
bed. "*Whose* hi-fi? There isn't a house . . ."

There wasn't a house for a quarter of a mile in any direction.

The music rose waveringly, as if produced by a weary organ-
grinder.

"I'm having hallucinations," he said. He strained every faculty to make out the music, which was fading; he half expected it to be followed by a chilling announcement. *Your attention please. We are about to have an atomic disaster.*

"You know what I think?" said Doris. "The refrigerator or something is attracting radio signals. That happens, Arthur, it's not so unusual." The sound of the music stopped entirely. "But if you're frightened, I'll just cuddle up closer. If you promise to be good." How could she chuckle at such a moment?

"No, no," he said. "I mean, it's gone, it's quiet now, I'll be all right."

"I'd be glad to . . ."

"No, no, go to sleep, Doris. You need your sleep."

"It's all my fault. If I hadn't gotten you started with the noise in the basement . . ."

"No trouble," said Arthur, "don't you worry. Wake me if anything else makes noise."

"I will, Arthur. I'm so glad you're right here beside me. Give me a goodnight kiss?"

He puckered his lips, feeling absolutely ridiculous, and she pressed her mouth on his. Then he settled again. But he couldn't doze off. He read *The Portable St. Augustine* until 4 A.M. and just as he lost consciousness he heard—on which side of the threshold of sleep who can tell?—a thump, as of a muffled gong.

He wished he could feel something for her. There she was, warm beside him in the bed. He was getting middle-aged. Maybe he should think about divorce? What else was he going to do with the rest of his life?

And then he was awake, the sun was shining, seagulls cawed, and shortly Doris appeared, fresh and bustling, bearing sausages and eggs and toast and coffee. "Wasn't that weird last night?" She rested her hand for a moment on his shoulder. She was very cheerful, she smiled as he ate. But he ate sullenly. "I hate this house," he said. "And the college, what am I doing at this crazy college? I don't know what's happening to me, I can't think

56

straight anymore. Maybe I'm getting pa
that somehow everything is out to get
mean? Do you ever have the feeling t
some kind . . . ?"

"No. Don't talk like that, Arthur."

"Maybe I should see the college anal
"Don't be silly."

He ate for a while. "Why do you su
sure I'd eat lilies of the valley? I mean

And then: "Did you ever notice th
movies people come in as soon as I sit
as eight people come and sit behind m
all the way through? Haven't you n
each other what's going to happen ne
picture."

"I don't understand," said Doris. "
"The Organization," Arthur said.
all of a sudden they start sawing d
God's truth, don't you remember?"
the one time she'd visited Arthur's
row. What was he teaching? It w
dreamy faced, looking more undern
in his corduroy jacket, tilting his
along, stopping to consider a faked-
girls, gazing out the window, pursi
a great deal on the rhythm of the sy
if you could read the sentence alou
tion as you go along? Let's get the
People, would you simmer down
posed a very interesting question a
his semicolon here. People. Class
encouragingly. The class, the peopl
it was just before the mid-semeste
busy drawing doodles in the mar
others were whispering, chewing
one of them, unconscious of Dor

57

"Everybody's physical," she said. "You've got a body. People who won't exercise just make me furious!"

"Oh my God," Arthur said, leaping up, "what time is it?"

"Just about ten. Where are you going?" He'd jumped out of bed, but at her question he stopped in his tracks. "I have no idea," he said. "No idea whatsoever."

"You wish you hadn't married me, don't you? Don't you? Yes you do. Yes you do, only you won't admit it." She sat down on the bed, in tears. Arthur stood with his arms akimbo as if his engines had stopped just at the point of take-off. And a hundred and eighty-seven miles to the north, Harry Zissel, riding along in the back of a station wagon otherwise occupied by five insurance agents on their way to a convention in Atlantic City, gazed happily out the window. The insurance agents are in mufti; from merely looking at them you would have no way of determining their occupation, or the fact that they each expect to be sleeping with a young woman not their wedded mate by midnight. The driver, a sprightly middle-aged man named George Gans who will not appear again in this narrative, is telling his friends a joke, a joke concerning a man who wandered until he was very old seeking an oracle to reveal the secret of life. When he found the oracle at long last he was told flatly that life was meaningless. "Life is meaningless?" cried the old man. "It *isn't* meaningless?" inquired the oracle.

And off to the west by a considerable amount, in San Mateo, California, where it is much earlier, not yet dawn in fact, a distant tugboat sounds its hooter, and considerable numbers of young people of both sexes lying awake and full of desire in San Mateo are moved to a terrible nostalgia for places where they have never been, stirred and saddened and even frightened, thinking of the sheer physical size, the sheer extent and mass and specific gravity of the nation, spreading away through dark miles under the stars.

SIX

Harry's favorite fantasy has as its theme *starting afresh;* all his clothes and possessions are burned up in a fire, and carrying the insurance money in his hand he goes naked into a high-class haberdashery and begins from the skin out, twelve pairs of underwear, eight or nine of slacks, two dozen Brooks Brothers shirts, a new watch, a new wallet, a new name, address, family, century. He'd emerge from that shop into a cool, green season, wearing a white suit, black shoes, black belt and watchband, lighting up a cheroot, letting the blue smoke rise, contemplating his work and finding it good, strolling off down deserted paths flicking the ash from his cheroot and nodding encouragingly to the beasts of the field and the birds of the air, to the grass and the ants and the trees. And where would the other people be? Nowhere. Burned up in the fire. And he'd take his time, too, filling the vacancy.

So all morning he amused himself, as he whizzed along from highway to highway, by picking out his underwear, his suits, his watchband, spending the first few rides in a mindless enjoyment of the unseasonably warm weather, the hitchhiking bringing on the glow of recaptured youth, infinite possibility, brushing through the roadside weeds, picking up the tang of auto exhaust, the sun soaking its way into his limbs as the big semi-trailers thundered by and he moved a short way down the shoulder where the chances for a lift might be better.

But by three o'clock he was stuck in Cordelia, New Jersey, and by just-before-five he was still there, hot and angry, sitting on the curb at the intersection of Main (US 19) and Cross (N. J. 320), getting less hopeful by the minute. What was he doing in New Jersey? He was waiting, waiting for a ride, waiting for someone or something to move him on. And no one would give him a lift. He'd be discovered when they excavated the place in the twenty-fifth century, still with his elbows on his knees and his chin in his hands. That would pose a problem for the archaeologists: what was this member of a distant tribe doing in a town like Cordelia, New Jersey, five miles from the beach? His voice said to him, *Zissel, take up your Danish and walk.*

Where? he said. Which way?

The voice shrugged, and Harry sat, exhausted, glum. There was no future in hitchhiking. And what if Miriam did something violent to herself when she found him gone?

What could she do?

Plenty, he replied. She could throw herself down the stairs to bring on a miscarriage, for example.

Miriam?

Well, she gets hysterical, doesn't she?

Then phone up, check if she's all right.

She's at work till 8 P.M. Besides, I'm running out on her.

But you want to make sure there are no hard feelings.

Right.

And that she's okay.

Exactly.

So phone her at work.

No, she'd hang up.

Why should she hang up? Maybe her period started. All you have to do is explain you're worried about her.

Long silence.

Okay, so don't phone, said the voice. *Do what you want.*

61

Maybe I should, said Harry.

But he sat, gazing at the telephone company building on the opposite corner. What was there to explain, that he was stuck in New Jersey? What kind of explanation was that? There wasn't any use calling her unless he had something to say, and all he could think of as a subject for conversation was the fact that he couldn't get a ride and didn't want to wind up living like cousin Sheila, telling children to drink their milk to the bottom. Was Miriam likely to be sympathetic? Probably not.

And if he got a ride, what good would that do?

He thought of going across country to see his brother, but he already knew what sort of advice Gordon would offer him. Gordon would say that he should give up smoking, go back to Connecticut, marry Miriam, return to school and study something practical, work at night, join the P. T. A. It would all be as simple and as endless as that.

No, Gordon couldn't do him any good, not unless he was ready to give up altogether. If he were ready for the sort of advice Gordon dished out, would he be where he was, stuck at the corner of Main and Cross? What he needed was a ride, a change of scenery. If someone would only pick him up he might think of where he wanted to go as he moved along. Maybe he should make himself one of those signs people hold up when they're hitchhiking? His could read ANYWHERE. But his heart isn't in it. Even his interior dialogue seems to be coming to a halt. Poor Harry, he's down to his last Danish and he's losing his sense of humor and it's not so funny, he's been in Cordelia for hours, it's a very serious frustration, as five o'clock approaches he's hundreds of miles from where he might have expected to be at such an hour, and who knows how many miles from any place he'll rest easy in, and nobody will give him a lift. He has no real sense of where he wants to go, and no idea that he'll be running into Arthur Thompson again in exactly seventeen minutes from now. All he knows for sure is that he could continue hitchhiking forever, moving around and around the board in short spurts or long like a counter in *Monopoly:* "Advance to

GO. Collect two hundred dollars." That was always such a nice moment, when you got the two hundred dollars. But then on your next turn you'd land on Oriental Avenue and somebody would have three houses there and that would cost you $270. He remembered all the prices in the Monopoly game. Boardwalk cost the most and then nobody ever landed on it. His favorite was the Short Line Railroad. He loved that game—it allowed him to be whimsical about money, and he badly needed such an outlet, because sooner or later every image in his head revealed the fact that it really had a frame around it, sometimes way off at the edges but always there, a frame composed of dollar signs. There was a money-price on everything these days; even Miriam was set off for him that way: he could never quite forget that she was paying the rent, and what kind of a thing was that for a potential novelist or playwright or sculptor or film-maker or whatever to be thinking about? Well, it was a funny family he came from—money was the only thing they thought was real. It was like each little dollar became a pat on the head from God. Everybody wanted praise most of all, but since there wasn't going to be enough to go around, God invented money instead. It seemed to Harry that the tone of his whole life came out of the way the adults talked when he and his brother Gordon listened at the top of the stairs after bedtime. Formed for life by other people's conversation. And it wasn't just the family, it was everybody, everywhere, money was the element you lived in, you took it into your lungs instead of air. If he were running things it wouldn't work that way, he'd give everybody a clean, fresh start at the age of twenty-two. How come Gordon didn't find it depressing, living for the daily drip of coin? Gordon, in the one letter he'd ever written to Harry, claimed to be happy as a chiropractor; married, two children, straightening the broken backs of the movie stars. But money *was* depressing, it made Harry sick to think of his father spending fourteen hours a day in that store for twenty years, toward the end losing even the impulse to smile or look a customer in the eye. And yet there was Gordon, virtue running down his back like an iron rod,

63

absolutely humorless, counting up the coin, the little pats on the head. He and Gordon had started off the same way, how come they'd turned out so differently, both originating in the standard Jewish homestead, playing touch football on Nevada Street, studying the violin with a lesson every Saturday morning at the Howard Building in Rockville Center and a brownie with ice cream and fudge sauce for lunch at Sadler's if their mother wasn't along to rule that out? Harry had branched off, gone to the university on a scholarship, forcibly exchanged that for the army, and now, for almost a year, in a sort of daze, doing this and that, back at school, no work getting done, a few women mixed in here and there and the enthusiasm thinning and the confusion pounding about his head, until he'd come to feel that though he was marked forever by his origins, he had no apparent source or direction; that somebody had raised him in a window box and then quit watering, and there he was, still rooted, drying out, with his voice saying *So become a chiropractor. Join a movement. Be an artist.—Only let's cut down on all this complaining.*

He thought about himself, which kept him from thinking about Miriam. The closest he could come to understanding his persistence as halfhearted pariah, gray sheep, convention-bound outsider, was to note that gradually you got hooked, that having fiddled around with a lot of romantic schmaltz in high school he'd more or less taken the bait, which in his case was a grotesque admiration for Rimbaud, Thomas Wolfe, Hemingway. Taking the bait, not even noticing at first that the hook was gaining a tighter and tighter grip on the resisting jaw, hoping like crazy that whatever did the fishing would keep on pulling. And then to find that the line had gone slack, that nothing was scooping him up, that all he could do, the hook still being there, was to swim, trying to get somebody's attention, flipping up out of the water, making a splash, swishing the tail and so on, anything to win back that tug again, to be landed, to be a *writer,* a *painter,* an *intellectual,* a *student,* a *pot-head,* anything, anything but a chiropractor counting the children, the movie stars, the coin. He remembered some of his writing buddies that first year at the university, how they used to worry about the "selling-out" problem, very idealistic. He'd already discovered by then that selling-out wasn't the problem at all, not for him, because there were no takers. And the grand alternative, eventually, seemed to be Gevner's Armored Cloud, Marriage and the Family—that was the only thing you were reasonably certain to find a market for. He could tell those old creative-writing buddies something, that the problem wasn't selling-out, it was buying-in. When the university took away his scholarship over the radio business he told his mother she'd had a bad break, that sometimes a man goes crazy, only not quite crazy enough, and then you just have to forget about him, write him off. He was a disappointment to his mother; for the life of her she couldn't understand why he refused to be the president of U. S. Steel. She knew he had a calling for it, so the reason he wouldn't answer must have been pure spite. And his father had never said a word. His father had merely sighed. Harry thought of him as he sat on the curb in Cordelia, thought of his father's calloused hands, of the neatly sewed-up rip at the shoulder of the orange and yellow striped robe his father had worn to the beach sometimes on summer Sundays. Izzy Zissel had been a sad, stoical, meticulous man; if he'd had literary leanings like his younger son he would have translated Horatio Alger into Yiddish, only with unhappy endings. A slow-moving, unillusioned character; Harry had looked at his closed face in the coffin a year ago and seen for the first time a beauty there, a dignity in the wide brow and heavy chin that he had never recognized in life. His father had always worn a brown felt hat at work, dragging sacks of potatoes from the rear of the store or standing absorbed at the counter that slanted down into the front window, carefully brushing the fuzz off the peaches with his nicotine-stained fingers. In his coffin his head had been as bare and round as a stone. He seemed so pleased to be there at last, his hands folded on his stomach, his best suit on. A place for everything and everything in its place. Outside the store when Harry was a child a row of upside-down baskets on the sidewalk against the front window formed the base for a counter made out of the tops of orange crates; a scale was hung from the awning pole, and here in warm weather beans and peas, rectangular boxes of Concord grapes, pears done up in groups of fives or sevens with tissue wrappings tucked into the crevices, kale and dates and mushrooms were sold. Certain fruits and vegetables had no place on this counter. It wasn't only the expensive items that went outdoors; the kale, no more than nineteen cents a pound even during the shortages of the 40's, held a choice position next to the entrance. Plums and blood oranges and grapes might be placed outdoors, but never peaches or cherries. They were in the front window. Or cucumbers. The cucumbers were set out next to the spinach in the back. When he and Gordon used to come down to help out in the store early on Saturday mornings, they were always taking the wrong things outside. All his life Izzy Zissel had been very strict about the cucumbers. They went in the back. Next to the spinach. *How* could he have hated such a man? It was inconceivable, but for years he had hated him. For what? For doggedly earning a living? For working without complaint, going on year after year dragging sacks of potatoes? At the cemetery they had all plucked grass to throw on the mound of the grave, and back home, before going up to the living room above the store where a caterer had set out food and whiskey and all the mirrors were draped with pieces of sheeting, they had ritually washed their hands with water from a milk bottle, and his mother, her eyes still red from weeping, was already worried about the caterer's bill.

I could die right here on this corner, he said to his voice. I really could. And who would notice? What possible difference could it make?

Everybody's got troubles, the voice replied.

Poor Harry. He doesn't remember this, but once when he was four years old, on a particular Sunday afternoon deep in childhood when the entire family was in residence for the weekend at a summer house in Atlantic City, he came down to the living room after his nap, rubbing his hair, his dark eyes standing round and at attention. He'd wandered into the empty living room with its scattering of sand on the hemp rug, still feeling a bit starched from the long morning on the beach, and there were the adults at the dining-room table drinking coffee, a visitor, a distant lawyer cousin who was reputedly a millionaire telling them a story, an endless story, a millionaire's story, and all of them, Flora, Raymond, Izzy, all of them dying with the tedium, looking forward to the laugh, urging on the punch line with every muscle. Struck by that polite, tense silence at the table, made uneasy by that unaccountable tableau, not seeing the story-teller himself and wondering if they were all hypnotized, he'd switched on the radio, a battered Philco upright, and with the click of the knob the lawyer happened to come to the end, happened to be saying: "I told him I *liked* his wife all right, but the bar association just didn't allow that kind of payment!" And they all laughed, naturally—a four-year-old boy, how would he know what makes them laugh? He immediately figured it was somehow or other his turning on of the radio knob that had done it. So what did he do then? He was all smiles to see them go on like that, and when they toned down he proceeded, like a workman, like a scholar, to turn *off* the radio, which was still warming up, and approach it again in exactly the same way. Who could tell which gesture had done the trick? Did they laugh at the hunching of the shoulders? the scuffing of the feet? the hesitation at the last instant, hand already reaching for the knob? He put them all in again. He hunched, scuffed, hesitated —clicked, and in the dining room there was silence. Nothing. If any of them had even seen him, what was so funny about turning on a radio? Another child might have blushed, might have giggled, getting the point, letting it go. But not Harry. Ah, Harry, switching off the Philco once more; meticulously, slowly, twitching the shoulder just so, scuffing the feet, calculating the exact instant of hesitation, cold-faced and already a little sick in the stomach from the failure of cause and effect, twisting that humorless knob again and again!

I could just die, he said to the voice.

They'd walk around you crossing Main Street.

67

Right. And then on Monday when the street cleaner came along, he'd shovel me up on the end of his shovel, which wouldn't be much of a job.

Because by then you'd be shriveled up like a gourd.

Exactly! That's it. Light as a gourd, or an empty beer can.

So he could lift you up just on the end of the shovel, using the other hand for the broom, you see.

Right! It would be early in the morning. He'd light his cheroot. There wouldn't be any traffic to speak of, it would be nice and quiet and he'd appreciate the fact that there was something a little unusual to pick up.

Maybe he'd take it home and show his wife.

Sure. That's good. Keep that in. It wouldn't be the first time somebody dried up in this town, but still—

Still, it would be something. It would make his day.

It is just before five, and as we see, he's feeling uncharacteristically low. Among other things, he may break the world's free-style record for not getting a lift on a major highway. Records are made that way, by people persisting without any particular purpose, without even realizing they were in competition. Two and a half hours ago a kindly Oldsmobile had plopped him off at an Esso station at the northern edge of town, and he had stood there for fifteen minutes. Then he'd begun to walk, gradually slogging to the center of the business section and setting up shop permanently at the traffic light across from the telephone company. By now, if a public-spirited iconoclast ever tore that building down with his bare hands, Harry could restore it from memory, pilaster by pilaster.

But he hadn't been depressed at first. At first he had worked at hitchhiking like a professional entertainer. Sometimes the light would catch several cars and he'd go back from driver to driver goosing the air with his thumb, smiling at them, speaking through an open window. And either they'd look straight ahead, contemplating the remains of a squashed insect on the windshield, or else they'd shake their heads or gaze right through him at the bedpan display in the window of McCarty's Rexall Drug —he went in there at one point for a lousy milkshake—or some

68

would stick up a single finger (what did that mean?), or point in the opposite direction—and pretty soon the sun had started to weaken and the spring day was cooling and he was disgusted. For a while he smoked a cigarette and ignored the traffic. He studied the telephone building, its fake marble pilasters and its Renaissance windows and the gargoyles on the roof. Town cars kept pulling around the corner into the parking lot. People were shopping everywhere, so many darting in and out of the drugstore you'd think McCarty was running a special on contraceptives instead of bedpans. The drugstore window was filled with instruments of suffering. There was a wheel chair with a pair of crutches leaning against it at the back of the display. A sign read—it actually did—WHEN THERE'S AN INVALID IN THE HOUSE, MAKE HIM COMFORTABLE. The drugstore smelled of comic books and spilled syrup. They served up coffee in pink plastic mugs, and at the back of the window display, under the sign, he saw a list of charges which he copied down on a napkin, thinking he might be able to slip it into his play or his novel or a short story somewhere. Maybe even a poem. It already looked like a poem.

RENTAL RATES

Deluxe Model Wheel Chair	$15/mo.
Reg. " " "	10
Children's " "	8
Walkers	7
Walkerettes	5
Hospital Beds	10
" " w/sides	15
Crutches (Aluminum)	3
" (Wooden)	2
Canes	1

Commodes and Mattresses Cannot Be Rented

Morbid. What is it with him? Why can't he be like everybody else and stop moaning and trying everything at once and get down to some useful work, resist ruining everything, wise up and be cool and make hay? Why can't he marry a nice girl and go off to the Greek Islands? or take up parachute jumping? or write his short story or his novel or whatever. Or be a bum? A hipster? Something! *It's a question,* his voice would say. *I could offer theories if I wanted to; I know a great deal about the case.* But then it begs off. *Listen, am I an expert in social diseases?*

In Harry's condition there's little room except for hope, and so he continues to hope. In other words, he's normal, like anyone else. During the year he lived with Arthur Thompson he remembered one discussion when he was terribly depressed. He had just finished a long popular novel about the Arab-Israeli war that Arthur had warned him was junk. But the book hadn't upset him in his aesthetics—he didn't read books for that—it had made him feel terrible specifically because even the least sympathetic character, an American doctor, a kind of sex maniac who was ruining the kibbutz, even this doctor in the long run turned out to have more courage than Harry could find in himself. As a touchstone for his emotions in those days he would sometimes imagine dying for a girl who didn't care for him. He'd go over all the girls in his art history class, the Jewish girls and the Gentiles, the five Negro girls and the three Puerto Ricans, sick with lust for all of them as he held off the enemy with an old-fashioned machine gun and the girls escaped in a helicopter, one by one, without a word of thanks. Sick. Sentimental. But at least at that point he'd wanted to accomplish something, if only to impress all those girls. Arthur had told him, full of enthusiasm, that he was beginning to understand original sin, and besides it really *was* a lousy novel.

"So if you understand original sin, what can you do about it?" Harry wanted to know.

"Nothing!" Arthur had laughed. "That's what we call the human condition."

"Some condition."

"Well, I didn't make it up, did I?"

"Things might have been better organized."

"Okay, give it a try, get yourself some firmament and a little protoplasm and see what you can do."

"Yes," said Harry, "I see what you mean. Religion, that's one answer, I guess."

Arthur said it was better to settle for knowledge. That was humanism. In exchange for suffering you learned a little about why you suffered.

But it sounded somehow like religion to Harry, and it made no sense to his emotions, because he was planning to conquer himself at that point, he was going to make his life come straight like a rider rearing with a tightened grip on the reins. The books he read in the freshman year convinced him that man was a creature meant to fly magnificently right into the sun. But at the same time as he was finishing Arthur's *Don Quixote,* weeping, literally, over the beauty and sadness of the Don's aspiration and the brutality of the world—at the same time he was also dipping into a paperback called *Chalk Up Your First Million!,* because he'd be damned if he was going to have to work like a horse for the rest of his life. He threw away *Chalk Up Your First Million!* at the end of *Don Quixote,* but then he fished it out of the bin again before the trashmen came.

It's a hard case. And is he getting sad! All these energetic New Jersey people are passing him and none of them will even give him a nod. Nobody stops. Nobody looks or listens. Harry sags on the curb like a frog in an experiment; Haly's experiment, in which the frog's spinal cord is severed at the neck and it is demonstrated that the reflexes continue even so, an electric shock making the leg kick. Dr. Gobine, who taught Harry freshman psychology, still concludes in a sepulchral voice when he does this demonstration from Royal Society days for his first year kids: "So *can* we say when life ends?" And why is it that New Jersey should break Harry's spirit so, sever his emotional spinal cord? Why does the ride seem to end, or perhaps—as Gobine would say—maybe not end, in Cordelia? Cordelia doesn't seem to want him to pass through. Is he supposed to settle down and open a fruit store? To Harry it seems the town wants to teach him a lesson, which is that he is not there. His thumb, before he became morose, was going a mile an hour trying to communicate with the drivers of Cordelia. But no soap. And maybe it's true. Maybe he isn't there. A whistle blows, and then another, off in the distance. Five o'clock. He sits on the curb at dog level, and a young pregnant housewife stands right next to him talking to another one, all bundles, going back to their cars, waiting for the WALK sign, and he looks up and takes in their nice long legs. He and they are living on two different planes of existence, like in a novel he'd read the first chapter of once where there was a city of the dead and a city of the living, both going along at the same time, both the same city, but the ones who were alive couldn't see the dead ones and vice versa. In Cordelia their main street was his highway, and he could have the highway, they'd take the street and the Safeway Supermarket and the U.S. Post Office and a walk on the Boardwalk and a Coke in McCarty's and the hell with him. Outside the bus station up the street an old man was washing his cab, pottering around the gleaming old Buick with his hose. And on the quiet, tree-shaded streets away from the shopping section Harry imagined a few kids slowly riding their bikes and talking, and everything looking so clean, so peaceful and orderly. Nearby would be a golf course, and beyond it some woodland where paths would weave toward municipal fireplaces, to which fathers would come at the end of the day with their families, with their dogs and picnic things, throwing the babies up in the air. He saw a series of Norman Rockwell covers from *The Saturday Evening Post,* scenes of resort-town humor, well-groomed settings with happy, tanned, sly-witted, easygoing citizens, pleased or exasperated, coming to life in his mind, becoming solid, four-dimensional. And yet, was Cordelia real? Was it more than a mock-up composition-board Hollywood back-lot model of a town? If he went behind the facades, would he find that the houses were solid after all? Would he find a Harry Zissel there in a junk-strewn yard, crouched up in the fetal position?

A teenage girl passed him on the sidewalk, wheeling a baby. A baby-sitter? An older sister? She smiled at him—amazing! She was humming to herself and he realized as she went down a leafy side street that he'd picked up the song, a hymn that had come, perhaps, from last night's prayer meeting at the Baptist Church. *What a friend we have in Jesus, all our grief and sin to bear.*

Which were the living? Which were the dead?

He saw the baby-sitter or the older sister, back home, sitting on the porch, rocking in a glider; the lawn sprinklers would be on and the husbands would be coming home with their evening papers and an ache started in him that became a dryness of throat and tongue and a pounding of the temples. He felt dizzy, dizzy with longing; and at the same time he wanted to run.

Which were the living?

It's a question, said the voice.

And then, all at once, the girls began to descend from the telephone company building. They poured out the double doors and floated down the five wide steps in platoons, in flurries, dozens of them, gabbing and laughing and meeting and walking and waiting—a burst of girls, an explosion of girls, all of them so confident, so sure that the land of the living was really out there as they came through the doors. It was as if they'd been tossed like confetti, scattered chattering or sulking, all in different-colored April dresses. He stood up for a better view. They were amazing; beautiful. The whole shift came out at once so that anyone who might be interested would know that Wednesday had come to an official end, that the telephone company was through with these females for a while, that they could go home and get dinner ready or wash their underwear or catch an early movie or worry about the erogenous-zone problem, or not worry about it, and suddenly Harry had an honest-to-God vision, he saw all these girls, some of them pretty and young and gentle, the kind who in the fall will wear cashmere sweaters with brown tweed skirts; and some of them all painted up with dyed hair, and one who had a walk like a flamingo and carried a long blue umbrella rolled up English-style—he saw all of them come in a rush of expectation to the doors of the telephone company building . . . to find that there was nothing outside. Nothing left.

73

Not a thing, not even the five steps they'd mounted when they'd come to work. It was all gone, the town of Cordelia, New Jersey, was gone, turned to a powder-blue void while all day long they were talking on the telephone!

The expressions on their faces! Like something out of Hogarth, every mouth at a different angle. Oh, the poor girls, they deserved better! All girls deserved better, all the girls everywhere. Harry wore an astounded smile. Maybe being stuck in Cordelia was a sign. Maybe it all meant something, winding up in Nowhere, Main and Cross, the bedpans in the drugstore window, the girls coming out like that, as if it had all been arranged. And crazy overdue Miriam, she might jump off a bridge just for the experience! But what could he tell her? He'd think of something. He'd make it up as he went along. They'd get married! Why not? What could they lose? And suddenly he felt a flood of energy: life was sweet! There was too much talk about love, not enough action. A little fan went on when he closed the door to the telephone booth in McCarty's, and he thought, wasn't that nice of them, to put in a little fan for the springtime? He set a handful of change on the shelf, scooting the pennies back in his pocket. "Beds-'n-Things, Operator. It's a furniture shop. Maybe it's listed under John Hughes, he's the owner."

"Did you say Hughes?"

"I did, my love."

"Hughes," said the operator. "I'll give you Information."

"That's very good of you," Harry said. "I love telephone operators."

But Miriam wasn't there.

She hadn't come in.

They hadn't seen her all afternoon.

"What do you mean, Johnny? Sure she's there, look around a little. Where else could she be?"

"She told me to tell you that, Harry," Johnny whispered. "She doesn't want to talk and she doesn't want to see you anymore. Where the hell are you?"

"In New Jersey."

74

"Really?"

"Listen, I'm coming back, John. Will you tell her?"

"It won't do any good, Harry. She said she's through with you. She's disgusted. She's moving out."

"But she can't! Put her on the phone, John, she can't be through, we're going to have a baby!"

"You bastard," said John, "did you knock her up?"

"That's an ugly expression," Harry said. "Besides, I want to get *married* now. Be a pal, Johnny, go tell her. Tell her I'm ready to get married, okay? Propose for me, will you?"

"I'll try, Harry. Hold on."

He held on. "Forty-five cents for the next three minutes, please." He bonged in two quarters and told the operator to keep the change.

Johnny came back. "I told Miriam you were ready to get married, Harry, but she said who asked you?"

"Oh God, it's worse than I thought."

"What are you doing in New Jersey?"

"Talking to you on the telephone."

"Boy, you sure did fuck up this time, didn't you?"

"Yeah."

"She says to tell you your name is Polonius. What does that mean?"

"It means I'm a rat."

"Well you are, aren't you? She sure doesn't like you anymore. She really hates your guts."

"Thanks, John."

"That's okay, Harry. Say, what's it like in New Jersey?"

"They're having a special on crutches and bedpans."

"Is that right? Will you be back in time for my party Friday? Say, how come Polonius means you're a rat?"

"It means anything you want it to, Johnny. It's a Persian word that means anything you feel like."

"Your time is up, sir. Will you signal when you're through?"

He was through. He was through all right.

"Well, Polonius, John."

"Polonius to you, Harry. Is she really pregnant? She doesn't look so good, I noticed. Should I tell the other girls in the shop you're ready to get married?"

"Thanks, John. Just tell them *Polonius,* will you?"

"Be glad to."

Harry cradled the phone. It rang violently and he paid for the overtime. But he didn't leave the booth. It struck him that he was always facing himself in enclosed, coffin-shaped spaces, in showers, in closets—what a way to live! But he felt safe there in the phone booth.

It seemed like a nice place to stay.

All he'd need would be curtains for the window, a few books, a hot plate—he could sleep sitting down.

Out in the drugstore a boy entered with a bundle of evening papers.

So now he was free, she'd let him off the hook. Thrown him off. Probably her period had started. In any case, he was a free man. And what was he going to do about it? What were you supposed to do after you finished running away?

Sitting in the phone booth he tried to start up the beginning-afresh fantasy, but it wasn't any good. What could he do with twelve pairs of underwear shorts when he didn't have any place to live? He could hardly expect Miriam to continue paying his rent if she never wanted to see him again.

It would be a good time to join the army. But he'd already done that.

He counted his money. Four dollars and eighteen cents. Ah me. He'd just stay on in the telephone booth, that's what he'd do. *At least you'll be cool with the fan,* his voice agreed. *Also, you won't have to put in a telephone.*

On the other hand, she really should marry him if she was going to be pregnant all the time. She really should, he should insist. But it would take so much emotional energy. It was so hard to do anything with women, you had to go at them with a bulldozer and even then they held solid. Mountains, that's what they were. You couldn't budge them an inch, and they wouldn't move on their own either. And then suddenly they'd go and do something absolutely insane. He got exhausted just thinking about it. Miriam. She was undoubtedly still overdue. It would be just like her to move out of the apartment at such a moment.

Exhausted, just thinking about it.

He sat in the narrow phone booth, the little fan droning on and on, playing *Perdito*. That memory was usually nicely repressed, he and Arthur Thompson up at dawn to broadcast *The Morning Watch. Perdito* for seventeen days straight on the campus station until they threw him out of school. Six in the morning, imagine! No wonder no one listened. In theory there were early risers out there, people with morning classes, farmboys from the midwest still hearing the sounds of cockcrow from the corn fields of their dreams. *The Morning Watch* was supposed to comfort earnest seekers stumbling toward books through the half-light; late bull sessions were supposed to pick up some Charlie Parker to counteract the apathy of morning, no solutions found; campus lovers were offered music with their instant coffee. But Harry had discovered what the campus really did in the early mornings, which was to sleep. Where desk lamps glowed behind a few windows on the small quad, where pages were turning on Eastern Avenue, where fingernails were being bitten, where typewriters trudged line by line across the endless white parade ground of a freshman theme, no radios sang. If a rich girl in a private room in Sandol Memorial Hall with a clock radio and a teddy bear and a framed photo of the family in sombreros from their Mexican trip, if such a girl happened to be awake at that hour doing her hair or her Plato, she'd tune in to a professional disk jockey from Hartford, not *The Morning Watch*. So it was a good program for a novice broadcaster: the audience small and sleepy, or nonexistent. Music from six to seven. "You may remember this little number," Harry would say again and again as the long-suffering Arthur at the controls behind the glass partition waited for his upheld arm to fall. "It's the same little number we just played. In fact, it's the same little number we've been sort of playing all semester, students. So phone in your complaints. Or requests. And now, Dizzy Gillespie and Per*dito!*"....

He'd light a cigarette and go round through the hall to the sound booth. "It's eerie, Thompson, it's like God brooding over the waters. There's not a human being out there."

"Minute to go. You'd better get back. You want me to play the same side again?"

"Damn right." He'd go through the hall to his microphone. "That was Ray Noble, mothers, with 'Alice Blue Gown.' We'd like to hear from you, you know? It's a request program. Like the philosopher said, if nobody sees the tree falling in the forest, it stands right back up again. So phone us at extension 473, okay? This is station WFUM, broadcasting from offices in the Student Union. The time now on *The Morning Watch* . . ."

"Who wants this job?" he would say. "It's absurd. We're tossing Perdito into the void. We have nothing to give the world but Perdito."

"How'd you introduce it this time? I had the ears off."

"Great—there goes the only audience I've got. I told them it was the Westminster Boy's Choir singing Molly Bloom's soliloquy. By God, I'm going to make those bastards say something. One mothering phone call, that's all I ask. Give me a listener and I'll break my balls for him. How much time do we have left?"

"Nineteen minutes."

"I'm going to give them a nineteen-minute commercial for atheism, how's that?"

"Been done."

"Sodomy? Inter-racial marriage?"

"Commonplace."

"Communism?"

"Now let's not run away with ourselves, Zissel. They'd pick that up all the way in New Haven with their radios off."

"They'd hear it through the bloodstream . . ."

"By ESP . . ."

"Dean Brady would be in here with a hydrogen bomb . . ."

"To eject this noisome pestilence."

"Who could blame him?"

"Abuse of the airlanes, eighty years in Sing Sing."

"Back to New York. Back to the ghetto."

"Damn right! How can our women be safe? How can we trust our drinking water?"

Back to the farm in Wisconsin. Back to Russia, noisome element."

"Back to the fruit store, by God. Thirty seconds. What's next?"

"Play it again. The Tokyo Samisan Quintet with their best-selling disko . . ."

"Perdito!"

So then, said the voice, *then there was the interview, right?*

"Look who's just wandered in, listeners! It's Dizzy Gillespie! What you doin' here man?" "Well man you know I mean I got me a big club date here in town . . ." "Right, Dizzy! Talk at the microphone and tell these college students what you think of them." "Oh, shit man, I can't do that." "Sure you can, Diz, come on now, speak right out, what do you think of all these mothers in the audience?" "Well man, you know, I mean like all these mothers is, they impress me like, well, I mean *shit,* man, we're on the *radio*" "That's all right, Diz—this is Dizzy Gillespie, listeners—now tell us, Diz, how do you feel about these deans and faculty and *that* jazz?" "Well now, Mr. Zissel, I'll tell you— I never seen a more thick-assed bunch of mammyjammers . . ."

And then the others started coming into the studio, said the voice. *Who did you say was there? I can never remember.....*

You played those parts, Harry said, how come you can't remember? Let's see, there was Einstein, I know that.

Thomas Mann. Samuel Gompers. Ella Wheeler Wilcox.

Right! Right! Oh, what those bastards were doing to Ella Wheeler Wilcox!

And then you finished up with Jesus.

Poor Jesus. That was going too far.

Oh, I don't know. You were pretty gentle with Jesus.

Maybe. Boy, those were the days, doing all the accents, all those guys in there arguing and Thompson rushing in to stop me when I started to do the fire engine at the same time. Gosh, I was a one-man fire! "The place is stifling with smoke. Listeners! Nothing will make us stop broadcasting! Phone in your comments: extension 473. Let's have your criticisms! This is a request program! The time now on *The Morning Watch* with the fire beginning to spread rapidly to the rest of the campus and down Eastern Avenue is 6:53. And now another word from Jesus . . ."

And nobody phoned in, that was the remarkable part. He was called before the Disciplinary Committee, he lost his scholarship, so somebody must have heard, but nobody phoned in. Nobody really noticed.

There was the one girl, his voice reminded him. *What did she say?*

Remembering the girl as he sat in the phone booth, remembering her serious face, the face of his audience, he began to laugh within. Because the girl had said . . . she'd said . . . "Don't you play *Perdito* an awful lot on that program of yours?"

But his smile quickly wanes again. He's getting lonely. *Perdito.* They wouldn't let him stay on in the phone booth; they'd kick him out sooner or later, he knew that, and he decided to go quietly. Don't shove, officer, he said to the voice. We support our local police. He plunged out into the world again, lifted his thumb, not even checking its direction, and there was Arthur Thompson in his '58 Chevy, caught at the red light, gazing at him with a look of horror through the fly-specked windshield. Coolly and without hesitation Harry opened the car door, settled himself, slammed the door shut. Thompson looked three hundred years old. The light changed. The car stalled. The drivers behind began to beep. "God, he was crazy, that Dizzy Gillespie," Harry said. "Completely out of his mind."

"Should I play it again?" said Arthur. "It's got a nice beat."

"Why not?" Harry said. "Sure, go ahead. *Perdito.* Our song." And then he grinned, shouted, punched Thompson on the arm.

"Isn't this a *son*-of-a-bitch! Where'd you *come* from, Thompson? Who sent you?"

"The Organization," Thompson said.

"Is that right? Well listen, you're not looking so good, do you know that? How come you stopped writing me letters? What the hell are you doing in Cordelia, New Jersey, Thompson?"

"Suffering."

"Of course. Say, you don't seem pleased to see me."

"I'm ecstatic," Thompson said. "My cup runneth over."

"That's more like it. Where are you taking me, anyway?"

"I don't know. Home to my wife for supper, I guess."

"You're *married?* Godalmighty, when did this happen? The last I heard . . ."

By the time they arrived at Inlet House Harry had heard more. But to him the wife seemed fine, a handsome Southern girl, and she put out lamb chops for supper. Harry explained that he was just wandering, it was Easter vacation, what a coincidence to run into Thompson, on and on in that vein, he couldn't bring himself to get started with the Miriam situation, it was too depressing, there'd be time for all that, he was going to spend the night. In fact, he began to think that he might just move in altogether, because Doris went off into town to get something special for his breakfast. She seemed excited that someone had arrived for Thompson to talk to; she followed their conversation back and forth across the dining table like a judge at a ping-pong match, smiling happily. But when by mistake Harry refused more coffee, she took his cup and as a matter of course carried it right to the sink, where she proceeded to wash it, dry it, hang in on its hook before returning to the table to listen to them recount old times, observing them in turn like a sparrowhawk. Harry was careful not to set his cigarette down, he feared that if he stopped smoking with clear visibility she would snuff out his butt, lift him, wash him, dry him, hook him up. An efficiency model. A wife. She probably didn't mean any harm, she was just automated, like Miriam's mother; each time a cup was rehung, a sentence spoken and bitten off at the end like a piece of thread, a day nicely packed away on the shelf of night, a pleased girl-scoutish grin would undoubtedly be seen to appear. She had a neat figure; her face was as heightened by color as a child's, or a child's doll. She had beautiful red hair and the few tiny freckles about her nose were appealing, and the bright grin. But what in the world was Arthur thinking of? Had he gone out of his mind? Why had he *married* her? She was running on tracks, you'd have to hold her upside down to make her blink!

He and Arthur talked on into the night, while Doris made up a couch for him in one of the upstairs rooms, made it up very nicely as a bed, the sheet drawn back, a towel and washcloth over the arm, apologizing that they didn't have anywhere near enough furniture yet to fill the house. The couch stood alone in the room, but there was an ashtray on the windowsill. He was tired, depressed by what he'd seen and heard of Thompson's homelife and all his strange teaching troubles. As if he didn't have enough worries of his own, now he had Thompson's to think about. He stripped to his undershorts, stretched out with a sigh, and immediately his mind returned to Miriam. Miriam. She was crazy. She couldn't be through with him—how would she feel when she was all big and pregnant and they clamped her in a Salvation Army nursing home and started singing hymns in her ear, or sent her back to Chicago to her mother, or threw stones at her on Beachum Street? Wasn't it against the law to get pregnant like that? She was only nineteen, a minor after all. But they'd throw *him* in jail, that's what they'd do, or make him give her so much a week to support the kid. How much? It couldn't be much, a kid doesn't eat anything.

And what about college? said the voice. *Do you have any idea how much it costs to put a kid through college these days?*

I'll train him. He'll win a scholarship.

Sure. Listen, you'd better not get involved with support payments, you know? It's easier to get married.

I'm willing! Didn't I tell her? Didn't I tell Johnny to propose to her for me? She wouldn't even talk on the phone!

82

Because her feelings are hurt. Listen, go back, show her you're
serious. You'd better get a job, that would impress her.

But my play! My statues! My construction! What about my
artistic career?

He was drifting off. Miriam. Mrs. Harry Zissel. Selling encyclopedias. Middle-age. It didn't bear thinking of.

A room full of screaming infants. Two rooms full, all girls.
Future telephone company girls. He began manfully making the
rounds, wiping noses, changing diapers, forcing them to eat their
carrots. Then he heard from somewhere in the bowels of the
house a strange noise, a thump: it sounded like a dinosaur giving
birth. He shrugged and settled deeper into sleep. His dreams will
be pornographic in part, but not really all that interesting, so let's
move ahead to Thursday morning and catch up with Arthur and
Doris. Doris is going to surprise Harry with lox and cream
cheese for breakfast, and everything will get a bit hectic and
complicated for a time, but for the moment Harry sleeps like a
fish at the bottom of a well. He really needs his rest, it's been an
exhausting day, hitchhiking from Fear of Reprisals, Conn. to
Cordelia, N. J.

Thump.

Double thump.

SEVEN

"This is great," said Harry, spearing a piece of lox and insinuating it around the cream-cheesed half of a bagel. "What a nice welcome! This sure must be an enlightened town!"

"It was entirely Doris's idea," said Arthur. "I don't believe in indulging you."

"Was it? Really? I love you, Doris. Divorce this jerk and let's get married."

Which achieved a smile out of her. He began to speak to Arthur about Miriam.

"You're smoking a lot," said Arthur. "You've already smoked four cigarettes this morning. Why don't you quit?"

"I did," said Harry, "I just tend to start up again when there's a crisis."

"Every day is a crisis."

"Exactly. So I'm smoking all the time."

"I suppose you think that's funny? Very funny. Don't you realize what smoking is? It's the death wish, ever think of that?" Arthur seemed even more grumpy this morning than he had last night, and ten times as bad as four years ago. Doris gazed at her husband. She'd seen *him* smoke at least ten cigarettes when he went down to search for the thump again in the small hours.

"Thank God for the death wish," Harry was saying. "How else could a man survive? The reach must exceed the grasp."

But Arthur continued grim. "Is that supposed to be funny too? Well it's not. It's not funny." He shook his head disgustedly. "You haven't changed a bit, Zissel. You always feel so sorry for yourself you can't *think*. The army didn't mature you at all."

Doris leaned forward at the table. She wished she had a friend like Harry; Arthur seemed to be building moral muscle right before her eyes. He was starting to look like a village elder. And Harry was smiling. "You two do each other a lot of good," she told them. "Oh, I knew he'd straighten me out," Harry said, "the minute I saw him. Good old Thompson! I'm going to settle here for the rest of the semester and hire him to holler at me every morning."

"Very funny. Who do you think you are, a character in a comic strip?"

"I'm the Dogpatch ham," said Harry. "You're Mutt and I'm Jeff." But he wished Doris wouldn't take away his coffee cup as soon as he set it down. "Of course, I'd rather be L'il Abner, like any normal American boy, only I've lost some of that innocence somewhere along the way. I'm not the same ambitious, studious fellow you used to know, Thompson. If I'm going to be in a comic strip I'd better settle for Charlie Brown, they tell me he's an anti-hero, an existentialist."

"Do you identify with Charlie Brown?" said Doris. "I think he's just—"

"Heaven forbid!" said Harry. "I wouldn't presume. I'm just a plain *non*-hero, humble as pie."

"Look," said Arthur, "let's stop all the quippery. What made you run out on this girl? Go on, give me the sordid details." He slumped down in his chair. "Farewell the quiet mind."

"Who would I be," said Doris. "In the comics?"

"I have no idea." Tillie the Toiler, Harry thought, but didn't say so. "Feel free," he told her, "how about Daisy Mae?"

85

"Oh good," Doris cried, "that's lovely."

"And Arthur here can be Mammy Yokum. Or Mary Worth's Family."

"What are you talking about?" Arthur inquired belligerently. "Do you always say the first thing that comes into your mind?"

Harry sighed. "I'm grateful when anything comes into my mind."

Doris looked at Harry closely. He seemed to be enjoying himself, but he wasn't really, she could see that now, it was Arthur who was getting a kick out of the conversation, and he looked as grim and as somber as a lamppost. Nobody in her family ever talked much at meals. In her family there were whole days when nobody said anything at all except please pass the sugar.

"Please pass the sugar," said Arthur. "Listen, if you just up and leave a girl without a word it's clear you don't give a damn about her, so what's all this marriage business? You don't want to marry what's-her-name any more than the man in the moon. No wonder she wouldn't talk to you on the phone. Think of the shape she'd be in if she *did* marry you!"

Harry thought of the shape she'd be in if she were truly pregnant. As soon as he got Arthur alone he'd have to tell him the whole depressing story. "Go on," he said, "bawl me out, I'm feeling better already."

"Sit up and *think*," said Arthur, "will you? Be sane for a minute and stop the joking and act your age. When you wrote me at Stanford you were going to be a sculptor, remember? What happened to that girl, the one you were sleeping with when you got out of the army? What was her name? Mary-Ellen Something. The one from West Virginia."

"Mary-Jean. Her name was Mary-Jean Howard. That wasn't anything serious, Arthur. She just slept with people to be friendly."

"Exactly!" Arthur shouted, and Doris's attention swept back to him like a ping-pong ball.

86

"Easy," said Harry.

"But that's the point. It's not that simple. As soon as you get bored, you take off. Who do you think you are, a tomcat?"

"Tomcats," said Harry. "What a life they lead!"

Doris laughed, looking rapidly from one to the other. She began to clear the table, taking up the dishes one by one, washing them, drying them, stacking them away without missing a word. "You're in fine form, Arthur," Harry said, "for a man who's going out of his mind." But Doris's laugh stuck in his side. What made her so feverish with enjoyment? She listened to them with the breathlessness of a Roman matron watching her first encounter between the Christians and the Lions. Who was this Doris, anyway? She reminded him of a happy power-room with a single janitor in attendance; she gave off the same kind of hum. Inside her he imagined all sorts of complicated machinery going without a hitch, absolutely spotless, lit by fluorescent tubes. Women.

"So there she is up there in that crummy apartment without a friend in the world," Arthur was saying. "I know that town—it's depressing. What if she does something to herself? You told me she's fascinated by suicides—don't you realize that *means* something? Have you thought about that? How come you *always* get involved with these neurotic women?"

Why was he so concerned? Harry wondered. What was eating old Arthur?

"She's all right, she's just pissed off," he said. "She'll be all right once I talk to her. Listen, Arthur, she's, let's see, fourteen days overdue, you follow me?"

"Oh God," said Arthur, "so that's it! And you say she's just pissed off! Nineteen years old, living with a man, he gets her pregnant, and one fine morning he just disappears—how would *you* feel? You may not take your own life seriously—"

"Could you, if you were me?"

"Of course not! But who makes it that way?"

"Me," said Harry. "Continue."

87

"Well, how would you feel?"

"If I were Miriam? And she called me up on the telephone from New Jersey? I really don't know. It wouldn't bother me. At least I'd *talk* to her."

"Have you ever been deserted?"

"All the time. But let's talk about something else for a while. This is getting kind of dreary."

"Listen," said Arthur, "what if she has a mental breakdown? These neurotic girls do that all the time when they get involved with sex and it doesn't work out. Have you ever thought about that? You may already have done her some permanent psychic damage. You can't just desert people!"

Who was he really preaching to—Doris?

"We must be boring your wife," Harry said.

"I'm not bored," said Doris. "Not at all. I'm fascinated."

"I'm sorry, Doris," Arthur said. "Here you made us a wonderful breakfast and we just—"

"I'm *fas*cinated," she said, and looking her full in the face Harry saw that she observed him with the expression of a person watching a horror movie, just at the point where the mad doctor is scrubbing up for one of his clever operations. But her little smile was there all the same. A silence fell at the table. Harry gazed at the shining rows of pots and pans hung with perfect symmetry on the length of red pegboard above Doris's stove.

"Well," he said, "I guess I'd better hit the road if I'm going to be in South America by bedtime."

"I envy you," Doris said, her eyes bright. "Nothing seems to bother you. It's your ethnic background, I suppose. It's just . . . so rich."

"Sure," said Harry. "Like humus. Great stuff for burials, ethnic backgrounds."

"But it's the way you talk. It's kind of an *atmosphere* you have. You'd envy it too if you'd grown up in Tennessee."

"They don't have atmosphere in Tennessee? It must be hard to breathe."

"Oh, is it," said Doris. "Is it ever!"

88

"You hear, Arthur? I don't appreciate. I come from so much Long Island ethnic background it could kill you, but I fail to appreciate."

"Very funny," Arthur said.

Doris told them she knew it must sound silly, but she loved the way they argued with each other.

"Love is cheap," Arthur blurted, and that really silenced her. She rose from the table and began returning things to the refrigerator.

"Why did you say that?" Harry asked. "What's *wrong* with you, Thompson?"

"I'm sorry," Arthur said. "I'm just a little upset. The house has been making me nervous. I'm sorry I snapped at you, Doris."

She nodded, cleaning up, thinking that men were such cowards, they only attacked when you were being pleasant, that's when they went right for the throat; but if you'd only be snarling and dangerous, then they'd respect you. Jungle law.

Meanwhile Harry took out the little notebook he kept in his wallet pocket. The napkin on which he'd recorded McCarty's wheel-chair prices was tucked in at the back. Under the entry reading *telephone girls* he wrote: *love is cheap*.

"But what if she does decide to commit suicide?" Arthur asked. It was turning into another beautiful day, in the high seventies. They were walking on the ocean beach, Arthur in trunks and Harry with his trousers rolled above the knee. Doris came along behind, collecting shells. "Or what if she takes it in her head to try to abort herself? What if she's lying there right now, in a pool of blood?"

"Will you please stop talking that way?" Harry splashed along at the edge of the icy surf. In the past hour he had phoned Miriam four times. No answer. The phone just rang and rang. She really must have moved out. "Maybe I'd better call the police. You're getting me awfully nervous with all this suicide business, Thompson."

"Well, she might be lying there slowly bleeding to death, you see, and not be *able* to answer the phone."

89

Doris picked up a shell. It looked as if she were making an effort to houseclean the beach.

"Miriam wouldn't do anything bloody," Harry said. "That's not her sort of thing. If she hasn't moved out she's probably off somewhere playing her banjo. I mean, if she started to commit suicide she'd probably get distracted and forget what she was doing."

"Very funny," said Arthur. "Sure."

"Well, you'd have to meet her. She's like me in some ways. I mean she wanders around, it's hard to describe, you remember how I used to be? One week she's modeling at the Art School, then all of a sudden she's taking banjo lessons, and then the next thing you know—"

"She's having illegitimate children."

Harry ignored him. "You know how a kitten gets all involved, boxing a pencil all over the floor or something? And then suddenly just leaves it flat, like somebody'd thrown a switch? Well, that's Miriam. In some ways."

"Your type," said Arthur.

"She is," said Harry defensively. "I mean, she was. She's fine, really. A little mixed up, but who isn't?"

"I'm not," said Doris. "I'm the only sane, normal person I know."

Harry gave her a look. The way she had of talking, as if each word were a newly-minted dime. But he had to admit that Doris was really something in a bathing suit. If her posture weren't so perfect she'd look absolutely wonderful, except that when she straightened after reaching for a shell, she stood with her head up as if she were going down the aisle to be coronated. He knew these Southern girls, they were all football queens at heart. But then she gave him a smile, apropos of nothing, absolutely free of charge, and he relented a little. It was an impressive bathing suit all right, even if she did seem to get gooseflesh, wearing it in April. Two piece, light yellow. A very thin fabric, he doubted that you were ever supposed to get it wet.

There were a few people on the beach where the Boardwalk

began. They were passing the second-rate hotels now. A bald man in a long, striped beach robe, his flesh shrimp-pink, sat on the wet sand in their path and Harry jumped over his outstretched legs. "Hey, Beatnik, watch what you're doing," called the man in the striped beachrobe.

"Everybody gives me advice," Harry said.

He returned after letting the phone ring twenty times, and discovered that Arthur, crazily, had gone into the water. "Who does he think he is, a polar bear?" He sat on the sand next to Doris. "He said he had to get more excitement into his life," she told him. Harry shrugged. Two muscular boys were setting up a few beach umbrellas nearby and farther back toward the boardwalk there were rows of canvas chairs, some of them occupied by Easter tourists wearing sun-visor hats. But it began to look like rain. The sea air touched wet against his face. Off to the right a fully-clothed family group piled into lunch and a woman screamed that Mitchey hadn't brought fruit for the children. The children. There seemed to be children all over the place. Two little boys came running by toward the water with great clamor and a spraying of sand, helicopter blades spinning atop their beany hats. They were chasing a little girl who giggled wildly; they wished to dunk her in the ocean, no doubt. Children. But at least they knew what they wanted—namely blood, he thought, as the male helicopters landed on the giggling girl.

"Why don't you go in the water, too," he said to Doris, considering the bathing suit. "Be brave." She sat hugging her knees, watching Arthur, who seemed to be having a seizure. "It must be too cold for him to jump under and get wet," she murmured. Arthur appeared to be coming out, but then he changed his mind and ran headlong into a high wave, found his feet again, and rubbed himself with his long arms crossed. He began riding the waves like a kid. He caught a tall one, leaping up just as the crest reached him, flailing with his arms until he was pulled down into the charging force of the water. If it didn't kill him it might wake him up. He found himself ending against the shore, freezing, out of breath, and stumbled back for another ride.

Doris and Harry ignored the first light drops of rain. "What's this Miriam like?"

"Sort of a dreamy tomboy, if that makes any sense. She works in a furniture place. Beds-'n-Things."

"Is that what it's called?"

"Yeah. Isn't it awful? But she really wants to be an actress. She's not all that good I guess, but she's all right. She's very pretty. In a way. She may be too much of an intellectual to be a really good actress, though—too self-conscious. She quit college. She didn't have time to do any reading at college so she quit so she could get an education. But she's sure too much of an actress to be an intellectual."

Doris was paying attention, but at the same time she seemed to be lifeguarding Arthur as he rode the waves. "We'd better get him out of there—it's going to pour."

"She's strange, I guess," said Harry. "I mean erratic, you know. Her mother was a great disciplinarian, but her father's an advertising man, he tried to make her flexible. He sends her money every month. So she got caught between them, that's her theory. They're separated, her mother and father. Anyway, she goes at things like crazy, but then she stops or she gets distracted. You've never seen anything like it when she gets going, though. Like reading a book. Where do you start when you read a book?" He saw that Arthur was coming out.

"At the beginning."

"And read right straight ahead?"

Doris nodded. Arthur ran up to them from the ocean, wrapped himself in a towel, and was shaking water out of his ears while Doris's head was nodding *yes-yes,* so his at the same time was going *no-no-no.*

"Where do *you* start reading a book?" she asked Arthur.

"Actually," he said, "I always start a book with the blurb and all that, and then I go back and read the notes. Or if it says something about the type it's set in, I like to read that first. Or the index. I start on the outskirts."

"Maybe I'd better go right back up there," Harry said. "I still can't get her on the phone."

"I even read the copyright notice. I suppose that's sort of compulsive—I never thought about it before. Say, it's raining!"

"Yes?"

"Then I read the book."

"The whole book? From front to back?"

"Unless it's Hebrew."

"One book at a time?"

"I should hope so," said Arthur.

Doris's head stopped following the conversation back and forth. She smiled. It was Arthur's point.

"Miriam reads from the middle," said Harry.

No response. Doris was packing up their things.

"I was telling Doris. She gets an impulse to read a book and nothing can stop her. Suddenly she's off to the paperback place and if they don't have it she can't get to sleep till the library opens, and if the library doesn't have it she goes up to the main branch or over to the university, except by that time she's usually on another kick already. But she'll come walking in, you know, and she's already practically through with it. She sort of wanders in there and works over the middle for a while and then she leaps up to the front and then she flips around and then she's reading the last page and all of a sudden it's over."

Doris and Arthur remain unmoved, ducking under the Boardwalk, setting off toward the car, the family groups on the beach either packing up or huddling under their umbrellas.

"Does she read the copyright notice?"

"I guess so. Sometimes she has hundreds of books going at once. Some of my friends think she's a little affected, you know. A little stagey. In the fall she's supposed to play Camille with the Little Theatre.

"Hmm," said Arthur. "No answer?"

Harry shook his head. "It rang twenty times."

"Do you think she'd really move out?"

93

"I don't know. I really don't understand women, Arthur. Do you, now that you're married? I've heard they always change for the worst once you marry them."

"Come *on!*" said Doris with a little laugh.

"Well, I can't help it, that's what I hear, they're supposed to become exactly like their mothers, it can't be avoided, it's like some sort of gland women have."

"Well, I just hope your woman hasn't done herself some harm, that's all I've got to say," Arthur told him.

As they moved rapidly along the beachside street through the mild rain Doris brushed the sand from her legs and bottom.

"Maybe I'd better go home and have a look," Harry said. "Irrational things do happen."

"I thought you wanted to move in with us?"

"No, I think maybe I'll get going, Doris."

Arthur gave Doris a glance. A long glance. "Listen," he said to Harry, "do you want me to drive you back to Connecticut?"

"What for? You have work to do."

"That's all right," said Arthur. "I'm feeling sort of irresponsible. There's no teaching till Monday anyway. I sort of feel like a change-of-scene somehow, I haven't done anything just for the hell of it for years."

"You've got sand on the back of your pants, Harry," Doris said with a sad smile.

"Who'd water all your houseplants?" said Harry.

"I don't know. Maybe if Doris . . ."

"Are we going up to Harry's?" she said. And then: "Aren't I invited?"

"It's not that," said Arthur. "What could you do up there?"

"Let her come," Harry said. "You can be the best man and I'll be the miserable bridegroom and she can be the maid of honor. That is, assuming we can find Miriam to be the bride."

"Matron," Doris said.

"But where would we both stay?" said Arthur. "It's not—"

"There's plenty of room," Harry said, enjoying the situation. "These things can be worked out."

94

"Well," said Arthur, "I don't know. I just thought I'd have a look round at the old campus. But maybe it isn't such a good idea." The rain was coming down more heavily and they hurried to the car. "Of course, if *you* want to take a little vacation—" Arthur said to Doris.

"You can go alone," she told him with disgust. "I'll retire gracefully. There's no need for the electric cattle prod."

"Come on, Doris, don't be like that."

"Like what? I've got the message, so you can turn off the record. I know when I'm not wanted." They were in the car, stuck at a red light. Arthur turned to look at her in the back seat. "Don't be like that. You come along if you want to. I'd be back in a day or so in any case. But suit yourself."

"Thanks." Grimly she looked away at the people waiting for a bus in a drugstore entryway. A much-corseted woman, heavily made-up, dressed all in white, held her little son by the hand. The boy was clothed like a midget, a complete mimicry of a man to the tiny Panama hat on his head. A group of teenage girls in flowered dresses waited there too. One of them, slightly apart from the rest, ran a comb languidly through her long, wet, mouse-colored hair.

"I can take the bus back to the house," Doris said. "There's no need to drive me home. You and Harry can just—"

"I'm still in my bathing suit, for God's sake," said Arthur. "Listen, I didn't mean to hurt your feelings. Did I hurt your feelings? I hurt her feelings! I'm sorry, *mea culpa,* I only . . . if you really want to come, okay. I mean, that's fine. I just thought . . ."

And Harry was thinking: connubial gray, that was what it was like. Struggle. Interference with the lifeline. Marriage. He felt personally acquainted with all the couples moving down the side streets away from the shore. On the beach they were rapidly dismantling umbrellas and folding up chairs, and as the sky darkened further children would be gathered up from their castles at the verge of the pockmarked ocean. He could see how the first large drops had splattered down to spot the dry wood of the old-fashioned boardwalk, and then the sudden downpour, as if blown in off the sea, and people running for cover with newspapers over their heads and a motorcycle cop roaring down the empty boardwalk, hunched over his machine. There would be the sound of the rain, and hard rubber balls bumping under the glass of the Pokerino tables, and couples with their children standing under the awnings all the way along the Boardwalk, looking out at the ocean.

Arthur increased the speed of his windshield wipers. "Why *don't* you come along?" he said to Doris.

"You really mean it? Are you just *saying* it or do you really mean it?"

At the next intersection Harry caught a glimpse of the beach in the distance, a cross-section of silvered Boardwalk-railing and a flicker of dark water beyond. An Army-Navy store was running a fire sale, and he wondered how the fire had been set. Down the side streets of this run-down part of the Cordelia seafront he read signs that would probably be there forever: ROOMS; APARTMENTS; LIGHT HOUSEKEEPING.

"I really would like to come along," Doris said, "if you *want* me to."

Twenty minutes later she was all packed, using her vacuum cleaner so the house wouldn't smell musty when they returned. She finished with the crumbs under the coffee table in the living room, stopped the machine, changed the attachment, and humming started to vacuum the coffee table itself. The vacuum cleaner makes a great roar, and Doris is full of happy concentration. She's sure a change of scene for a day or so will do Arthur good. Upstairs in the bathroom Arthur is taking a fast shower after his daring April-dip in the ocean, and Harry sits on the toilet lid keeping him company. The shower creates a considerable din, a sound different in tone from the vacuum cleaner but with the same spirit. It is impossible to make out half of what Arthur is shouting from behind the curtain. "Boy," says Harry, "it sure is misty in here. Tell me something, Arthur—I may never get a chance to talk to you alone again. What's with this wife of yours?"

"Doris?" The rest is lost in the slamming of the water against the tub.

"Who else? Don't get me wrong, she's fine. But sometimes when she looks at you it's like you're something tasty she put in her shopping cart at the supermarket."

"She's—," Arthur said. "Her father's a justice on the Tennessee Supreme Court."

"You don't say?"

"A little repressed. They never communicate in her family. So dignified they don't talk."

"Tell me," said Harry, "are you happy in your work? I mean . . . being a husband and all?"

"What? What did you say? She's sort of domestic at heart, I guess. I don't think she's really all that interested in teaching. I think she'd just like to run the house."

"That's what you think, do you? Listen, Arthur, do you know what's going on out there? She's cleaning the place and it's not even dirty!"

"What?" The shower suddenly stops and the sound of the vacuum cleaner is distantly heard.

"This is just like you," Arthur says, drying himself. "Two minutes ago we were talking about you, and all of a sudden we're talking about me."

"How come you're so anxious, old buddy?"

"Me?"

"I mean, would you say you were a happy man?"

"Okay, so you don't like my wife. Let's talk about something else."

"Come on, Arthur, play fair. I never said that."

"Sure you did. Not that I give a damn—"

"You're reading things in. It's just the way she looks, like a . . . like your mother or something. No, take it easy. In my situ-

97

ation, you see, being a prospective *father* all of a sudden . . ."

"That's kid's stuff. We're adults. That's your kind of thing. Messy."

"Greasy kid-stuff."

"Right."

"Gosh, you're in worse shape than I thought, Arthur."

"You think so?" A serious question.

"You're in *awful* shape, worse than I am. Listen, you've got to get a grip on yourself with this being grown-up business, Arthur—you're getting hysterical. Who do you think you are, Nathaniel Hawthorne? I mean, which side are you on, old pal?"

"I've seen the way you live, Harry. I've tried it. Big deal. I may not be happy, but what's the alternative, living in a rattrap on Eastern Avenue? And if this Miriam of yours is really suicidal, I mean manic-depressive or whatever—"

"Dirty pool!"

"Well, you said yourself—"

"I never said 'suicidal.' "

"If the shoe fits," said Arthur.

"Listen, she's about the least morbid girl you've ever seen. She's so casual sometimes it drives me out of my mind."

"Yes. Well if she's moody, like you say—"

"She's impulsive."

"All right. You said it now. So why can't you get her on the telephone? Where is she? If she's erratic and moody and impulsive, like you say, aren't you a little worried that when the irresponsible father of her unborn child—"

"Oh, come off it, will you? You talk like a lady's magazine."

"If the shoe fits . . ." said Arthur, combing his hair.

"You'd better hire somebody to write you some new lines, Nathaniel."

"All right. I don't even know the girl. I don't give a damn about her. But she tells you she's pregnant—"

"Overdue. Overdue."

"—and you disappear within five minutes. No wonder *you're*

98

not unhappy, *you* just disappear. Do you think everybody can live like that? I may be anxious, but at least I've got some—"

"*I'm* anxious, all right. I'm just as anxious as you are. I'm going back aren't I? You're taking me back, aren't you? And what are *your* motives? You want to get away from your wife for a minute so you can take a breath of fresh air without supervision, now why don't you admit it?"

"Okay, I admit it. Now what?" They were moving down the stairs toward the sound of the vacuum cleaner. "At least I wouldn't just simply . . . some people in this world try to create a little decency around them, did you realize? If this girl of yours has done herself some harm you're going to feel like . . . like a sex-maniac."

"Harm, harm! You have the imagination of a Sunday-school teacher. Harm! What do you want me to do? What am I supposed to do, for God's sake, she doesn't even *believe* in marriage and here I am off to the rescue! It I waited a little maybe the rain would stop, maybe she'd marry somebody else or just die or go in a convent or something. I mean, what do you *want?* I don't even like the girl anymore, yet here I am. . . ."

Doris was working the couch over with a thin blade-like attachment as they entered the room. The couch was perfectly clean, but she'd decided to give it a treatment anyway. Once she started vacuuming it was difficult not to run through the various attachments, the one for the venetian blinds and noisy one for rug-vibrating and the one for table-tops. There were actually eleven attachments, you could dry your hair with Doris's vacuum cleaner, or spray paint, or sharpen knives. Her mother had given her the machine, a huge, cast-aluminum thing, when she first went off to California to college. Doris felt deeply committed to it. But she stopped poking between the cushions and clicked it off when Harry and Arthur appeared. They were shouting at each other. Violence of any kind stirred her, but sheer noise especially, which might have been why she spent so much time with the rug-vibrator. And Arthur was swooping his arms against his sides exactly the way Harry did, she'd never seen him do that before, it brought color to his cadaverous cheeks. She had no idea what they were arguing about; it made no difference, it was the style she appreciated, beating at themselves like children in a tantrum. That's what she needed, a nice refreshing tantrum—but she didn't have the temperament or the talent or whatever it was that let you do it, that let you go swinging back and forth around the room banging your head and saying over and over "A sense of responsibility, that's all—a goddam sense of responsibility!" And Harry shouting back, striking his chest, "To what? To what?"

One may pause to wonder exactly why they are carrying on this way. Obviously they are getting something out of it, just as Doris does by watching them, the vacuum cleaner hose held in her hand like a limp spear. If we turn down the sound for a moment, merely observing the silent contortions of lips and jaws and arms and legs, the scene begins to take on a certain clarity. Why flap the arms as if trying to take off, as Arthur is doing? Or collapse on the couch, all limbs agape, as Harry collapses, only to leap immediately back up and hit oneself with both fists on the head? Doris wears a dazed smile; she looks like a street cleaner who has wandered into the middle of the French Revolution. If we read lips, it would seem that Harry is saying "no" a great number of times, while Arthur faces him full on, mouthing "yes-you-are, by-God, oh-yes-you-are." We may be tempted to conclude that self-defensiveness on both sides is responsible for the curious intensity of this discussion. But the interesting thing is the way their hands and arms and legs keep moving. It's not self-defensiveness at all. They are hitting themselves—striking, slapping, gouging, punching themselves. Climbing Everest.

And meanwhile Doris says nothing. She'd never be able to let herself go like that. It was all in where you came from, all a question of upbringing; she could see her mother's demure little mouth and folded hands, her father's perfectly round spectacles and tiny false teeth. How come her parents were so small? And dignified? A few years ago she would have thought that Harry was hopelessly vulgar. Now she still thought so, and envied him.

It wasn't fair: either she should take after her parents or not take after them—not both at once.

Arthur had his eyes shut. He sat on the newly-vacuumed coffee table swishing his head back and forth like a metronome while Harry barked at him. Harry is saying, "Puritan! That doesn't sound like the welfare-state to me!" and Arthur is saying, "Shut up! Shut up! Let me finish!" And Doris is thinking how strange it is, that she actually envies Harry Zissel, of all people. He makes her feel exactly like she does when she's using the rug-vibrator.

EIGHT

They left the rain behind on the Garden State Parkway. Twice, once on the Parkway and again just west of New York on the Jersey Turnpike, they stopped for Harry to phone. No answer. But he'd find Miriam, all right. He was going back to face the music—the wedding march. He just couldn't think of anything else to do. He was going to become a mature, responsible creature, a husband, a citizen. It made him sick to his stomach. "You've got me all stirred up," he complained to Arthur. "Now I don't know *what* I'm doing!" In the back seat Doris worked at a piece of knitting, a sweater for a cousin's new baby. Harry felt that he was coming out of the trance he'd been in since he spoke to Johnny on the phone the evening before. Some of Arthur's crazy suicide talk had gotten through. "Can't you drive any faster? She may be lying there this minute in a pool of blood." Arthur mumbled something. "What?"

"Sixty's the speed limit."

"Oh, for God's sakes!"

An hour later we find them moving over the Dunnbar Street Bridge in the gloom of dusk, the tires zizzing on the grillwork. They are at the Square; passing Johnny's shop, which is closed on Thursday nights. They are moving up Eastern Avenue. They are caught at a red light and Harry puffs tensely on a cigarette, hunched forward, as a few people cross the street. It is deep twilight. As they turn the corner onto Beachum he half expects them to run over the loaf of bread he left behind. A distant sound of fire-fighting apparatus becomes louder and fades away.

Awaiting Harry, as he leads the way up the dark staircase to the fourth floor, tucked into the roller of his typewriter, is a blue envelope containing a three-page document which will prove on examination to be the last will and testament of Miriam Barbara Hippolyto.

"*Open* it," Arthur says.

Harry holds the unopened envelope and does an unaccountable thing: he smells it, lifts it to his nose. Then, trembling, he rips it open.

Wednesday, April 14, 1965

Being of sound mind and disposition, I, Miriam Barbara Hippolyto, here set down my last will and testament. I wish to be immediately cremated and buried at the direction of my father, Mr. Franklin R. Hippolyto, of Lake Forest, Illinois.

I declare that I appoint Mr. Harry Zissel, of 96 Beachum Street, the sole executor of my worldly belongings, to be disposed of as follows:

To the Ford Foundation, New York, N.Y.:

> All my clothes and shoes (including my sari but excepting what is listed below), my steam iron, my Picasso and Modigliani prints, my white bead purse and my white kid gloves.

To Mr. N. C. Nardiman, 96 Beachum Street:

> My banjo, my photographs, my Mah-Jongg set, my Victory of Samothrace, my birchbark, my Lincoln Imp ashtray, my Venetian glass pig, my donkey that nods, and my sea-fossil stone.

To my mother, Frances Lehrman Hippolyto, of Chicago, Illinois:

> My paperback, annotated edition of *The Selected Poems of W. B. Yeats,* and my unicycle.

It went on for three pages, names he recognized and names he didn't. He kept saying "Oh-my-God." Mr. and Mrs. John Hughes of Beds-'n-Things, Inc., received her tiger-tooth necklace; somebody in Queens got an Indian silk scarf, white with golden hinds. To her brother, all her books not otherwise bequeathed. To a certain Gary Lehrman in Gary, Indiana, her grimlin [sic], her brass buddha, a $20 gold piece. To Mrs. Martin Benjamin (formerly Wilma Zinn), her porcupine quill jewelbox. To Mr. and Mrs. Sheldon Suberstein, her green tonette.

And to him, to Mr. Harry Zissel of 96 Beachum Street, Fear of Reprisals, Connecticut:

a note on the floor of the main closet at said oft-mentioned residence, and a sigh of farewell.

[signed]

Miriam Barbara Hippolyto

Dear Harry:

Had you scared, didn't I? Admit it, you were scared. I forgot to say in the will: you get all my cash on hand, anything you can scavenge from the corpse go ahead, help yourself, feel free. Poor Harry. My period started *last* Tuesday morning—normal, no discomfort. Odd, isn't it, how I'm always right on time? Not that you notice. Ah well. The truth is, I don't know why I told you that about being overdue. To see how you'd take it? Like a man? My father used to say, "When in doubt, lie." So she is gone, poor lady, she is gone, more sinned against than sinning. Forgive the style—your influence. I leave you with all admiration and distaste. You never bought any bread, you bastard, I had to eat saltines for breakfast! You can always find a girl to live with you, and we were in bad shape anyway. But that wasn't very original, running away—pretty bourgeois, petty bourgeois—if you ask me. So I assume you'll be back soon enough, that's the whole point, isn't it, working up a head of guilt so you can come back and get married and be deadly dull forever? Poor Harry, I wouldn't be you for all the world.

He turned to the second page of blue notepaper.

But what if you never get this message till thirty-eight years from now? Gosh! Thirty-eight years, I'll be in the menopause. It's possible you joined the Foreign Legion.
Do they still have the Foreign Legion?
But if you're quick about it you will find that I have gone out of my way and sprinkled some Arpège—thank you, that was very thoughtful of you, the Arpège—and if the smell is gone the drops may linger on. Girls are emotional and they like to chatter constantly about sex and suicide and Italian movies, like you say. So don't take them seriously, Harry, that's my final advice to you. Why not buy yourself a dog or something? Some fish? They're simple and loving.
I'll get the rest of my stuff out of here one of these days. Twirl your mustachioes.

M.

Harry boosted himself up on the half size range in the kitchenette, saying the word "wow" intermittently, as if the burner under him were lit.

Arthur laughed, then shrugged, passing the letter to Doris. "She wasn't even overdue, much less pregnant. Some sense of humor."

"Wow," said Harry, "I'm exhausted."

"Well, you're off the hook then. Your problems are solved. Are you feeling all right?"

"What?" Harry distractedly observed Doris's grin as she read over the will.

"Are you . . . ?"

"Jesus! That Miriam. Why'd she do that? I thought for a minute there she'd really killed herself."

"Well," said Arthur, "you've got to meet her, she's like a kitten . . ."

"She'll be back," said Harry. "Her things are all over the place. I'll kill her!"

Doris finished reading, replaced her reading glasses in their case and put the case in her knitting basket.

"Should I make us some supper?" she said. "Does she really own all those things in the will?"

"Who can eat?" said Harry.

Arthur opened the refrigerator and looked in. A lime, a carton of milk, a bottle of Dijon mustard, three eggs, a few wisps of salad greens on the bottom, like dejected weeds. Something in a dish that Harry told him was haddock casserole.

He closed the door.

"I'm not hungry," Harry said. "You two go out. Go over to Hulbert's. Live it up, this is your Easter vacation."

"How are we going to sleep tonight?" Doris asked.

"There's a bedroom. I'll sleep on the couch."

She went to look.

Arthur moved about fingering things. "How come you're so sad?"

"I don't know."

"I thought you *wanted* to get rid of her?"

"Did I?"

"Well, forget about it. She sounds pretty childish to me. Superficial. I mean, it doesn't look like she gave much of a damn for you in the first place. She was probably just waiting for an excuse to take off."

"Yeah."

"So you're lucky it's over."

"Oh, sure. Lucky," he muttered. "Look, Arthur. I'd sort of like to be by myself for a while."

"Okay."

"It's funny. You just about had me convinced I should get married."

"I did? Don't worry, she's not the only woman in the world."

Doris returned. She wanted to know if there were any clean sheets around, she'd looked and couldn't find any. "Do you suppose your friend took them with her?"

Harry jumped down from the stove. "I bet she took the pot-jar," he cried. "The bitch, I bet she did!" He went into the bathroom and returned with a dripping Hellmann's mayonnaise jar which contained a small brown paper bag, which contained his pitiful supply of marijuana, a few leaves and seeds and stalks.

"A woman of honor," he said.

And she hadn't taken the sheets either. They were found at the bottom of a plastic bag full of washing back from the launderette.

"What's a potjar?" Doris asked Arthur as they made up the beds.

The heat was still coming up from below. What an apartment—in the wintertime the radiators remained stone cold. Harry switched on the rotating fan on the windowsill behind the couch and looked out through the open, barred window. It was finally getting dark. In the john Arthur was freshening up before taking Doris out to eat and to see old friends. Doris, permanently freshened, sat across the room, which has even more than usual a look that could be described as "lived-in." On the floor, on the chairs, on the mantel, on the table, a debris of books, food-stained dishes, newspapers, a bronze waterpipe, a record player, scattered clothing, Harry's construction, ashtrays holding wads of Kleenex and banana skins. On the walls, fastened with thumbtacks or friction tape, a few reproductions, two of them Modigliani women, one a Picasso sculptor-and-model. Also newspaper photographs and portraits in pen and ink done by Miriam of Harry, a sequence of these on large ragged sheets of sketching paper running along the cabinet doors in the kitchenette. A Wildroot Cream Oil advertisement, or rather a barber's calendar, hangs just behind the plush chair where Doris sits studying the place with an appraising, amused expression. On the calendar above her head are pictured in profile the heads of a dozen men and boys demonstrating various styles of haircutting. The one whose curly hair most approximates the look of Harry's is labeled *English Tweed*. Arthur fits in somewhere between *Butch* and *Ivy League,* though at the moment as he stands at the mirror in the john, his hair is slicked down as if it were short, wet thatch. On the calendar, slightly to the side and behind each male profile appears the shadow-drawing of a woman, an admiring woman or girl suited to the particular style of man or boy or haircut. *Cadet* has a cheerleader, *Butch* a high-schooler (freckles), *Executive* a simpering-type twenty years his junior, *Hollywood,* of course, Female Hollywood, and *Roman Nights* a nymphomaniac. *Young Master* has an audience of two, a pig-tailed girl-friend and a Mother. All the male faces are very smug. There is one called *Commuter* who reveals a touch of anxiety shading the eye and brow. Maybe worrying if he needed a haircut?

Harry, deep in thought, was not prepared to hear Doris speak. In the first instant, with her voice coming from across the dim room, it was as if Miriam were there.

"I hope we're going to be real friends," Doris said, so quietly that he was startled, and then she added quickly, "But you don't like women, do you? I mean, Arthur was right, wasn't he, about you and Miriam? As if it's any of my business."

He looked at her, and the rotating fan came to the edge of its cycle and buzzed and began the trip in the other direction.

She looked very nice across the room, her skirt just above her crossed knees. She seemed embarrassed now. Her head was leaning back against the scabrous plush of the armchair.

"I'm a great admirer of women," Harry said, "only they confuse the hell out of me."

"Do I confuse you?"

It was just this sort of thing that worried him about women— the way they were always manipulating, fishing for something, arranging. After all, it was none of his business if Arthur wanted to be married to this cheerful, orderly girl. Joy to their sheets. But when she saw that he himself wasn't so hot on her, why force the issue? She must have realized he was feeling low, glum and vulnerable: why stick the little penknife of her affairs into him at such a moment? *Because* he was feeling low. Of course. When else? She was a politician, like all of them. Even the lighting, the absence of lighting, was working for her. Even the crossed legs, the shadowy thigh-show, could hardly be entirely inadvertent, because at a certain moment in his statement of how, of course he liked her and any wife of Arthur's was a friend of his—as he was saying that, that she seemed to be taking good care of Arthur and Arthur obviously needed care all right, *he* didn't even *know* he was confused—at a certain moment she pulled her skirt down a bit, as if to remind him that she had, being female, a certain power over him.

"It's nice of you to say that," she said. "I guess I'm a little paranoid today. Arthur's been acting so strangely."

"Oh yes?"

"Well, he hasn't really been happy at Cordelia at all. It's sort of hard for him to settle down. And then . . . didn't you think he was a little strange about my coming up here?"

"Strange?"

She laughed. "I thought maybe he was getting tired of me already! I thought he wanted to get away."

Harry translated: "Do I have a major husband problem?"

"This started when?"

"Oh, it's been going on for months. But what I mean is just after the beach. Suddenly he got, I don't know, sort of quiet. When I wanted to come up here with you."

"Well, that's not *my* fault, is it?"

"I don't mean anything is anybody's fault," Doris said sadly. "I'm just talking off the top of my head."

He looked at the top of her head. Her hair was a reddish presence in the dusk of the room. He looked at the Wildroot calendar. It was too dark to see all the women on the calendar to identify her type. He had a sense that she was a cross between the little girl and the mother behind *Young Master.* But in the dimness of almost eight o'clock the drawings of the women had faded away altogether. They were hiding back there, smiling through the darkness at *Butch,* at *Cadet,* at *Roman Nights.*

The rotating fan turned its attention to him briefly and moved away. The room was cooling off.

"Should I put on some lights?"

"Not for me," said Doris. "This is very restful. Aren't you

going to eat with us? You must be starving. Come on. You don't want to be all alone, do you?"

A silence grew between them.

"I'm coming in," called Arthur from the john. "Are you both decent?"

"Very funny," Harry said.

It took ten minutes more to convince them that he wanted to be left behind. His stomach was producing audible cries of hunger by then, but it was beneath his dignity to eat at such a moment.

It was the first time in his history that he could remember preferring to be left alone for an evening.

He went to the refrigerator and ate a vitamin pill.

He began to wander, opening a cabinet above the stove and eating some raisins. He ate some Sugar Pops directly from the box, which claimed to contain a toy moon rocket.

He sat again by the barred window, thinking that the bars were merely pretending to keep the local junkies and burglars and rapists out, that really they were intended to prevent the alleyway from being splattered all over with despondent, falling bodies.

He is feeling sad.

The window directly across the alley has its blinds closed.

He smokes a cigarette in the dark.

He is very sick.

He thinks that probably he has at least forty more years to live.

He thinks of maggots.

Of grass.

Of worms.

He decides to take a shower and shave.

He turns on a light.

He closes the barred window.

He turns off the rotating fan.

Standing in the shower, he begins to make an effort to put his life back together again, to figure out where it all went wrong, where his enthusiasm had gone, the burst of energy with which he'd returned to college, all his plans? Was it Miriam's fault? How could it be? He was a slob, that was all, no discipline, no real desire. And full of complaint. He felt ashamed even to be concerned over the failure of desire, when everywhere in the world people were suffering from great weights of horror, hunger, oppression. How could he take his own troubles seriously, what did they amount to in the face of the general disintegration of practically everything? People, his mother used to say, people are starving in Europe and here you waste all this good food on your plate.

Forty years to live. Had he lost his appetite *because* others were starving?

It would be a comfort to think so. But untrue; if he were more concerned about the state of the world would he feel like such a nothing in the first place?

So be concerned, said his voice. *Fine. Who's stopping you? Think of others.*

I haven't heard from you in a while, Harry said.

I've been around, said the voice.

He had lost his idealism, that's what it was, his sense of purpose, the goods of the intellect. What had happened to the sheet of paper where he'd written down all the wise-saws from Conrad and Hemingway, the nice up-lifty poem by Ella Wheeler Wilcox, the sheet where he'd copied out *Work, work, for the dark night cometh?* For that matter, where were all the sharpened pencils, the lined yellow tablets, the marble-covered notebooks? Where were they now, the Corrasable bond, the carbon paper, the onion skin?

Over and over again he had settled at his desk only to realize that he didn't know anything, want anything, love anything— could he write about *that?* Write about how he sort of wanted to be a writer, or a sculptor, or whatever, it didn't make any real difference, just so it would cause everyone to notice him, love him? Write about the failure of desire? how the whole world was in a frenzy, hemlines going up, pot coming in, movies getting dirtier than ever—all to stimulate some vague impulse to keep the reproductive habits of the race alive, a sea of aphrodisiacs and exhortations and sex manuals and girlie magazines, because nobody really loved anybody anymore, so there's a prodigal tide of stimulation to stir the faltering male, to wake up the terrified sperm cells so one at least might make the egg, keep things going a little longer.

The problem of love. Why a problem, anyway? Because there were dangers everywhere, people were obsessed with the self, with self-hunger, self-control, self-hatred, self-destruction. Or else the opposite, sheer chaos, oral or anal, anything but real Eros, and a man stuck with himself was screwed either way, tight or loose, he or Arthur, what difference did it make?

Screwed either way.

Depressing. No chance for love.

If he were rich, he suddenly thought, what he'd like to have would be a portable shower, a kind of shower you could walk around in, go out in the street with the shower stall around you, just have a nice hot shower going on you all the time, even sleep that way, standing up like a horse in the rain.

He soaped his groin, but with no particular interest.

He had to stop fooling himself, he wasn't going anywhere, he was standing in place, he was lifting one foot and then the other, wondering why there was no applause. He was *He-who-would save-his-life,* that's who he was: how come he hadn't set that down with the other wise-saws? Instead he'd written out a list of the crazy jobs he'd had, as if he'd gone deliberately to work to build up the proper impeccable, improbable background for the biographical notes on the dustjackets of the books he'd never write. The soda-bottling plant in the Bronx, unloading empties, just after the army: that was the best one, the symbolism was good. He should have stayed there, he might have been promoted to heaving on cases of fulls eventually. It was before he came back to Connecticut and started with the sculpting: unloading the empties from the soda trucks and in between helping out on the production line and sleeping at home with his head on his typewriter after work. They made two drinks, KooLKoLA and Woopsy, a kind of lemon-flavored blood. Unloading cases of empty Woopsy bottles. And at the height of the summer, when they were all working overtime, the syrup mixer had to break down, and for a week with three other guys at the end of the production line there he was shaking the bottles of Woopsy by wrist action, two at a time, spreading the beauty of the syrup around. At first he had just grabbed the big quart bottles by the neck and flipped them, but after a while his wrists tired and he'd be thrashing them out every which way, grunting, trying to keep up with the flow, praying the damn belt would stop somehow. Once his rubbery arms snatched up two bottles of Woopsy and swung them right into each other, glass crashing over the cement floor and the drink flooding him and his fellow workers.

He thinks: the story of my life.

If he went after Miriam, wherever she was, she'd laugh in his face.

And why not? Whyever not? Because he didn't love her, not really. And that wasn't something you could decide to change.

He makes a line of furrows in the bar of soap to get at the dirt beneath his fingernails. The shower he is under presents the effect of a jaded garden hose rather than a laughing spray. A few sad, curving strings of water splatter on his bowed head. Poor, hairy corpus, he thinks, studying his body. Poor fellow, what's to become of you? What has happened to the male animal?

He thinks: bodies are so sad, they plod along like some good-natured dog, everywhere you go they come along, always waiting for you to throw them something, a bone or something.

A chicken wing, said his voice.

But Harry ignored the comment. How did he get tied up with that voice, anyway? Some voice; the Village Explainer; going on twenty-three years old and without a brain in its head.

He was tired of being neurotic; it was losing its charm.

What about giving up and selling encylopedias? said the voice.

He looked down at his toes, tilted against each other like people at a turning on the subway. He smiled ruefully. He had a great affection for his toes.

Without Miriam he would have to go to work somewhere, he couldn't take any more money from his mother.

But he'd be damned if he'd allow himself to think of the Miriam situation that way. Moneywise.

He'd be damned.

What had he done to Miriam, after all? He'd gotten scared and then she wasn't even pregnant! What a hell of a thing to do! Why did she want to do that? So naturally he'd gone hitchhiking—so what? He'd come back and she'd left him, and he found that he missed her, missed somebody, wanted a woman to be there, that was all. That was simple enough.

Scared, said the voice. *Simple enough.*

There wasn't much left in his checking account. And what was he going to major in, the Mind-Body Problem? Twentieth Century Plight?

He would have to pick up a job. Leave school.

It follows, said the voice in funereal tones.

Sure. What was he doing with his free time anyway, what was he accomplishing that he shouldn't be a worker? But maybe he could start all over again on his play?

No, the play was hopeless, crazy, no coherence. What was he trying to say there? Why were all the characters on crutches? What was the function of the big scene when they pushed the boulders at each other? For that matter, what producer would stand for a stage full of boulders?

He might as well go back to work. After the shower. After the shave. After the pants that trail along the floor.

But it could be a great play, a new style, four stars, critic's circle, don't miss! They might even put in his name in small type on the advertisements, along with Julie Harris, Sidney Feltlife, Richard Burton.

Ella Wheeler Wilcox.

Quit it, Harry said.

But maybe something would turn up. A woman. Wouldn't

that be nice? Are you serious, Mrs. Guggenheim? But it's only a fragment of the finished . . . How *good* of you, but one needs so little, really, and there are so many other young novelists . . . of *course* it would be helpful to be abroad, of course—you really think so? Mr. Scribner? New Directions? You showed them my . . . ?

The telephone rings. Just when he's started to revive a little, when hope is beginning to bloom, when the hot water is picking up! Thompson's Organization, no doubt. No, maybe it was Mrs. Guggenheim. Or the Nobel Prize! The telephone continued to declare itself as he ran with a towel around his waist into the bedroom, cutting the sixth ring neatly in half.

Miriam.

"What are you doing?" she asked. Just as casual!

"Nothing." His heart is pounding. "I was in the shower."

"Sorry. I wanted to check about my stuff . . ."

He squeezes himself down on the green painted apple box tucked between the beds where the phone usually rests. A considerable pause occurs on her end of the wire. Then: "When did you come back?"

"Just now. I got your note. Some note. And the last will and testament." The towel has come undone from around his waist, but it goes ignored.

"I'm sorry. I'm hanging up now. I decided I wouldn't talk to you at all."

"Wait, don't! Aren't you coming back?"

"Of course not."

Like a pitcherful of ice water thrown in his lap.

An even brisker voice: "Look, Harry, when would be a good time to pick up my things?"

"Where *are* you? Where are you staying?"

Pause. "I just called to make sure nobody was there, Johnny said he'd drive me over for the stuff and I wanted to be sure you weren't around, that's all."

"For God's sakes, Miriam!"

"Well, what's the matter?"

"Don't you have any human feelings, none at all?"

"Your next line is: 'How can you throw me away like this, like, like an old *shoe.*'"

"No, that's not the next line, Sweetie. The next line is FUCK YOU, MIRIAM! That's the next line."

"Fast curtain."

"Okay."

"Then why don't you slam down the phone?" She laughed.

"Why don't you? You've got the roles backwards. You're the one who's supposed to hang up."

"Okay, let's try it again."

"Right. FUCK YOU, MIRIAM! You hear? FUCK you, minx!"

"Very good, Harry, let's leave that in. Listen, before I hang up, when would be a good time to get the rest of my stuff?"

"You mean a time when I'm not around? Anytime." He was feeling true anger now. Refreshing. My, how it was refreshing to feel things. Anything. "I'm not even around right this minute, you could come over here and bump into me and think you just tripped on the carpet."

"Come on. Do I have to send Johnny by himself or will you kindly tell me . . ."

"You're amazing, Miriam, you know that?"

"I know."

"You're entirely out of your mind. You're entirely self-obsessed."

"Sure. I decided to get out. Of my mind that is, not your filthy apartment, though God knows . . ."

"Look, my old roommate Thompson came up with me and he has his wife with him—you might run into them, I don't know what they plan to do, there's liable to be *somebody* around here, but as far as I'm concerned I'm going off to a bordello anyway, I'll be out of here in fifteen minutes, *covered* with perfume. So come get your unicycle anytime you want. Overdue!"

"Are you *sure* you're going out, Harry?"

"FUCK YOU, MIRIAM!"

116

"Several have," she said, and slammed down the phone—he'd taken the precaution of holding the receiver out from his ear each time he spoke the curtain line.

The bedroom blinds were unclosed. From the window across in the next building a little boy in pajamas had been gazing at him, elbows propped on his bedroom windowsill. The boy seemed startled when Harry stood up and the towel fell at his feet, but then he held firm, fascinated. He was wearing a red and black cowboy neckerchief with his white pajamas and he had a long yellow pencil tucked above his ear. The boy was studying Harry intently, but pretending not to, and in spite of himself Harry felt his spirits slightly revive. Suddenly he scrambled across the bed to the window, five feet ten inches of naked Zissel, and gave the child such a look as might appear on the face of an old elephant sucking lemons. The boy held out for just a moment, but then he bolted, and in another instant an angry adult female hand swooped down the windowshade and Harry allowed himself a bitter chuckle. When in despair, he thought, there's nothing like the skillful frightening of children to bring yourself out for a breath of air. He closed the blinds and blotted himself philosophically with the towel. Then he began to move. He went back to the bathroom and shaved, then dressed carefully, in a fresh pair of khakis and a clean white shirt. After considering for a moment he put on a tie. He shut the blinds in the living room, had a handful of Sugar Pops and one of raisins, turned off all the lights, and settled down in the plush chair to wait for Miriam.

NINE

The steak at Hulbert's is a bit tough, but tasty. The coffee, as Doris predicted, is vile.

"Don't you think Harry has a queer attitude toward women?" she said.

"Queer?"

"Well, toward marriage. He acts as if it's death or something."

"Does he? I guess you're right. Maybe it is. I bet it kills more people than . . . than traffic accidents."

"That's very clever, Arthur." She smiles at him like a proud parent.

"I wish you didn't have to choose between being respectable or being alive," he blurted out.

She fails to comprehend.

"If there were only some middle way!"

"But isn't there?"

"No. Not any more. These days you're either a conformist or a nut."

"Who says so? Harry?"

He fails to reply.

"Should we use our spoons?"

"What for? They have spoons here." Walking to the luncheonette, Doris had spotted a curio shop open across the street and had dragged Arthur over. She'd bought a set of four small antique spoons in a case lined with worn blue velvet. The spoon-handles were monkeys, one hear-no-evil, one speak-no-evil, one see-no-evil, the last with crossed hands tucked under his armpits who must have been touch-no-evil. Each monkey stood on a tiny heart. They were nineteenth-century Dutch, the girl at the shop explained; in Holland such spoons used to be traditional presents for weddings or funerals.

"I wanted to look at them again."

"Suit yourself," said Arthur.

"You're still in a vile mood."

"Am I?"

"Ever since Harry showed up. Didn't you like your dinner?"

"Ah well. The steak was a bit tough."

"But tasty."

"Yes."

"Don't you want a monkeyspoon to stir with? They're cute. Take speak-no-evil."

"Mmmm."

"Arthur, what's the trouble with you? What are you brooding about?"

"I don't know."

"Is it Harry?"

"I don't know."

"Is that all you can say?"

"Yes. Isn't that sufficient?"

She lowered her head and stirred her cup contemplatively, gripping the hear-no-evil monkey between two fingers by its elbows. She had begun to suspect that she was pregnant, but she was afraid to talk to him about it. Betty, the older waitress, came to ask if they wanted dessert, and at the farthest table in the rear Roger Hulbert, forty-six-year-old son of the owner and a friend of Harry's, placed a bet with himself: dessert for the girl only, and for the man a second cup of coffee, black. Now, as for her dessert, ice cream, or blueberry, rhubarb, or apple pie were the long shots. The odds favored lemon meringue, a banana split, a fudge delight. As Roger watched the redheaded girl contemplating the menu her face seemed to become more cheerful, she'd put on glasses, she looked like the man's daughter, she could be going for anything from Boston Cream to Bread Pudding.

"When do you want to start back?" she asked tentatively. She'd decided not to eat the crust of the lemon meringue pie, a concession to her figure, especially if it might start swelling on its own. But maybe she was just being suggestible. It seemed to her that she would be roughly twelve days overdue, if she'd calculated correctly.

And Arthur, as if he had begun to float, as if he were a surfer who had finally caught a truly big wave, the wave of his career, found that he was telling her with perfect ease that he didn't plan to go back, that he might just stay. Of course, if she were anxious to return, well, by all means, they could take her over to the bus station . . .

"It's not that easy," she said. He was surprised that she wasn't shocked, or frightened, but rather immediately angry, a part of her emotional range he had never encountered. It made him tilt back in his chair.

"I'll be back by Monday, don't worry. I've got a job to support, I won't run away. *I'm* not Harry Zissel."

"Oh hell," said Doris. "When you use that tone . . . do you have to talk like that?"

"Like what?" Arthur said. "I haven't noticed anything special about my tone."

"No? Well you sound like a talking refrigerator, if you want to know."

"I see."

"No you don't."

"Don't what?"

"*See,* Arthur. You don't see anything, you don't see what's right in front of your nose!"

"Meaning you? I see you all right, Doris. But thanks for your opinion. I plan to memorize what you think of me, you know? Every golden consonant and vowel."

"Oh hell!"

She ate her pie. After a moment he said, in the same stiff tone, that he was sorry if he'd offended her.

"Ha," said Doris.

"Now what does that mean?"

"Nothing, nothing at all. Let's go back and get my things. Is there a phone here?"

"What for?"

"To call about the bus schedule."

"Now come on, Doris. I never said . . ."

"No, you never said!"

"Now listen, Doris, we're arguing like . . . like a middle-aged couple, for God's sake! You're being ridiculous, this has nothing to do with you. It's world-sickness. *World*-sickness!" He was feeling suddenly great again, articulate, easy, in perfect control. "Aren't I free to visit Harry for the weekend if I want to?"

"You're as free as you feel, Arthur."

"Exactly."

"Which isn't very free, is it?"

"Oh, I don't know."

"Well, *is* it?"

"Isn't it? Maybe not, maybe that's why I want to stay up here, I've gotten to feel like a . . . dray-horse. It's just been one thing after another, graduate school, writing the thesis, trying to teach at that godawful college, it's all so dull, so meaningless—" He saw that there were tears in her eyes. "Don't," he said. "Don't do that. Please, Doris."

"I'll leave you alone," she said. "We'll get a divorce. I'm sorry I've been . . . such a *bother*." She blew her nose on the smallest piece of Kleenex he had ever seen.

It was true, he had wanted to get rid of her all along, she somehow stood for all his dreary commitments. She was society, all by herself. And he didn't trust her not to do him in. Didn't trust her. They'd been married for over a year; he had kissed her lips and counted her freckles; his hand used to rest every night at the moment of sleep on her sex; and he didn't know her, didn't understand the first thing about her. He knew she had a rich cousin in Ontario, that her father had once owned a sporting-goods store before he turned to the practice of law, that her young Uncle Alex, at loose ends, had just joined the navy for a second tour. He knew that she had sung in a high school chorus that had won a state prize. He didn't know the first thing about her. What did she want? For him to be happy, she said. To have a happy husband and give assistance to the neighbors and be a fine cook and somehow sexy and profound and responsible and impulsive all at once, and it would all work out, all would be well, all manner of things would be well.

What did he know about her except that she had always seemed so calm, so cheerful? It was as if seeing Harry again twenty-nine hours ago had awakened him to the fact that he was one of the living-dead. Married. Respectable. Bourgeois. Sanity: it was somehow monstrous.

Was she a monster?

She looked innocent enough. She looked like somebody's sister. Like a girl scout. But he was afraid of her, that was becoming clear—there was something too persistent about her, when he started off for the john she was likely to ask where he was going, as if she liked to keep track. There was no telling what she'd be capable of in a few more years. She'd have him washing the walls.

She ate another bite of pie, wet-eyed. He gazed at her from behind the tilted rim of his raised coffee cup.

You're as free as you feel.

Well, true enough, that *was* his problem. Her freedom lay in her lack of concern for the whole concept of freedom. Women were like that. He could imagine her accepting the role of a martyr without even knowing there was any alternative—if the lions were hungry, Doris would feed the lions. And his own lack of freedom, did that come from being *overly* concerned? Then the only solution would be to say and do the first thing that came to mind, like Harry. Just be whimsical, live by chance, leap around, from one woman, one job, one mood to another. But a man had to be *civilized*. Just now he'd said the first thing that came to his mind, that he planned to stay on with Harry, but that wasn't any solution to the freedom problem, it was just giving up the problem, forgetting about it. And then what about the work-problem? And the morbidity-problem? And the thesis-problem? And the love-problem?

She glanced at him briefly and lowered her eyes to her pie. The stiletto look.

And what about the chaos-of-international-affairs problem, and the getting-older problem and the publish-books-and-articles problem? There were supposed to be two sides to every question, but he always found about seven. Following impulse solved nothing but the problem-problem. But then, didn't that contain all the others? *He* didn't know.

He was afraid he'd just ruined his marriage.

From the time Doris had spoken the words *You're as free as you feel,* exactly sixty-seven seconds have passed on the Rolex Oyster Perpetual worn on the hairy wrist of Roger Hulbert, the son of the owner, and in that time Arthur's moral surf ride has fetched him up in shallow, icy water, scraping bottom, his hair tousled, his breath gone. He told himself that after a while he might wade back in for another wave—the feeling of free flow was magnificent—but for the moment he'd better walk a little way up the shore.

"I didn't mean to hurt your feelings, Doris."

She smiled. Bitterly.

"It was just an impulse. We can go right back home now if you want to, both of us. We don't have to stay here."

"It's not that. I don't want to go back. I want to be . . ." It seemed for an instant that she was going to break down again. Half her pie remained on her plate. The little spoon with the monkey perched upon its heart, hands covering its ears, lay along the edge, still filled with a bite of meringue.

"You're sorry you married me, that's all. Be honest. That's

why you want to go away. And I thought it would be fun, sleeping in a strange room, in that nutty apartment. I know you'll laugh, so go ahead. I thought we'd stay up late, and talk . . . like when you're little and you spend the night with a friend and stay up till all hours, just whispering . . ." She sobbed. He began to trudge through the sand. The waves of impulse were already far behind. It was heavy going at first, but after he'd gotten the hang of it again it seemed as effortless as speaking out had been a moment before.

"I never said I wanted to leave you. That's ridiculous! I'd rather be with you than . . . just about anybody."

"Really?" She blew her nose again. "Really?" she asked, still sniffling, but with a hesitant smile.

"Really," he said. "I'm sorry, Doris. I shouldn't have—"

"I want to do whatever—"

"Yes, yes." He patted her hand.

She took up the monkeyspoon and licked it off with her tongue, her eyes fixed on his.

A stirring occurred at his groin.

What was going to happen to him? How could he ever get rid of her now?

A charmed expression appeared on the swarthy face of Roger Hulbert, the son of the owner. With the little spoon, Doris was feeding Arthur an enormous bite of lemon meringue.

How the hell can I get her back now? Harry was saying to the voice. You can't argue with her once she makes up her mind to switch around to something else. She's a force of nature!

A waterfall.

Or an iron mine.

Well, not really. An iron mine, that's not very nice. How about a gold mine?

Very funny.

Look, the voice said, *dominate her. Violent self-assertion. Be very male, she'll love it.*

Sure. She'd break my arm.

Miriam? That slip of a girl?

Some slip. What did her father claim about her mother?

That she was raising Miriam to be the first female five-star general.

Sure. So what am I supposed to do, keep her bound and gagged?

Why not? She'd appreciate the interest.

Sure.

She would. She'd enjoy being bound and gagged, it makes women feel free to be all tied up, then they don't have to think. That's why they get such a kick out of marriage.

Very clever. And when she has to go to work what am I supposed to do, take her over there on a leash?

Hold on, now, said the voice, *let's not get sadistic all of a sudden.*

At which point Miriam and Johnny began to climb the stairs at 96 Beachum, each carrying a large empty suitcase. They mount toward the dark apartment where Harry sits waiting, and as it happens, the first truly significant words he had ever spoken to Miriam were just then repeating themselves in his mind. It had been at the University Theatre, she was pulling a mild fit because he hadn't yet gotten hold of one of her props, a vacuum cleaner, after a week of rehearsals. When she quit complaining he'd said: "Why don't *you* try being the stage manager?"

Which led him to the memory of the February afternoon when he'd spied her in her low-necked red velvet through the window of Beds-'n-Things and she had said "Hi, Zissel—can I sell you anything?" and he'd told her that he was just looking, just looking around.

Miriam and Johnny have arrived on the third floor landing and pause for breath. Johnny is breathing particularly hard. He runs a long finger down the back of Miriam's neck, and she tells him to quit, and Harry is remembering the second time he entered the shop, to tell her he was interested in a bed lamp. She'd had the same dress on: later he'd learned that Johnny insisted it would double her sales. She'd led him through a maze of mirrors, through a forest of high-backed rockers, across the bedded fields. Her leg was bumped by a passing boudoir chair and she stopped to rub the hurt and his eyes fell uncontrollably into her bodice to trace there the line of her under-sheathed breasts. She straightened and caught him at it and an ambiguous smile appeared on her lips.

"Were you thinking of something in metal or what?" She'd only left school a month before, but she was already a pure shop-girl. And Harry, who'd been thinking not of metal but of her breasts, opened and shut with great rapidity several drawers of a desk he happened to be standing by, and then collapsed in a furry white swivel chair. This had seemed to confuse Miriam, who asked if he felt sick. He was already a drowning man at that point, drowning in desire, but instead of the past moving in review before his eyes, it was the future: work . . . fame . . . scorn of fame . . . more fame. He'd screened the vision again, trying to fit a female into it somewhere. There she was, Miriam Hippolyto, the lead in *The Respectful Prostitute,* leaning over him darkly, giving off the scent of Arpège, saying "Aren't you feeling well?" And immediately the future consisted of nothing except the two of them in a circular bed covered with simulated leopardskin.

"What's wrong, Harry?" she had asked.

"Nothing. It's just you've thrown me off-balance. I'm upset. I'll be okay in a minute."

"I've upset you?"

He'd nodded, shrugged, gazed at his feet, sighed. He hadn't dared look up at her. "Maybe it's your perfume."

"Really?"

"Yes, well, I'm very sensitive to smells—scents. I just got out of the army a little while ago, maybe I shouldn't get so close to women."

"You're allergic?"

"Highly sexed!"

That had done it for Miriam. Her smile had come alive. A

small seed rose by stages to a fine little tree of laughter. Others in the shop had turned to look at the dark-haired girl and the young man sitting despondently in the furry white swivel chair. The young man sitting in the chair had begun to laugh also, though without her assurance. A terrible thing was happening to him, his will was draining away, just draining away: his body felt limp, uninhabited, its machinery running without any supervision, without any brakes—

"Get up now," Miriam had said. "Come on."

He'd gotten to his feet.

"Look at me." She'd touched his cheek. The scent of her fingers had made him dizzy, made him close his eyes tight. He opened them to find her face two inches lower down—had she taken off her *shoes?*

"It's nothing to be ashamed of," she'd whispered affectionately. "It's a univeral instinct." She tilted up her head. The tip of her nose, as cool as air, was then situated exactly one-millimeter from his own. "Am I in love with you?" he asked in an astounded wheeze.

"Of course. It's perfectly natural. I feel sort of strange myself."

"Shall I kiss you?"

"Why not? Please."

They'd kissed. At length.

Coming up at last for air.

And in the shop the three other salesgirls, the two stockboys, Johnny, a young married couple from Meriden with their eight-month-old daughter in a collapsible blue stroller, the Paul McCobb sales representative from New York, two elegant local young men in suede jackets looking through fabric samples, all hesitated, like a provincial audience between movements of a symphony, and then, perhaps started off by the eight-month-old daughter of the married couple, there came a gentle round of applause. Harry still hears its echo in his mind as Miriam and Johnny reach the fourth floor landing, pause before his apartment, listen suspiciously, and note only the silence in which he sits, seven feet away from them on the other side of the front door.

"He must be gone all right," Miriam says. "Thank God."

"Wait," says Johnny, setting down his suitcase, "I'll see if I can tell anything through the old keyhole." There is an abandoned keyhole below the black doorknob. He kneels quickly, tries to kiss her leg at the back of the knee, and applies his eye. One can achieve a focused picture of Johnny if it is mentioned that he looks like The Ghost of Christmas Past after an extended stay in a concentration camp. A weedy type, with a mandarin mous-tache and beagle eyes. "It's dark," he says.

"Good." Miriam thrusts her key into the Yale lock above.

Which startled Harry out of his memories; they were advanc-ing into the room like conspirators. He switched on the lamp be-side him.

"You bastard!" said Johnny.

"I'm going," Miriam announced.

"Now just a minute—"

But she was out already, on the stair. He caught her by the shoulders two flights down. "Let go. You promised you wouldn't be here!"

"Should I rough him up for you, doll?" Johnny shouted from the landing above. He drooped over the bannister with his mouth pursed, like a mustachioed fish awaiting instructions.

"I have nothing to say to you, Harry. Let me go."

"I could say plenty," Johnny shouts.

"Go away, John. I've got to talk to Miriam."

"Don't you tell him to go away. He's my only protection."

"I'm everybody's protection." Johnny starts down the stair. "Except his."

"No," says Miriam, starting immediately back up, "we'll just take my things and leave, that's all. He can talk as much as he wants, I just won't listen. You told me you'd go out," she throws at Harry behind her, "that makes me so mad!" She goes into the apartment, taking up her suitcase, and the two men trail behind.

At the bathroom door she turns—"Do you *mind?*"—and slams it shut.

"You have no sense of decency," Johnny says. "You won't even leave her alone when she goes to the bathroom."

"Take off now," says Harry, "before you get hurt."

"Hurt?"

But Harry is talking to her through the door. "Miriam? Listen, Baby, I just hitchhiked down to see Arthur Thompson. I want you to come back now and stop acting ridiculous. I wasn't running away."

"Ha!" Johnny responds, and from Miriam the sound of the toilet flushing.

"Miriam? We love each other. Don't ruin everything. Why did you lie about being overdue? Not that I don't forgive you—"

They hear bottles being heaved into the suitcase. "Are you proposing marriage?" she calls out suddenly.

"Sure."

"Are you on your knees out there?"

"I'm on my knees."

"He is *not!*"

"You want your answer?"

"If it's convenient."

She bursts out the door and veers past them into the bedroom. "Fuck marriage," she says, "that's all I can say, there's a gentleman present."

"Now look, Miriam, I didn't even think of deserting you. I really didn't."

"Then why did you desert her?" says Johnny.

"Can't you shut this guy off? Stop making comments, Johnny. Go back to your goddam bed store."

"Making comments, that's my speech mannerism. Everybody's entitled to a speech mannerism. If you want to stop people from talking—" Harry makes a sound like a cat in heat and grabs Johnny hard by the neck; Johnny slips on the throw rug by the door and they both go down on Miriam's former bed. "I say," says Johnny, who has recently become convinced that he is essentially a homosexual still trying for a cure, "please!" Harry gets up, but Johnny lies there, his feet over the bed-end, his thin, pale, freckled hands crossed on his stomach. He closes his eyes. His mustache droops. "I think," he says, "I'll take a little rest after the violence. Harry? I'm glad you're back. Can you come to my party tomorrow?"

Miriam is busy grabbing up bits and pieces of clothing here and there. She picks up her unicycle and rolls the odd-looking, armless machine into the living room and leans it against the wall by the front door. She collects half the books in sight, piles her Mah Jongg set on top of her Go board, and ducks down on the floor to pull out a strapless bra from behind the bed where Johnny is lying. There is a dreamy expression on her face. Seeing the bra being handled so unceremoniously, Harry feels his whole being tilt with sexual pain. The nostalgia comes on in him so thick and unexpectedly that his nostrils dilate as if he is about to weep, and Miriam says to the brassiere "I knew I'd find you somewhere, stupid!" and brushes past him into the living room.

He goes around and sits down on the other bed. "I didn't mean to strangle you, John. I'm sorry." He is thinking: *Gevner's* ARMORED CLOUD.

"Then why did you strangle me?" Johnny says, not opening his eyes.

"Let's go," Miriam calls from the other room. "I've got just about everything."

Johnny rises, shrugs at Harry, and the two straighten their shoulders and march down the hall to the living room where Miriam is waiting.

What should Harry do, considering his condition; his emotional state; the whole situation? For one thing, he doesn't in fact understand the nature of Miriam's anger. After all, since she purely invented being pregnant in the first place, what does she expect? She preaches on about Lawrentian polarity and Sartrean good faith, and then, when she *pretends* to be twelve days overdue, is he supposed to start treating her like something out of the *Ladies' Home Journal? He* feels badly used. Why all the fuss? He needs a reprieve, time to get back on his feet from where she has him now, flat on his back. Maybe she was just indulging in the sulks, she was a great one for the sulks, and in fact she had seemed sort of glum for weeks before he left, now that he thought of it. Whenever he got permanently depressed like that he tended to ask somebody to marry him—maybe it just worked the other way round with women and made them mean? But what should he do? She won't even let him *talk*.

He does, in fact, what might seem a bit surprising if we hadn't witnessed his gathering melancholy during the past three days.

He begins, in a mild sort of way, to weep. This is perfectly authentic weeping, though it comes on without warning, surprising him; he is standing there and suddenly he realizes that this will really be his last look at Miriam; and the tears are in his eyes; not over her loss, but the finality of it, no chance for appeal; over the fact that they were executing the wrong man, that he hadn't done anything, that there'd been a mistake somewhere high up in the Organization.

He wiped the tears away with his fingers, but that only called attention to them.

"Ah, Harry," she said, "dirty pool."

He turned aside. Emotionally he was poised like a diver who has bounced a few times on the board, not really meaning to plunge, yet suddenly rising, toes unbending, arms swanning out —he fights against the full release, the dive into the bottomless ocean of misery, self-pity, the lack of control, the fear of never being able to come up for air. I'm hopeless, he thinks. His nostrils widen. It is like the long anticipation of a sneeze. It is like the hovering moment just before the top of the climb of sex. And before he knows it he's gone over, he's sobbing, Miriam observing him with horror as he leans against the wall beside her unicycle, then slides down to the floor, his head against his knee. "That's it, then," he says. "Go on," waving his arm at them, strangling the sobs, "I'm *sorry*." He gets control, but it threatens to begin again. He lurches up and touching the furniture along the way staggers to the bathroom, knowing that it wasn't even simply for the final loss of Miriam that he had wept; that it was for loss itself, for waste, for the strange law that everything, everything must turn out badly. The human condition. The Organization.

In the bathroom, over the sound of the water running in the basin, he heard the apartment door close. They were gone. He tensed against a chill that moved through his entire body, like a wave through a sieve. And he was all right, whole again. Drained. It had been like an earthquake, and now all was suddenly still within him. He dried his face and blew his nose. He was still weak in the legs. He shook his head like a cat with a mouse, drew a large breath, and smiled at himself wanly in the mirror. He tried out a grin showing all his teeth and realized that Miriam was watching from the shadow just beyond the bathroom door.

"Christ," he said, "you scared me!" It was just like her to change her mind. She told him she'd sent Johnny on ahead to wait in the car, she didn't have the heart to leave until she knew he was all right.

Now he felt shamed, in a way that he hadn't been by the tears.

"That wasn't about you," he said. "Don't act like somebody just *died!* I've been working up to that for about twenty-three years."

She nodded. He found that he felt perfectly cold toward her. He'd had his release, he was empty, now there was an edge of hatred because she'd shamed him, seeing him there at the mirror.

"Where's your stuff?" he said.

"John took it down to the car. He forgot the unicycle." She was holding the solitary wheel by its single, seat-topped limb.

"Want some coffee?"

"Johnny's waiting."

"Sure."

"I'll listen to you now," she said. "What did you want to tell me?"

"Nah," he said. "That's all right."

"Then I will have some coffee."

He put the water on to boil and poured himself some Cointreau in the bottom of a cup. She'd given him the bottle of Cointreau. A certain amount of feeling was growing up between them again, like a hint of musk in the room. When the coffee was ready they sat at the table in the kitchenette. It was strange. She was his guest. Johnny was waiting for her in the car and she was sipping coffee out of one of the big yellow mugs they'd bought one windy afternoon in the Square. They were together in the apartment as they'd been for three months, and now he wasn't allowed to touch her, ever again.

"Is there any sugar?"

He passed her the sugar.

It was very strange. His sadness began to return.

"Well," she said. "I guess I grew up yesterday."

Poor Miriam, it's clearly a hard job for her to strike the proper note. She's sad herself, though she'll be damned if she'll show it. And she's not at all anxious to rejoin Johnny; she had enough trouble with him the night before, and the prospect of seeing the eyes of Johnny's mousy wife again tonight sends a shiver right through her. It was a mistake to let Johnny take her home, she would have to change that arrangement fast. And meanwhile here she was, feeling like a bitch, staying on to console Harry. How could she help feeling sympathetic? Because she *was* a bitch. She thought of the Indian virgins who were supposed to sleep with their thighs roped together. To prevent rape? or the giving of sympathy? To give sympathy to Harry would be catastrophic. It was over, and she had drawn a line; it had been working up to being over for a long time.

And yet she was sad. He seemed to expect something from her now, their roles had been reversed, he was no longer in any way the villain of the piece, by staying to console him she condemned herself for being the cause of his pain.

133

It was hard to find the proper tone. She solved the problem by speaking in a low voice, the kind of voice one uses at funerals. It wasn't anybody's fault, the low voice implied. It was simply an act of nature.

It should be noted that Miriam has a beautiful voice. She speaks as if the sound were filtered through clear, cool water.

"I'm feeling very strong. Can you tell? It's just that things weren't going very well anyway, were they?"

"What are you talking about?" He'd spoken too sharply. They were both realizing that it had been a mistake for her to stay on like this. All of the emotions of the past few days had dwindled to nothing but an aggrieved embarrassment, this restrained feeling between them.

"I don't want to argue," Harry said. "I just want to understand. I thought we were doing all right. Isn't that a laugh? I know I shouldn't have taken off like that, without telling you anything. I guess I wasn't quite ready to get married."

"It wasn't that," she said.

He blinked at her, raising his shoulders.

"It wasn't that. It wasn't because you didn't like the idea of a shotgun wedding. Who could blame you? I would have done the same thing."

"You're kidding."

"No, if I were a man mixed up with a girl like that, like the kind of vicious person you obviously thought—"

"I see."

"I may be a bitch, but I'm not vicious."

"I didn't know there were various kinds of bitches."

"So now you know."

"Yes."

"But it wasn't only that. I've got to go," she said, rising. "I'd better go, Harry."

"No, don't. You can't go now."

"I've got to."

What do you have to lose? said the voice. *Rape her. Come on.*

He reached the door ahead of her, blocking the way. "Stop it,"

134

she said. Her voice, which was described a moment ago as sounding as if it were filtered through water, now sounds as if the water had become a little cloudy and agitated. "Let me by, Harry."

"Not till you tell me when you started to hate me."

They stood inches apart. He watched the complicated small movements of her lips like a hungry man studying the growth of his neighbor's garden. Slowly, softly, her lips formed what once would have been an unprintable phrase.

He grabbed her and managed to press his mouth upon hers, but it was like the contact of bone on bone. She felt sick at being so unmoved in his arms. For her it had begun to turn to nothing, whatever there was at first between them, long before this ridiculous week. She had only wanted to return some of the early sweetness, because she'd been needlessly cruel, and now he was making her sick of him. She pulled away from his embrace. "Are you trying to break my *teeth,* for God's sake?"

Why were all the men she knew so weak?

"Let's make love," he said. "Just one last time. Maybe it will change things."

"I feel like a sister toward you."

"Don't joke."

She shrugged her shoulders, then tossed her head. "Let me by, Harry."

"But why? Why did you say you were overdue?"

"You want me to tell you? Because I was tired of us, that's why. Because I didn't like the way you sounded talking to your mother while I was stored away in that closet. Because I wanted . . . I wanted something to *happen* for once."

"Something happened," he said.

"Oh yes."

"You caught a glimpse of the moral putrescence within. And then I ran away, which was terribly dull and predictable, wasn't it? Just what you thought I'd do."

"I didn't think anything. I tried to tell you—you've never had any idea of who I was or what I stood for, not the slightest glimmer. So I thought, if that's all he thinks of me . . . let's quit this, Harry, it's just too awful and depressing. Let me go now." She was holding the unicycle between them, letting it roll a bit from side to side.

"This is a hell of a situation," he said. He continued to lean against the door. *Try to kiss her,* said the voice. *Go on, go on, try. Kiss first, rape later.*

"Let me go, Harry."

He moved out of her way. She started slowly down the four flights, bumping the unicycle. When she was on the second stair he called out: "We should have made love!" and for a moment she stopped, looking back. "Yes," she said, and he gazed down at her then in total confusion.

"Only you didn't want to enough," she called up to him.

"Miriam! For God's *sake.*"

"You never really loved me," she said. "It's too late to start now. We don't know how to love people."

The unicycle bumped down, a step at a time, and the front door opened and closed.

His voice spoke to him very gently:

Have you ever really thought of killing yourself?

TEN

It is early Friday morning. For a considerable time in its slow turning the earth has revealed little more to the sun than an occasional steamer bound for Livorno or a school of dolphins humping along a cold eddy of the Atlantic tide. But the sunlight beams down with a bland intensity, beams on everything, regardless of race, creed, or place of national origin. And everything seems in its usual state of receptivity: New Hampshire fishermen greet the first rosy wave of dawn with a starting of motors, and TV aerials on the roofs of oceanfront hotels in Atlantic City, Myrtle Beach, Fort Lauderdale, and Key Largo, bristle and flash. The light brings the rumble of semi-trailers along the Jersey Turnpike out of busy hiding, and brightens the aluminum glitter of ten thousand identical screen-and-storm windows in the housing development below Hartford, Connecticut, where the Subersteins live. It pleases early walkers along the tidal flats up and down the coast, and sweeps over the neo-gothic spires of the university in Fear of Reprisals where Harry and Arthur at this very hour approximately four years ago were sending *Perdito* pounding out into the mild morning air. Off to the west by a considerable amount, beyond San Mateo, California, where it is still dark, still night in fact, a distant tugboat sounds its hooter, and great numbers of young people lying awake and full of desire in San Mateo are moved to a terrible nostalgia for places where they have never been. But in the living room on Beachum Street where Harry lies in fitful sleep the sunshine nudges its way, first as a pale rectangle on the windowsill, then spilling over to the floor at a sharp tilt to form a plane in which dust motes dance, entering at this uncomfortable angle because the eastern window of the room has its blinds down practically to the sill; then, so impeded, the light makes a patient progress across the cluttered floor, riding up and over books and shoes, over oddments for Harry's construction, over crockery and cooking utensils, fingering the plaster bust of Leopardi, always on the move, climbing the record player to inch across its grainy plastic top and down the other side. Now, going on ten o'clock, the sunlight stretches out, works up the foot of the couch, advances gradually, ripplingly up the furrows of foxed brown mohair, and in a final, conclusive effort, flows over Harry, his mouth curved sweetly in a dreamer's incalculable ease. The light rolls over him, rises up the leprous back of the couch like clear water nearing the lip of a tub. And comes to a wavering halt as it reaches the buff wall, drawing a tide-mark there across the wall and the dusty window and its bars.

As if this had caused a reverberation, Harry's eyelids flutter. The Friday morning sunlight falls upon him, the world continues turning, in China in the dead of night a new Chinese is being born every several seconds; in India the Himalayas are covered with unmarred snow; in various parts of the U.S.A. patriotic families are reciting the pledge of allegiance to the flag before eating breakfast. Much, in short, is happening everywhere completely beyond the range of our narrative or the concerns of Harry Zizzel, who is scheduled to awake in a moment on the couch at 96 Beachum to discover a pain commencing at the soles of his feet and concluding in a headache that probes experimentally at the occipital lobe.

This is the second night running that Harry has spent on a couch. Later he will weigh the qualities of the two, his couch and

Arthur's, and conclude that his, the couch of so-called luxury, has it hands down for size and overall softness, but that Arthur's is stronger on basic consistency of surface and freshness of smell. It will strike him that way later in passing—but for the moment his bare left shoulder twitches like the rump of a horse annoyed by flies; his muscles and tendons, despite seven hours' rest, register great resentment at being disturbed, and at the same time his brain is striving to retain a dream in which he is piloting a car without brakes along an empty highway. In the dream he controls the car not by a steering wheel but with a propstick, as if in an old-fashioned airplane. Actually the prop takes care of itself, which is convenient, for he is much involved, in a slow, frustratingly-satisfying way, with a young woman clad—somewhat clad—in nothing but a fur-lined cloak, rabbit or ermine, it's hard to tell. They go around a curve and start gradually downhill. The prop becomes difficult, he barely manages to control it with one hand and keep in touch with the girl with the other, dangerous work, cars and trucks zooming by, the girl drowsy, not noticing the danger, and no way to slow down. Luckily vehicles ahead and to the side keep veering off onto exit ramps, he's feeling confident, the road is even going a bit uphill, more uphill, which slows them—maybe the hill will solve the brake problem, his only worry. He figures his luck is looking good enough to get him there (where?), but how to stop is the big question. Travel uphill, is that the answer? The girl in the dream is suddenly wearing an Arabian veil, and he realizes that it is Doris. Doris? Uphill and slowing, life becoming sweet, until it strikes him that at a certain point they were bound to roll over the top and down the next hillside, or begin rolling backwards down this one. But the hell with it, let people get out of the way behind or ahead, he turns his full attention to the fur-lined Doris, the car is like a room, like a boat, a bed, a couch . . . he rolls over on his side, facing the sunlight, and the dream expires before he's quite through with it. He inches back over the curious terrain of the cushions, fighting to stay asleep, hunching, seeking comfort, his mouth working. He is wearing only BVD shorts from which a sizable portion of the anatomical region intended to be covered has escaped. The sunlight beams upon him. The tidemark on the wall and across the barred window moves with a slight movement of the opposite blind. He is awake, miserable, his tongue like the grass doormat of a beach house, his bones throbbing in a muted cadence, all of him producing the sensation of having been meticulously beaten the night before. For the space of two seconds, lying flat, he proceeds to give up drinking, smoking, women—especially women—self-pity, late hours, and artistic pretensions of all conceivable kinds; taking up instead early rising, cold baths, Great Fortunes. After Miriam had left last night, and before Arthur and Doris had returned, he'd knocked off the remains of the bottle of Cointreau plus a full pack of cigarettes. He eases up gradually. He sits for a long moment on the edge of the couch with his face in his hands, Doris in the dream forgotten, he himself feeling very strange, like some leftover part of someone he can't quite recall. Something Miriam once said comes dimly back. ". . . scared to death I won't get everything, so all I get . . ." Yes? he urged his memory. All I get . . . ?

Is the leavings, said his voice. *The dreks; the dregs. Also the snows of yesteryear, the unfinished, mangled, fly-blown . . .*

Did Miriam say all that?

Of course not. But you know what a dropout is? An ego-maniac. A life-hog. Wants everything, consequently gets . . .

Yeah, you just told me.

Life is a pseudo-problem, said the voice. *No solution in sight.*

Thank you, said Harry. Many thanks for your helpful advice.

Be my guest. Have you ever really thought of killing yourself?

He sits hung-over on the nut-brown couch; then rises, with shambling steps makes it across the room. He's certainly not going to kill himself without some breakfast in him. That's not the sort of thing you want to do on an empty stomach.

Not a sound from the closed bedroom door. Were the Thompsons still sleeping? The apartment is so quiet it seems to hum, but that turns out to be the refrigerator. He studies the contents.

Doris and Arthur had carried a few things back with them last night: a package of bacon, eggs; odds and ends. Haddock casserole still in residence. The chill refrigerated sub-world was a bit more populated now, like the apartment; it hums, beams with light-shine. Harry takes up the carton of eggs, seems to weigh it in his hands. It is heavier than he expected; he returns it to the top shelf. It strikes him that he hasn't had what you could call a meal for a good long time. Maybe that's why he's been so depressed. He consumes a handful of cheese crackers, and proceeds to fix himself a cup of instant coffee at the hot water tap. The coffee tastes like Guinness Stout, but at least it wakes him a little, it gives his stomach something to do, keeps it off the streets. Munching cheese crackers he takes up his khakis from the floor and slips them on.

Have you ever really thought of killing yourself?

Okay. Thank you. Now go away.

But wouldn't it be hilarious? and typical? I mean Arthur gets you all excited about Miriam *committing suicide, and then, as it turns out . . .*

Stirrings in the bedroom. A thump. A double thump. What are they doing in there all of a sudden? A sound as of someone chopping a hole in the floor with the front legs of a horse. Which continues—clearly nothing sexy, entirely too violent. For Arthur, anyway. On the other hand, it might be an emergency —maybe they're beating up on one another without saying a word. They've been bitching enough to need a good mutual maul. Suddenly there is heavy breathing, grunting—wow. As he stands before the door, about to shout *do you need any help?* Arthur emerges and passes him on the way to the john, washcloth and towel over his arm like an underclassman at a military academy. His former roommate shrugs before he disappears: "Doris exercises in the mornings."

The door to the bedroom remains open. She is fully clothed, down on the floor in front of the beds, and he watches with astonishment, with a growing respect and attention—fifteen pushups, before breakfast! She glances at him with a quick smile and

141

begins to do an incredible thing: arching her body, she balances briefly on one hand and one foot, the other arm and leg in the air, and then with a banging flick reverses, back and forth, again and again, arms and legs sticking out all over the place and her skirt riding high up her thighs, legs lovely, delicate but strong. Mindlessly he wanders into the room, sits on the end of Miriam's bed, smiling. Now Doris is doing sit-ups at an unbelievable rate, turned away from him, her wrists touching her toes, her head touching her knees each time, her blouse coming taut over her bra-strap, loosening, coming taut. Amazing. He's forgotten his troubles—when she is finished and sits drooping forward like a rag doll, he applauds.

"Thank you," she says. "Don't you exercise in the morning?"

"My imagination," he says. "My mind. Not this sort of thing."

Wouldn't it be funny? typical?

"Well," she is up, running in place, "you look like you *need* some exercise. You could have a fine body—if you took—some care of it." Stopping, panting, pushing back her hair. "I'll teach you the whole series if you want."

"I have a mongrel body, it's no use, I was put together by an amateur."

"With this system you start with some very easy things and gradually work up to your profile level. Okay? Want to try? Let's start with running-in-place."

"No thanks, Doris. Teach Arthur. I'm sedentary from top to bottom. Besides, I'm actually thinking of killing myself."

"Can't you even try running in place?"

"I could, my love, that's my kind of exercise, but when you come right down to it—"

"You're a snob," she said, "like Arthur. Another mind-snob." At least she was perfectly cheerful about it. "You're a victim of this mind-body thing."

"It's Plato's fault," said Harry. "Plato and Aristotle. They sure got everybody completely fucked up, those boys."

"What does Plato have to do with it?"

. . . hilarious, if instead of Miriam . . .

"Harry?"

"Plato? Nothing, nothing really, it's just something to say, I sort of like to say words, keep my mouth moving."

"Okay, move, I want to make the bed."

"You don't have to make the bed."

"Oh yes I do. Up. Get *up,* Harry!"

He shrugged and stood as she straightened the beds, with a sudden conviction that she had *slept* fully clothed. There was some essential, unmoving part in her, despite all her efforts at smiles and banter. An iron core. Formidable. Also she seemed to know just what she wanted at all times—any normal male would contemplate rape after an hour in her company. Or, in a certain mood, murder.

Or suicide?

She finished with the beds and pushed back her hair. "What will you do now then? Find another confused girl to come live with you?"

"I guess first I'd better run up some breakfast."

"No, I'm the one around here who teaches the domestic arts. Just exercise your mind." She stepped into her high-heeled shoes and left him with a wave. "Stop *thinking* about her." The room had a hint of the earnest smell of a gymnasium.

Exhausted, as if he'd been the one to do the exercising, he stretched out on Miriam's bed. Arthur returned—either he too had slept fully clothed or Doris had had him up doing exercises earlier, because he looked very rumpled, even with a fresh shave. "Okay," Arthur said, "let's hear all the details."

"No," said Harry. He'd given them both an account of Miriam's visit, late into the night. "Who cares anymore? The hell with her. If I could find a nice, normal girl, a girl who wasn't so distracted, who really liked men or sex or whatever it is . . . who was willing to blow her cool and *feel* a little something for somebody . . ."

143

"Yes?"

"I'd marry her, is that it? Become an encyclopedia salesman? Ah, the hell with it."

"It's not the girl," said Arthur. "It's you."

"Naturally. Tell me, why'd you go to a movie?"

"Nobody's around on campus. I didn't see a single face I knew. The town's really changed in four years."

"Has it? I keep wondering about that. I mean wondering what's changing, me or it."

"It," said Arthur, "don't you think? You're the same as ever. But it's unbelievable, some undergraduates were practically copulating right there in front of Sandol Hall last night. I mean, standing up! About ten couples, trying to beat closing hours. You'd think you were in Tahiti or something."

"They don't have closing hours anymore."

"You mean the co-eds just stay out all night?"

"For Godsakes, Arthur, did you sleep with your clothes on?"

"Doris did."

"Did you?"

"Well, I thought Doris would feel, you know, in a strange place . . ."

"No, I don't know. Did she make you sleep—"

"It was *my* idea, if you have to know. When you're in a strange place you get nervous, you never know when you might—"

"Jesus! And I expected you to teach *me* something!"

"Not so loud, Harry, she's right in the next room."

"Arthur, what's happened to you?"

"There you go again."

"No, no really, is it that bad to be, what, what are you now, thirty?"

"Just about. So I'm trying to lead a mature existence."

"Sleeping with your clothes on? A mature existence. Boy! I mean, you still must be down there underneath, Arthur, we'll just have to blast a little to get under all that accumulated bullshit. What you need is artificial respiration."

"Thank you. Did that make you feel better?"

"It made me sick to my stomach. Boy, you're some example for the next generation."

"Who said I'm supposed to be an example? Am I accountable to you? Listen, if I were *free,* with what I know now, I could really get some living done, believe me. But as it happens I make you sick to your stomach, and I stand here and let you insult me, it's a great mystery."

"Why aren't you free?"

"Ha," said Arthur.

"Because of *her?* Don't be ridiculous, she'd follow you anywhere, like a faithful dog, anybody could see that."

"Okay. But the more you understand the other guy's point of view, the harder it is not to sort of start functioning in terms of what he, or what she wants. That's what marriage is like. I mean, I'd be much better off with Doris if I were an egomaniac like you, then I'd just carry on without even noticing—"

"—Yeah, like I do, right over the Alps with my elephants! You talk such *crap,* Arthur. Why do I expect that everybody who's five minutes older than I am *must* have something to tell me, some lifesaving word he could toss out if he'd by God only take the *trouble?*"

"I can't tell you anything, Harry, not once you get started. I never could."

"No," Harry said with a sudden grimness, "you'd better tell me, Arthur. If you've got anything for me you'd better start coughing up right away. I'm depending on you. Seriously, what am I supposed to do?"

"You want advice about Miriam? Doris thinks *I* should go talk to her. Get her to come back here."

"About everything. I'm scared, Arthur. Listen, it's not a joke, I'm starting to feel a little I don't know. Suicidal."

"Yeah? Well cut that out!"

"Okay."

"Did she take all her belongings this time?"

Harry nodded, half sitting up in bed.

145

"Stop and think—why did you ask her to marry you on the phone that time?"

"Who knows? I thought that was supposed to be the thing to do. I felt lonesome, that's all. *I* don't know why I do things."

"You felt lonesome?"

"Okay. Because I love her. Is that the right answer?"

"Love her! You don't love her anymore than you love . . . Doris, for God's sake!"

Have you ever really thought . . . ?

"Maybe you lust after her, though I doubt even that. So if you want advice . . ."

Doris appeared in the doorway. "Orange juice," she said, handing Arthur both small glasses. "How can you two fight so early in the morning?"

"We were talking," Harry said with grim emphasis. "We were just trying to have a little uninterrupted man-to-man talk. I mean if you could spare us like thirty seconds all to our—"

She turned on her heel and slammed the door behind her. "Excuse me for existing!"

"Now *you've* hurt her feelings," Arthur said wearily.

"Of course. What do you expect? Everytime I open my mouth I hurt somebody's feelings."

"Come on, get up. She made breakfast, the least we can do is eat some of it."

They settled at the table in the kitchenette. Stiff as steel Doris served their plates with bacon and scrambled eggs.

"I'm beginning to gather I'm not wanted around here," Doris said. "I mean maybe you two want to run off with one another."

Arthur chewed at top speed, like a tunnel-digger, trying to open the way for speech. "Of course you're wanted," he told her. "Let's not start that again. You're very much wanted, Doris."

"I hate to feel—sometimes it strikes me that men aren't really—"

"Oh, you're wanted, you're wanted all right, Doris, don't get excited, please?"

"I'm sorry, Doris," Harry said. "I talk too much."

"He's sorry," said Arthur. "You can see it in his face. We're both just a little distracted these days. But you're wanted, all right. Jesus!"

She began to eat. They all ate. The refrigerator hummed. She refilled their coffee cups. "Go ahead," she said at last. "Talk. I'll wait in the bedroom. I'm sorry I didn't bring earplugs with me." Without warning she was in tears again, despite a mouthful of eggs. Arthur gazed at her in horror as she continued to chew. She dabbed at her eyes. "Talk," she said. "I couldn't be more uninterested. I'll catch the next bus to Cordelia. And you," she threw at Arthur, "you can go to Reno."

She took her dishes to the sink and left the room.

"There," said Arthur. "See what they're like? No wonder everybody's out of his mind. And you ask me why I don't feel free!"

"She seems to think you want a divorce," Harry said. He picked up a monkeyspoon and toyed with the eggs on his plate. "Where'd she get that idea?"

"From me."

"What?"

"You heard me. Only I always wind up feeling sorry for her."

"I won't say a word."

They sipped their coffee. Puffed on their cigarettes. Arthur seemed to be contemplating the idea of invisibility.

"What kind of spoons did you say these were?" Harry stirred his cup with one.

"Monkeyspoons."

"Why the little hearts?"

"For the monkeys to stand on."

"Of course. Which do you have?"

"Speak-no-evil."

"That's appropriate: Doris's is hear-no-evil. If Miriam were around she could use the one with its hands in its armpits."

"Touch-no-evil."

"Right. That's Miriam's kind of spoon, it just washes its hands of the whole business and goes sleepwalking."

"Women are strange," Arthur said.

147

"You *told* her you wanted a divorce?"

"No. Not exactly. I wish I'd kept my mouth shut."

"Poor Arthur. She really gets at you, doesn't she? We'll all be better off when they get this parthenogenesis-technique perfected."

"They've been doing it with frogs for years," Arthur said. "They make a tiny hole in the egg, just a pinhole, and it's fertilized."

"Simple enough."

"No mess. No bother. You don't even have to sever the spinal cord."

"The male frogs could just sit around all day in the swamp."

"Croaking," Arthur said. "Do you suppose they miss the lady-frogs?"

"They're cold-blooded."

"True."

"But they probably do miss them, they're only frogs, what do they know?"

"They've got this other thing, too, the chromosome-code stuff, all the microbiologists are working on it. Eventually they'll create life all wrapped up like at the supermarket, untouched by human hands."

"And the sperm bank," Harry said, "do you know about that? They want to freeze the sperm of great men and use it by artificial insinuation, centuries later."

"In*sem*ination, Harry."

"That's a joke! Only you in all the world, Thompson, wouldn't know that was a joke!"

"It would sort of be hard on the great men."

"Exhausting. There'd have to be rationing or something. But then women could raise lots of little Bachs and Beethovens. They could choose any brand of kid they wanted and never have to sleep with a man. Talk about efficiency!"

Arthur tilted back in his chair. "Listen. Our sex life has just about entirely gone to pot. There's something wrong with me, Harry. I mean, I've got wonderful theories—"

148

"She's sexy enough, Arthur."

"I know it. It's me. I'm falling apart. And she says 'Toast the bread, Arthur—all you need is some secure family life.'"

"That's a very good imitation, you know? That's exactly how she sounds."

"Oh, I've studied her all right. What do you suppose she's doing in the bedroom? Should I go knock on the door?"

"I have a better idea. This is the moment of truth, Arthur—do you think you can take it?"

"Shoot."

"Go get yourself another woman. No, I'm not kidding, it'll sweeten your disposition."

"There's still a law against bigamy."

"Only if you marry them, right? Listen, go fall in love with Miriam, she's perfectly free at the moment. Ten minutes with Miriam and you'll appreciate what you've got."

"I've never even seen Miriam. Can't you be serious for once?"

"I'll show you a snapshot and you can fall in love, what's wrong with that? People are always getting crushes on Miriam anyway. They see her down the end of the block and they come up and offer to lick her feet, like on a twenty-four hour basis. It's eerie. She says it's always been that way, it's because she's sort of cold. They can't offer her enough. They want her to walk all over them."

"Who are we talking about?"

"God knows. Strangers, usually. Her teachers at school. Anybody. They get this urge."

"And what does she do about it?"

"Oh, sometimes she kicks them in the teeth, which is no doubt what they deserve and are really after in the first place, or sometimes she lets them lick the feet, or she walks on them, it varies with her mood."

"I understand."

"Sure," said Harry. "I mean, we're all people here, there aren't many surprises or new positions."

Arthur lit another cigarette, took a long drag, settled down in

149

his chair. He placed his elbows on the table and contemplated his cigarette tip. "I guess I'd better take her back to Cordelia."

Doris entered the room and they saw that she had changed her clothes; she wore a yellow print dress and looked as fresh as a flower.

"You all right?" said Arthur.

"I'm stupid," she said. "I thought I'd go out for a walk around the Square and maybe do some window-shopping and let you two talk. I'm sorry I'm always butting in like that."

"No, no," they cried in unison.

"There's nothing you shouldn't hear," Harry told her. "Arthur was actually just going to sketch out the rest of my life and then you two were going to take off for Cordelia and water your houseplants and live happily ever after."

Doris sat down with them and shook one of Harry's cigarettes out of the pack. "Talk to Harry," she said. "Straighten him out. I'll just watch, I won't listen to a word."

Mid-afternoon. For hours they've been straightening Harry out. A rectangular cloud of tobacco smoke hangs just under the ceiling and Doris sits on the floor next to Harry's construction, her shoes off, her legs tucked under her, the sepia print of Strindberg gazing down balefully through the cracked glass as if to focus his hatchet face exactly at the top of Doris's head. Arthur is pacing up and down. Harry is stretched out on his back on the couch as if he had never left the spot where he'd spent the night. "All right," Arthur sighs, "so life is completely worthless and meaningless. You've proved it. We're all so sick it's a waste of energy even to hope that things might pick up a little."

"What are they going to pick up *from?*" Harry said. "The salt hath lost its savor, right?"

"And the daughters of music are brought low," said Arthur.

"And desire," said Harry, "desire shall fail."

Arthur gulped. "Talk about the *lost* generation," he said, "this one just stays home in bed, lost or found doesn't make any difference and they know it. This is the comatose generation. The dustbin crowd. Life is—"

"Meaningless? Not meaningless? Come on, Arthur, fight a little, put up some kind of a struggle, can't you? It's not funny anymore."

"Now look," Doris put in, "I know this must sound simple-minded, but if Harry could decide on *anything* he wanted to do, anything at all, just so it was some kind of real work, well that would be a starter." She looked up at Harry. "You could finish your Plato and Aristotle paper, couldn't you? Or your play, even if it is as terrible as you say? Just finish it even if you burn it up after?"

"Why?" said Harry blankly. He gazed at the ceiling. "Why waste the paper?"

"I give up," said Doris. "Life is meaningless."

"In a way he's right, you know," said Arthur. "I mean, where will the energy come from? I could tell him lots of things, I suppose. As a teacher of humanities I spend a lot of time thinking about such things and pushing against them and theorizing—"

"—and over*coming* them, Arthur!" Her eyes were alight. "I mean you're *wonderful* at overcoming—"

"—no, no I'm not, Doris, but that's not the point. I have some kind of vision of the good life, I guess, only it doesn't even work for me, so what's the use of spreading it around?"

"Now God damn it, that's selfish," Harry shouted. "You always did have a goddam tight asshole on you, Thompson. I mean, here's an old friend dying before your eyes and just because your own life isn't—"

"—isn't what?" said Doris dangerously.

Harry paused, then stopped. "Nothing," he said. "That's it. We've come to the end of the line. Motorists! You are leaving the State of Zissel! Drive with care."

"I don't know," said Arthur, "maybe you could make it if you could only think straight. Maybe I'm just a coward, you know, like the guy in the Bible, the guy who broke through on Christ but first he wanted to get all his affairs straightened out—"

"—like a Sunday pot-smoker," Harry said.

"—bury his dead," said Arthur, "and Christ said, 'Come, follow me, let the dead bury the dead.' I mean, break, change, carry on, right?"

"With your morality and my vanity, Thompson, we could rule the world."

"Yeah, but who wants to?"

"Why do both of you always give up?" Doris asked. She turned to Harry. "If you were a different sort of man, do you think Miriam would have treated you so casually?"

"What sort of man?"

"The sort who *does* things," Doris said. "Tell me, what's your play about? Read us some."

"Who knows? If I knew what it was about, I'd be in the clear. It's full of Dante's Inferno, among other things, But then somebody—"

"Do you *want* to finish it?"

"Do I want to? Sure. I guess so. Except two other kids in the class are writing a play about Dante's Inferno. And I found out a couple of years ago there was an off-Broadway play that was *called* 'Dante's Inferno,' and then there was going to be a movie, and then last week I read a review of a novel called *Virgil at Bay* so nothing seems like my own anymore. It's Arthur's Organization, that's what it is. If I put a note down in my notebook the next day there'll be a movie, a statue, a happening, an epic poem based on the identical idea. It's invariable. Somebody up there doesn't like me—or else He's got one sadistic sense of humor!"

"Well, what's the problem?" Doris asked, clearly unable to comprehend. "You *don't* want to finish it?"

"The play? It's awful. Besides, all those other fellows can do a much more professional job."

"Jesus! Okay. But you do want to get married, is that right? That's something you seem to want, isn't it? Stop and think. Do you? Do you want to get married?"

"Are you proposing?"

"Come on, Harry. The point is you don't seem to understand yourself at all."

"It's Miriam I don't understand." Sulkily. "Other people."

"Why? I understand Miriam, and I've never even met her. She wants the excitement of living with a madman and the security of his turning out to be not *that* much of a madman. It's what girls want, both things at once, a poet who's also an insurance company executive. I'm giving away one of the trade secrets."

"Some secret," Harry said.

"If that's what women want," said Arthur, "what about men?"

"I guess they want just about the same thing, don't they? Danger and safety?"

"No no," said Harry, "just the opposite. It must be the opposite. Everything's arranged in terms of opposites with that damn Organization. No, look, Doris, I appreciate your interest but it's hopeless. Even Arthur can't think of anything to say to cheer me up."

"I'm destroyed," said Arthur. "Even saying 'life is meaningless' is meaningless is meaningless."

"All I could ever take seriously is art," Harry said, "so I don't take anything else seriously enough to be an artist. That's really the center of my whole trouble, right there, only what can I do? The dinosaurs died out and we're getting along without them, aren't we? If evolution doesn't want me it's nothing to get excited about, I'll go quietly, no need for a purge trial. It's the sort of thing that happens, a creature comes along and there's nothing you can do, who needs him?, he's just supposed to sink down quietly and turn into coal."

"Everybody's life has value," Doris said intently. "Everybody's important or else nobody is, you've *got* to believe that."

"Oh sure. It's the lesson of history, isn't it? People killed off like flies year after year for centuries and ergo each individual life is sacred. I mean, we make human soap, and lampshades—"

"I'm feeling sick," said Arthur. "Do you think we could change the subject for a while?"

"I mean, what do I need, if I'm supposed to come to something? Simple: the courage of a great revolutionary. It's as simple as that. Courage. And a gift, a gift to force down the world's throat. Or else a shave, a bath, an education, a profession, a family tree, business connections, what else? An easy conscience? Confidence? A big lily-white house with a horse of my own, a set of Longfellow in the library, an Irish setter dog and a Phi Beta Kappa key? But since it happens that I can't supply most of these items and I'd only probably write obscenities in the margins of the set of Longfellow anyway, and be thrown from the horse, and be pulled on the leash by the dog who'd also shit all over the Persian rug in the library—"

"Can't we *stop?*" Arthur said. He was lying on his stomach out across the middle of the living room floor between Harry and Doris.

"I can't adapt," Harry went on. "I can't. Read Darwin—it's lethal whether you fight it or not, if you haven't got the stuff, the flexibility. I mean, look at the way I went through my artistic career. I never finished a single thing. Amazing, I must have set a record. Statues, paintings, plays, poems—you start wanting to create when you realize how much there is to say and you don't know how to get it down, and you're finished with art when you realize it doesn't make any difference anyhow, whether you get it down or not—and for me there never was any space inbetween, I had both realizations at once, all along. So that's it and I'm all straightened out and thank you and it's all been interesting and the solution is exceedingly simple, so now you can go home to Cordelia, finito, and be a happy academic family."

"What's simple?" said Doris.

"We've narrowed the alternatives right down—the only logical step is for me to commit suicide."

"Quit it, Harry," said Arthur. "You know how I feel about that particular kind of joking."

The rotating fan on the windowsill, turned on to get some of the cigarette smoke out of the room, came to the end of its cycle and gave a little sound—ti-ti-ti-titsch—before moving the other way.

"Who's joking? I've been feeling more or less dead for years, I might as well make it official." He started pacing around the room. "We'll have a party, you know? Get everybody together, a suicide party? Do it right, refreshments, music, maybe Arthur will give us a sermon. Tonight at Johnny's? Why not? He'll be glad to let me be part of the evening's entertainment. Should I phone and ask, or just make it impromptu?"

"He's off again." Arthur raised up on his elbows. "We'll just have to wait until he runs down."

"I'm serious. What we need is invitations with black borders. Hanging would be the most interesting, don't you think? Then you end with a nice comic hard-on. Listen, maybe it shouldn't be at Johnny's place, because really it should be formal, black tie, you don't do this kind of thing every day."

"He'll stop after a while," Arthur said.

"Will you come to my suicide party, Doris?"

She laughed. "I wouldn't miss it for the world."

"You see, you see, Arthur? At least Doris knows when I'm talking sense. It might become a national fad, I'll be a pace-setter, a hero, it'll solve the population explosion. They will say of me, 'In death, he arrived.' Only somebody else will probably get the idea first. You watch, next week in *Life,* the newest teen-age fad, suicide parties."

Actually, despite his fevered air, he was feeling worse now than ever, if that was possible. For one thing, in the talk of the past hour he'd gone right through what seemed to be his last surviving illusion, which was that when he came right down to it somebody adult, somebody who took the world seriously like Arthur Thompson, would be able to point out the path to him, show him the light, get him through the dark wood one way or another. But just the opposite had happened, he'd gotten Arthur so confused and dizzy by attacking all of his own not so sturdy commitments, offering Arthur a variety of nihilisms, a potpourri of sophomoric arguments against the usefulness of teaching, scholarship, living itself; blasting away at Arthur's pitiable apologies for his own so-called "values," denying the appeals of public service, taste, progress, joy—he'd gotten Arthur so depressed that gradually he himself had become frightened, for Arthur had sat there taking it all, actually agreeing with him, looking paler every minute. "And what about *you?*" Harry said to him now. "Why shouldn't this suicide party be a double ceremony? You're not happy, you just keep trudging along like an undernourished ox, what good is that? Love and work—ha!—it sounds great, love and work, but how do you do it? Other people are involved, and they'll be damned if they're going to cooperate. But at least I *know* I'm hopeless. I know I'm sick, so I lie down. You're worse, you're a hypocrite."

"I'm lying down," said Arthur, stretching out on the floor. "What do you want?"

"I want you to tell me how to *do* it! How to live!"

"By loving people!" Doris blurted with a sob, "that's how."

"Sure, sure, I know, but who's willing to be loved? I mean, look at Miriam."

"That's right, *look* at her!" Arthur shouted. "Did you? Did you ever really get outside yourself for long enough to even see her for a *minute?* For God's sake! I mean, go kill yourself if that's what you want, but don't act like everybody else comes from some inferior specie. The Last Lover, surveying the swamps and the dubious creatures of the future as he prepares to sink down—"

"—and become coal," Harry concluded in a whisper. He went on gently, quietly: "You're right. Of course you're right. If you want to feel about something you've got to really attend to it, give it some respectful *focus.*"

"Good, now maybe we're starting to get somewhere," Arthur said, with a teacherly lilt of encouragement.

"No we're not. It just keeps getting worse. You see, at my best moments, when I can think a little—I mean, I know all these things, or I keep remembering them, anyway—but the point is that I can't *do it,* I can't stop hearing—"

Have you ever really thought about killing yourself?

"Shut up!"

"Harry, who are you talking to?" Doris grabbed him by the shoulder and gave him a shake. "Arthur, do you think—?"

"No, no, fuck your strait-jackets!" said Harry. "I don't have the courage to go insane either. I'm going to be the most logical suicide since Hemingway, you wait and see. I mean, even Professor Gobine would agree in my case. Once the spinal cord's been cut, you might just as well go all the way and make frogburgers out of the remains."

"Stupid!" said Arthur. "This is stupid, disgusting talk."

"Sure, then what are *you* doing? You're dying running in place. Go on, tell me you like your life. Tell me you're fulfilled. Tell me some more about love and work and passion and perception and life and art and centers of tenderness and the happy few."

"Is it Arthur's fault if you want to kill yourself?" Doris asked quietly.

"Listen," Harry said in a thin voice, "how about if we smoke the last of my pot?"

Arthur shrugged. "What good would it do? Life is meaningless."

"Now just quit," Doris cried. "Just stop this, both of you."

"Thank God for women," Harry said. "Wow. Only the thing about women—"

"Stop! Will you *stop?*"

Silence. For the space of seventeen seconds there is silence in the cluttered apartment. Zissel and Thompson look at Doris like starving birds in the nest. "She's going to straighten us out, Arthur. I can see it. Boy, thank God for that! Go on, Doris, let's go, hit it, we're all ears, what's up, where'd we go wrong? Tell. Onward!"

Doris looked from one to the other in a feverish state. But then the edge of her thrust seemed to dull, right before their eyes. Her brisk air faded. "What was I going to say?" she mumbled. "I can't remember."

"Oh no!"

"All I can think of is the same, simple—"

"Go ahead then, Doris. What? Say it. I'm going to chain you to the wall and every morning you can say the same simple whatever, okay?"

"Wasn't it something about discipline or something?" She sat up straighter and tried a more confident tone. "Something about hope? Life for life's sake? Nothing to fear but fear itself? Something like that? Very up-lifty?"

"Yes? Was it one of those?"

"I *think* so. Wait, I've got it. You've both got to commit yourselves, that's all, get really interested—"

"In what?" said Arthur tiredly. "Everything turns out awful, doesn't it? If you're honest about it?"

"Best of all," Harry quoted, "is never to have been born."

"But when there's someone you love," Doris cried, "or some kind of work that's . . . oh, I don't know. You two are making me *so* sad."

"I've got to be more like Arthur, right? More stern and moral? Isn't that what he's supposed to be telling me, that I've got to be more like him?"

"But look at him—he's flat on his back."

"On his stomach," Arthur said. "I feel like the Book of Job."

"Now why are both of you always piling dirt on your heads, why is that? Do you realize that the kind of people you really are has just about nothing to do with the way you go on about yourselves?"

"Oh boy, Doris, you're getting started, I can feel it, you're getting up some of that old female steam, I'm straightening out already, let's have it, right from the hip."

"There. Now there's an example, a perfect example of what I mean, what you just said. Why should other people have to tell you what to do? Why do you always call for help, Harry? Are

158

you trying to make everybody believe you're an idiot so they'll pity you?"

"Not necessarily. I'm just realistic about it. About being an idiot."

"There, that's another example. An idiot! What do you think being realistic is, just emphasizing the *negative?*"

"I'm afraid to answer, Doris. If I say something you'll just tell me it's another example."

"There," said Doris, "you see? You're doing it *again.* And you"—she turned to Arthur—"if I didn't know you, what would I think? I'd think you were all one festering wound or something, wouldn't I? Without a single talent or any energy or anything?"

"Answer her, Arthur. I'm afraid to open my mouth, whatever I say just turns out to be another example."

"You see? What you just said, what you just *said,* Harry, there's a perfect example of how the two of you are always writing yourselves off. What is it? Are all men like that? I mean, what about when you think up your jokey ideas, Harry, isn't that you? Or when you're all jolly and full of enthusiasm and being hopeful?"

"When I'm—?"

"Men are self-destructive, that's all. Puritanical and, and rapacious and self-pitiful and—"

"Right," said Harry. "Go, Doris, go!"

"—self-demeaning and self-mangling."

"You're darn right! Self-mangling!"

"And what else? Self-misrepresentative."

"Shellfish?" Harry asked. "I mean, selfish?"

"Shellfish," said Doris.

"Boy, the way you describe them, men sound like real shits. But if that's what you think of us, Doris, I guess it's true."

"You're just hopeless," Doris said. "Both of you."

"But that was my point in the first place," said Harry. "Tell me, what would be good refreshments for a suicide party? Deviled crabs? Black bread and Bloody Marys?"

159

"Hemlock," said Arthur from the floor.

"Woopsy," said Harry. "Lemon-flavored blood."

"Okay," said Doris, "I know when I'm whipped."

"Oh for God's sake don't give *up,* Doris, I thought you were just *starting.* Listen, you give up too easily, you know? I mean, that's a perfect example—"

"Okay," said Doris, "okay."

"There," said Harry, "you see? What you just said. You lack confidence. You won't commit yourself."

A considerable silence, broken at last by Arthur, who rolls over on his back and puts his hands behind his head:

"It's true. I've never had the guts to try anything really new, to get some excitement into my life—"

"Oh God," Doris exclaimed, "are we going to start that again? That's an example of just what I mean. I give up!"

"You give up?" said Harry. "Well, *that's* an example—"

At which point they began to laugh. Arthur said, "Now laughing at such a moment, what an example . . ." And they laughed until they became hysterical.

"My stomach!"

"*Your* stomach?"

"Quit. Sssshush."

Lips clamped shut, like over-filled balloons. "Now trying *not* to laugh," Harry blurted, and they were going again, limping around the room, holding pillows over their faces. "I'm—" Doris gasped. "We're—" said Arthur. It slowed, surged up, stopped. Came again.

And then they were finished, blowing noses, wiping eyes; they were exhausted, and from somewhere church bells were tolling. It was three o'clock.

"Crippled for life," Arthur moaned.

"Wow. I haven't laughed like that since—"

"Don't," said Doris. "Don't say it." She clamped her hands over Harry's mouth.

"Mmrumpf," said Harry. "G'bemmpf. Lesjanngk!"

"There's got to be somebody around here to shut you up,"

Doris said. "Come on, Arthur, let's go see Miriam and make her come back."

"To wash the corpse?" said Harry.

The church bells stopped, than began again. Doris pulled Arthur to his feet. "You know," he said, "I just realized: it's Good Friday. Isn't that awful?"

The bells continued to toll.

"Yesterday the income tax was due," Harry said. "Nice timing."

"Poor Jesus," said Doris.

"We spent the whole day talking."

They sat, smoking, listening to the plangent, strenuous clangor of the bells. At last there was perfect quiet in the room.

ELEVEN

Parties at Johnny's always took a good while picking up steam. For one thing, the host himself often wasn't there till rather late since the shop stayed open into the evenings. There were times, if Johnnny had neglected to tell his wife that people were expected, when guests would arrive to an empty house, make themselves drinks, wander into the garden or down to the basement den where Johnny keeps his hi-fi and broadcasting equipment; later they would notice that the harried woman who let them in was working rapidly preparing canapés, and since Johnny passed out invitations by impulse, often to complete strangers, the guests might never discover that this was Marjorie, Johnny's wife. It was into this household that Johnny had taken Miriam when she'd decided to leave Harry, and last night the two of them had been together in his den until all hours working on his problems, which are rather complicated, since he's been married for ten years, has four children, finds Marjorie revolting, and hopes that Miriam will go bed with him to save him from the suspicion that he's essentially homosexual by inclination. It wasn't till late that he'd sprung the homosexual bit on Miriam, plainly disappointed that she wasn't shocked or for that matter even surprised. Actually, what she was surprised by were the four children, and she was shocked to meet Marjorie, so small and eerily mild, as unaggressive as a vegetable, a seedless grape, perhaps, or a tiny cucumber. Marjorie was delicately made, with a waif's smile. The word *frightened* offers a reasonably accurate description of her. Johnny confessed to Miriam that making love to Marjorie, when he used to do so, had been like trying to knead crumbly cookie-dough. On the other hand, the four children were the most violent human beings Miriam had ever seen. If Marjorie seemed frightened of Johnny, she seemed positively terrified of the children. Donald, the oldest, six or seven, came up behind Marjorie as she was serving breakfast the morning after Miriam's first night in the house and bit her with decision right through her madras slacks on the left buttock. "Donald," Johnny called out wearily as Marjorie screamed and tried to push the child away, "can't you stop biting your mother?" Marjorie pushed back a wisp of hair, smiled nervously at Miriam, and served their eggs. The two girls, five and three, ate cereal with their heads in their bowls, using their tongues like cats. "They're on some kind of cat-kick," Johnny explained. "Isn't it disgusting? *She*"—indicating Marjorie with a jerk of the elbow —"she can't control them." Marjorie allowed herself a tiny grin. The baby, John junior, was a head-thumper. They'd tried everything to stop that. He'd thumped his way right through the crib-pad, it seemed he only wanted to exercise his little cranium at one particular spot on the headboard, just where little Miss Muffet was sitting on her tuffet eating her curds and whey. Johnny threatened to cut a large hole through the headboard at that point, but the crib was already as tottery as a house of cards and tinkering would bring it down altogether. For hours every night John Jr. would work at his thumping, knees up under him at the top of the crib, moving like a piston, thump, double thump. The pediatrician claimed he'd eventually grow out of it, though it would probably affect the shape of his head.

"It's a matter of life or death," Johnny had told Miriam in the den. "You could save my life, it's as touching and simple as that. But you won't do it. Obviously. Obviously, you're female, so your human function is to frustrate, to build strong bones and sound teeth, it's perfectly clear, I know you're disgusted with my weakness, I shouldn't have told you so much, that's just my speech mannerism, I shouldn't have been so honest." Even through the soundproof door of the den a distant thumping could be heard. Johnny grabbed up the microphone of his house intercom, pressed a button at the base of the mike, and shouted "Marjorie, do something with that kid, I can't hear myself speak."

"I guess everybody's dishonest, really," Miriam told him. "I divide people up by how honest they are in admitting their dishonesty." At that point she'd been fighting John off for hours, from one side of the padded den to the other, ever since Marjorie had gone to bed and John had invited her down to try his broadcasting equipment. At first all he claimed to desire was to be permitted to kiss her feet, but gradually, by broad implication, it became clear that he wanted her to arouse him in ways which her imagination simply refused to contemplate. He made the nature of the contact he was sure would save his life gradually more plain, but she'd be damned if she'd let on that she understood what he was talking about.

"Women can't endure true intimacy," Johnny said sadly. "That's what's turning me away from them. They don't accept the body at all. They deny the body. They starve it to death."

"Don't John . . . please." He was like a mythological creature, thousand handed—it was impossible to control him, he moved like an eel. The den had walls padded with a plastic material, dark beige, which also covered the door; the ceiling was of white acoustical tile. Johnny's hi-fi and ham equipment weren't the only reason for the room's being soundproofed, that was becoming clear. Miriam eyed the collection of fossils and statuary on the library table in the far corner. If worse came to worse she'd at least have some artillery. She found herself even wishing she were back with Harry, recalling how he had stood tragically at the top of the stairs as she bumped off with her unicycle. At least Harry didn't have a wife sleeping in the same house, or four children any of whom might tumble out of bed and break down the door to bite her on the rear. She would manage to get John calmed and sitting behind his control-table playing her a record, but soon he'd be all over her again. Did Marjorie know what was going on? Miriam was in terror that Marjorie would appear in the doorway and just stand politely watching them. And Miriam used to be so proud of her trim figure and boyish haircut! Her mother had warned her about the sort of men those features would attract. But the few real homosexuals she'd known had all been so childlike, so clever, so charming. John, of course, was older, he was probably close to forty. She'd been crazy to move in, even for a single night. The worst of it was that finally he actually managed to get her a bit heated up, and then she despised herself; if she hadn't, she would have had to despise him, and he had enough troubles as it was. "Quit," she'd say, "you're out of your mind! You're sex-obsessed." "Come take a shower with me. Come on, it'll be refreshing. I won't bother you, I swear. We'll just wash each other. Come on!" One end of the den was devoted to a steam-room and shower enclosure. It turned out he had a waterproof bed in there, and a hi-fi speaker. It was terribly late to go to a hotel, but she warned him she'd have to if he didn't leave her alone. He hadn't even shown her to her room; she half expected to be invited to crawl into bed with him and Marjorie. "I don't understand," she said at the breathless end of another struggle, "I thought your problem was that you liked *men*."

"I don't have the courage for that," said Johnny. "You have no idea what I go through to follow up my appetites. The young are *so* cruel!"

"What you need is a psychiatrist."

"I've tried it, it's no use, it always leads to the same thing."

"You've gone to an analyst?"

"Three." He ticked them off on his long fingers. "All I do is fall for them. Did you ever try to make out with an analyst?"

"My uncle's a clinical psychologist," Miriam said.

"Yes, but did you ever try to make out with an *analyst*? It's murder. It's unbelievable. They're not human, they're made out of stainless-steel."

"Poor Johnny," Miriam said, looking at her watch. It was two-fifteen and she wondered what Harry was doing. There was a time a few weeks back when he'd started getting up at 2 A.M. to try to work, which usually led to his waking her up about 2:30 for some consolation. Men had such troubles; she wouldn't be one for the world. Was sex really that important? She knew you were supposed to think so, but was it really? Her uncle the clinical psychologist had told her that the rabid classical Freudians didn't check your pulse or your breathing to see if you were still alive, they asked about the quality of your orgasms. True genitality: if she understood it correctly, that was the ultimate goal of the times, roughly equivalent to salvation in the Middle Ages. But if that was so, how come she invariably ran into people with strange sexual needs, people who didn't appear to want to be saved by true genitality at all? And it was so hard to refuse them without feeling like cast iron. After all, who was she to be prejudiced? But there was no end to it, people would ask you to do anything if you seemed compliant enough and uncertain. Once she was waiting for a bus in the Loop after a cello lesson—she was sixteen—when a college boy approached her and asked if she could help him, he was being initiated into a medical school fraternity and there were several rather strange things he had to do as part of the hazing, and ten minutes later she found herself standing, *standing* on his chest as he lay full length on his back in an alleyway with his shirt off. They hadn't said a word to one another while it was going on, she just stood on him, he grunted when he first felt her weight and then lay there with his eyes closed and after awhile she got off and went back to the bus stop and her bus came and only then she'd begun to wonder how he could have hoped to prove to his fraternity brothers that he had really been stood on.

It was always like that, no one ever hurt her but she continually felt used. People saw something in her, an inability to be shocked, a willingness to lend herself to something new. Or was it only her superficiality they saw, the nothingness in her that depended on the curious and unexpected to create a sense of happening which she couldn't supply from within? What was it that made people want to be stood on by a sixteen-year-old girl with a cello? And what made the sixteen-year-old girl willing to stand?

"Poor Johnny," she said.

"God," said Johnny, "if only females weren't so *squeamish!*"

The shop hadn't opened till three-thirty the next day, in deference to Good Friday, so Miriam spent the morning hunting for new quarters, but nothing seemed right. She wondered if she should consider trying to get back into college somewhere in the fall. At least then she'd be living in a dormitory, she wouldn't have to fight for a chance to get some sleep. When she arrived at the shop the three other girls were already dusting off and removing covers. Johnny came up to her with his long stride and spoke in her ear: "You wouldn't throw a life-preserver to a drowning man!" She told him later, when there were no serious customers around, that she wasn't coming back out to his place. She claimed she'd found a new apartment. Actually, she'd have to stay at the University Arms Hotel. "Is it because of me?" Johnny asked. "Because I said that about self-abasement? Don't be ridiculous, Miriam. What about my party, you can't miss my party. Didn't I *promise* to leave you alone?" He'd promised, all right, on at least four different occasions he'd promised, but when she'd awakened at 5 A.M. to find him making passionate advances to her left foot at the edge of the bed, she knew for sure she had to get out of there. She had no illusions about male promises, they were handed out the way women used social smiles, not meaning anything except to seem civilized. "You're going back to Harry, I can just tell," Johnny said, looking very glum. She shook her head. "I wouldn't think of it. I may just go into a nunnery."

167

While they talked the other salesgirls glanced at one another and at Miriam with luxurious amusement. All three of them had been through a version of the save-Johnny's-life campaign. When Miriam moved out of hearing, Marcia whispered to Betty in imitation of Miriam's sympathetic tone: "Mr. Hughes, I'm afraid your fly's unzipped"—and they twitched their brows and giggled. When Miriam spoke to them the lewd smiles were there, just behind the eyes, but they all received the message of her dignified manner and said nothing directly to her about Johnny. "She went down for him," Marcia insisted later, when things were quiet during the supper hour. But Betty told her to take a closer look at John. Johnny's face each day was like an official bulletin on the state of his sex life.

"She's a terrible snob for a kid," said the third shopgirl, whose name for some unknown reason was Kempis Smith. "I feel sorry for Johnny, he's got that weedy beagle expression on him again. Look how his moustache is drooping."

"There are ways of expressing your sympathy in this organization," said Betty, who was the local wit. "Talk is cheap. Put your bottom where your mouth is."

They all felt toward Miriam like the discarded members of a run-down harem. They'd each taken a turn explaining the Johnny situation to her when she'd first come to work there, but she'd only listened politely and smiled. Now that she was obviously in the thick of it, there was considerable gloating and bitchy bawdry, but also a certain jealousy, though none of them took Johnny with any kind of seriousness. On the other hand, Miriam was prettier even than Kempis, and it looked like she might be holding her own.

"I bet she's still a virgin," Marcia insisted.

"Don't be crazy," said Betty. "What about that dark-haired fellow who's always in here? She's just the type that sleeps around like a fish."

"Sleeping around doesn't prove anything," said Kempis. "She's an old-fashioned iceberg with a burning tip, they always sleep around but nothing comes of it. Look at poor beagle-eyed

John! You've got to hand it to her, it takes genius to be a virgin with that kind of style."

"Poor unfulfilled Johnny!" Marcia said.

"Poor John," said Betty, "his fly remains hopelessly unzipped."

"Poor Johnny," they repeated to each other through their giggles. The fact was that though they attended all of Johnny's parties he'd never invited one of them to *move in* with him and his wife.

Supper time. Doris and Arthur are window-shopping. This is their second tour around the Square. "I thought you wanted me to talk to Miriam," Arthur said, as they stood before the window of a tiny shop displaying stamps and coins and engraving plates for marriage announcements that had been turned into ashtrays. Doris told him she was still trying to work up her courage. "But *I'm* the one who's supposed to convince her to come back, aren't I?" Doris said yes, but somehow she wasn't quite—"You're bored, aren't you?" she declared as they moved on, "just taking a walk with me?"

"Of course not."

They looked in at a dress shop. The skirts on the mannequins barely reached mid-thigh. "Admit it," she said, "you're bored."

"Don't be ridiculous, Doris!"

"You're bored," she said.

They were approaching Beds-'n-Things again. She wondered if they should just wander one more time around the Square? "If you want," Arthur said. "Why not? There's no hurry."

"You're a dear, Arthur. This whole business makes me terribly nervous." He told her it was *her* idea. What could come of it, anyway? Could they ask Miriam to move back and take care of Harry as if she were a registered nurse? "I know," said Doris, "it was just the only thing I could think of. It's my vice, I'm always trying to find *solutions*. Should we go in and look at the beds and all?"

"Then I'm *not* supposed to talk to her?"

"I don't know, Arthur. Let's wait and see." They were stand-ing now before the shop. "Maybe we should buy a new bed. Look at the crazy things they've got!"

"Listen, we've already got a perfectly good bed. I hope you don't expect me to transport a bed—"

"I was thinking about the guest room." What she was really thinking about was the nursery. "Now you're angry again."

"Okay," he said grimly, "I'm angry. Now let's go in and look at Miriam and her beds."

"No," she said, "tell me why you're angry. What have I done?" Through his mind a set of tableaux like stills from a movie were flipping over; various methods of mayhem: by axe; by bathtub drowning; by burial alive. The images passed through him with the speed of subliminal advertising: drown your wife in a Stanley Tub, all decorator colors. "I wish we'd never come up here," Doris said. "I wish I'd never seen that damn Harry Zissel!" Last night, just before they went to sleep, she'd made a curious comment; wouldn't it be funny, she'd said, if *she* were twelve days overdue? He'd told her it would be a riot.

Pushed from a jetliner without a parachute. Tripped into the path of an oncoming bus.

"Let's go in and look at beds," she said with a sigh.

Strychnine. Pillow suffocation. Bathtub drowning.

"Okay," he said, "I'm in your hands."

Miriam had spotted them through the window, the red-haired girl holding the tall, unhealthy-looking man by the arm. The man was very tall; he looked bleached, somehow, and as if he'd been stretched a bit beyond his normal height. "Pardon me," he said. "Is your name Miriam Hippolyto?"

"We've been dying to meet you," said the red-haired girl en-thusiastically. "We're friends of Harry's. We've been talking about you for three days."

Miriam failed to return the smile. "I hope it was all amazingly complimentary?" Then she asked how Harry was holding up.

"Not so good," said Arthur, "he keeps talking about suicide."

"Same as usual," said Miriam offhandedly. She veered into a

more professional manner. "Did you just come in to say hello, or can I help you with something?" Shopgirl smile. "I hope you're not going to try to patch things up between me and Harry."

"Oh," said Doris, "we wouldn't think of bothering you, we were just shopping. We just thought we'd drop in." From the tone of both women it becomes entirely clear that they are not going to get along. This could be scientifically proven by the set of each smiling mouth, particularly by the nature of the articulation at the corners of the lips, as well as by the degree of openness of the eyelids and the quantity of cold light reflected from each retina, if one only had the instruments and the methodology to perform such measurements. On the other hand, from a glance at Arthur's face it appears that he doesn't share Doris's view of Miriam. He already feels he's getting some more excitment into his life. "Harry's pretty miserable since you left," he told her.

"So I gather."

"He'll manage," Doris said.

Arthur and Miriam begin to speak of Harry in an undertone, as one does when discussing the newly dead.

"He thinks he may drop out of school and take a job."

"He must be really desperate then."

"Look, Arthur," said Doris, who had wandered off. "They have circular beds covered with leopard skin."

"Simulated," said Miriam.

"He claims he still loves you," Arthur said quietly. "Isn't there some chance . . . ?" Miriam could hear the violins swelling up in the background. She inclined her head. Somehow this Arthur person reminded her of her father. "I'm afraid," she replied throatily, "there's not a chance in the world . . . not for Harry . . . and me."

"That's . . . very sad," said Arthur, meeting her eyes. Why was she gazing at him like that? Where did the heady scent come from? He could hardly breathe, he was being gradually choked by an unfamiliar emotion. But Doris had fallen firmly into a role from an entirely different movie. "We can't take up

Miriam's time with personal matters when she's working, Arthur. Did you see the baby cot that folds up into a suitcase?"

"That's perfectly all right." Miriam said. "I was just going out for supper."

"I wish we could really talk about this," said Arthur. "I feel somehow that we could . . . communicate."

"He needs help, I know," said Miriam. "But isn't it always the people who most need it—?"

"I understand," Arthur breathed.

"He's like a child."

"Yes." They were still gazing into one another's eyes.

"If you two are going to keep talking about Harry I'll just wander around a bit," Doris said. "I hardly know him," she confided to Miriam with a fake smile.

Miriam returned the identical smile. Then she looked back at Arthur.

"You could have helped him so much," Arthur said. "Matured him. I can see that now."

Miriam tilted her head. "I'm surprised—weren't the two of you roommates? You look so—"

"I'm quite a bit older. I was in the navy before I ever came to college."

She nodded.

"You couldn't give him another chance?"

"You and . . .?"

"Doris."

"You two are . . . ?"

"Married, yes. It's very complicated. Our relationship."

"I'm sorry," said Miriam, still softly, "I don't know what makes me act if we were old friends or something."

"It feels that way, doesn't it? Strange." They sat on adjoining fur-covered swivel-chairs. "Honey," Doris called, "come look! They've got the cleverest little bedside tables!"

"We must talk more," said Miriam.

"Oh yes," said Arthur. "Where are you going for supper?"

"Your wife undoubtedly has plans."

172

"Undoubtedly."

"But if you . . . I'll be at Hulbert's . . . you know where that is?"

"Look," said Doris, "we couldn't afford one, but isn't that clever, a tiny little refrigerator built right into the side of the bed!"

"Very nice," said Arthur.

"Come over here and look at this," Doris called, "it's really insane, a bed that converts into a ping-pong table!"

"At Hulbert's?" Arthur asked.

"At Hulbert's," said Miriam.

Harry was at his desk in the bedroom reading his Aristotle, looking somewhat rabbinical with his head bent to the giant tome, when Doris crashed in on him without a word and picked up the telephone. "You startled me," he complained, "you shouldn't leap in on people like that. What did Miriam say?" On the phone Doris was inquiring about bus service to Cordelia. "What's going on?" Harry asked. "Where's Arthur?"

She didn't answer, but started folding her clothes into her suitcase. "Nothing leaves this town until two in the morning. I can't even get to New York."

"What is all this? Where'd he go?"

"He passed away a few minutes ago. Satyriasis."

"Come on, Doris, don't try to joke, you said yourself you weren't witty. Where is he? What do you want with the bus station?"

"He told me he needed some time for contemplation; to recapture his youth. He wanted to take a long walk on the campus by himself and figure out how to get some excitement into his life."

"So what's wrong with that?"

"He's not taking a walk. He's eating dinner right down at the corner with that goddam Miriam!"

"No!" said Harry. "Really? Arthur?"

"In any case I couldn't be more uninterested. I think I'll just go and wait in the bus station. Give me a cigarette, will you?"

"Has he left you? That's really overdoing it! Didn't he say when he'd be back? How do you know he's with Miriam?"

"Intuition," Doris said. "My gift of prophecy." She dragged too deeply on the cigarette and began to cough. He slammed her on the back until she stopped.

"Did you get anything out of her about me?"

"Not that I noticed."

"Not that you noticed. I thought the whole point—"

"Arthur talked to her. He asked her to give you another try, though it's beyond me what you see in that girl. She's just about the snottiest—" Doris laughed dryly. "She and Arthur seemed to hit it off so well I didn't want to interrupt—I discreetly wandered away."

"You seem different, Doris. Odd. Grim or something."

"Do I?"

"You're upset, I can tell. How did all this happen? You look like you've aged, you know? Since this morning."

"I've received the wisdom of the ages. I've learned my lesson —it sure took long enough."

"Lesson?"

"That the nature of a man is to run away. Tell me, how long does it take to get a divorce in New Jersey?"

"Now just a minute, Doris. If Arthur's eating with Miriam he just wants to talk to her some more about *me*."

"You're so *innocent.*" She threw the words at him. "You really are, it's sickening."

"But he's coming back, isn't he? They haven't eloped, have they? I mean, bigamy is still a crime in this country, so what are you worrying about? I mean, let's not throw stones, don't you think?"

"I couldn't care less."

And that was all she would say on the subject. But she didn't go to the bus station: instead she started cleaning up his apartment. After a time she went out to the Double-D for some oven cleaner and some food for their supper. "They're still in there at Hulbert's," she said. "Holding hands under the table."

"You've got a macabre imagination," Harry told her.

She spread newspapers on the floor before the stove and went to work furiously on the encrusted oven. The miracle oven-cleaner she'd bought claimed to be more powerful than the atomic bomb yet kind to the hands. "Don't you have a vacuum cleaner?" Shamefacedly he offered her a nubby broom. "Here are your shoes," she said, pulling them out from beneath the couch. "God, it looks like a mushroom farm under there!" How had she gotten involved with such a disgusting bunch of people? All men, she concluded, given half a chance, reverted to criminal types. Then what was she doing cleaning up Harry's apartment? It was instinct—she simply couldn't stop. He was following her around in a dazed way, asking her what she was doing. She produced some hamburgers for their supper; cleared the table; washed the dishes; put them away. Still no Arthur. "Look," said Harry, trying to lighten the atmosphere a little, "you and I could always run off to the Greek Islands—that would show him!"

"I bet you think I wouldn't!"

Harry whistled under his breath. He was feeling very dig-nified and calm. Like Miles Standish. Doris was powdering her nose in the little mirror of her compact, her eyes flashing. To Harry's surprise it seemed that they were about to go by cab over to Johnny's party.

"Shouldn't we leave a note for Arthur and tell him how to get there when he comes back?"

"You do what you want," said Doris. "I'll be damned if I'll leave him a thing. What he deserves is to find my last will and testament, right on the closet floor, drenched with Arpège!"

Harry looked in at Hulbert's while they waited at the corner for a cab. No Arthur or Miriam. Was it all a product of Doris's fevered imagination, or had *they* run off to the Greek Islands? He couldn't believe that Arthur would turn irresponsible—he couldn't have had that much of an effect on him, not so soon. But then, where was he? The '58 Chevy was nowhere in sight. Harry felt only the mildest twinge of apprehension, and even this seemed ambiguous in its source, he didn't know which he preferred to believe: that Arthur was at that very moment talk-

175

ing Miriam into returning to him, or that like John Alden he was speaking for himself. Maybe he was just driving around alone, trying to get a grip on his life, enjoying a moment away from Doris's supervision. On the other hand, at this very moment Arthur and Miriam—he could just *see* it—might be flying in a rented Piper Cub right toward Crete, Naxos, Cos. Ah well, he thought, past caring, joy to their sheets.

It was almost ten by the time they arrived at Johnny's, but only a few early guests were there, gathered in the garden where a makeshift ping-pong table had been set up to greet the spring. Johnny, wearing a beautiful lamb's-wool jacket with charcoal slacks, was supervising Marjorie as she prepared a tray of canapés. He had just come in from the shop, but without any Miriam hidden about his person, Harry noticed. Marjorie's little fingers worked rapidly washing parsley and smearing bits of bread as Johnny paced around behind her in the enormous kitchen. "Typical," he whined. "About once a month I have a few people in and nothing's ever ready, why is that? My wife's totally incompetent," he looked Doris over like an appraiser at a horse-auction. "She's absolutely worthless, a total loss, there's not a thing she can do right, I'd divorce her in a minute, but who'd take her off my hands?" He handed Harry and Doris a drink. "We'll have to have a little talk about that Miriam of yours one of these days," he said.

"Who's Miriam?" said Harry.

Marjorie was working frantically at the canapés. She apologized for being late, pushed back a wisp of dark hair, smiled. "The children were a bit difficult today." And in fact the attentive listener might hear, despite the conversation, a continued sound of thumping from little John Jr., busy at his nightly self-immolation. "He's going like crazy tonight," said his father. "What's wrong with that kid?" He put an arm around Doris's shoulders. "Say, where's that tall, sensitive-looking fellow you were with in my shop this evening?"

"He passed away," Harry said. "Nymphomania." Doris disengaged herself from Johnny's arm and with a wave to Harry walked out on the terrace and down into the garden. "Great that you could come, Harry," Johnny said, throwing an arm around *his* shoulders. "That's a very . . . stirring girl you brought along, where did you get her?"

"She's my old roommate's wife. Hands off, John, you hear?"

"Harry! As if I weren't a married man!" He draped his arm around Marjorie at the sink and she practically keeled over. "Where's the tall husband fellow? I saw him at the shop a few hours ago, talking to Miriam."

"He's off contemplating—I left him a note, maybe he'll show up later."

"Contemplating! Strange! I mean, Miriam—you know Miriam? Miriam Hippolyto? my employee? your more recent roommate?"

"The name seems to strike a bell."

"Well guess what? She took off from work early tonight. Right after supper. Now why, do you think?"

"Don't tell me. To go to a bullfight in San Mateo, California?"

"No, but you're warm."

"To a Roman orgy in Cordelia, New Jersey?"

"Getting hot."

"For a long, solitary walk through the campus, contemplating?"

"Right! How'd you guess?"

"I have my informants. I'm sure they'll make a lovely couple."

"Now go on out in the garden and have a great time, Harry, you hear? Remember that word of yours, Polonius? Well, Polonius, you know? I mean, have another drink and just . . . Polonius."

Harry moved among the guests, feeling dignified and numb. Had Arthur betrayed him? Could he even call it that? Was there such a thing as betrayal anymore? Not that he cared. Since the long talk of the afternoon, he'd felt as if the heart had been taken out of him, chewed on a little, then replaced, slightly off-kilter, a soggy mess, with him still under anesthesia from the operation. He hardly glanced at the people arriving. Johnny invariably invited dozens of strangers—the more new blood the better —but then there were also all the regular spongers who didn't wait for invitations. They were trooping through the house now and out by the kitchen to the terrace and lawn below, a motley crowd, business people with their wives or girl friends; Kempis and Betty and Marcia from the shop; a few college kids back early from vacation (one of these, female, wearing what looked like striped pajamas, had brought her zither along). Harry recognized three of the local painters, abstract expressionists. There were also two bookies and one solitary man from New Haven who said he worked for City Hall. The ping-pong table had been set up across a birdbath with two of the wire-backed dining room chairs for support at either end, and Doris was playing when he got there, the table slanting on either side somewhat uphill. She seemed to be trouncing the official from City Hall, who played without taking off his hat. After a minute Johnny came down and took up Doris's drink from the lawn and offered her sips between volleys.

Harry looked on, admiring the way Doris slammed the ball. *Who would have thought that Arthur had it in him?* said his voice. But even if Arthur was just trying to talk Miriam into coming back, Harry realized it didn't matter in the slightest. At which point the voice perked up considerably: *Tell me, are you happy in your work? Have you ever really thought of committing suicide?* To his right, trampling around in the young flowerbeds beside the fence, three students were having an argument. "The novel? What do you mean the novel? The novel's dead!"

"Ill," said the boy. "Merely ill, Sydney."

"This sure is a dark martini," said the third student sadly, tilting his drink from side to side. He was the only one of the three without a British accent.

"It's made with tar," Harry told him.

"Yeah? Who are you?" said the third student suspiciously. "Buttinsky!"

"I'm just the man who delivers from the tar store."

"Yeah?"

"I'm a student," Harry said, fearing violence. "I'm a sophomore."

"Well we're anti-students, see? So don't get familiar."

Harry felt that his day had somehow passed. And so quickly, while he wasn't looking. You could bend down to tie your shoelace these days and when you straightened up all the fashions had changed and they weren't even using shoelaces anymore. He couldn't keep up, it was all getting beyond him. Was this an anti-party? Were they all anti-people? He made his way to the terrace where he consumed a few comforting cream-cheese balls coated with chopped parsley and nuts. Delicious. Two women nearby, one in the identical yellow print dress that Doris was wearing, were trading market tips. At least that's what they seemed to be trading. "United Fruits," said one of the ladies. "My Phil, my sonny-boy, he just picked up fifty shares, preferred. Take a tip, United Fruits, they're bound to split, two for one."

Harry pulled out his wallet notebook. There was the napkin recording McCarty's wheelchair prices, a few unfiled dying-words, Arthur's little saying: "love is cheap." He wrote, without smiling, "United Fruits," and went down to the garden again. The three local painters were sitting on lawn chairs below the terrace. The one he knew, Billy Rupp, still wore his working clothes; it looked as if he'd been using his beard to clean his brushes. "No titles," Billy was saying, "just put on the date."

"I tried dates. Now I'm back to titles. I want you to have a look at the big canvas, Billy, it's called 'The Dyad Is The Bride of Chronos—So Go Know!'"

"What's a dyad, Harry?" said Billy Rupp.

"A double-chromosome."

"Yeah?"

179

"One half of a tetrad."

"Crazy," said Billy Rupp.

Harry drained his drink and went for another, smiling along at the people he recognized. In the dining room, Roger Hulbert, the son of the owner, was having a talk with a very large girl in a baby-blue bare-shouldered angora sweater and a skirt that seemed to be made of aluminum foil. "I got to hand it to you," Roger told her. "I would have given odds of three to two they were mainly foam rubber. Or silicone."

"Hi, Harry," said Roger, "we're making book on whether this here hunk is padded out or not."

"*I'll* never tell," said the girl.

Doris still played ping-pong ferociously, taking on all comers. It was a lovely spring evening. People were all over the garden now, in such bright clothing that if one switched for a moment to an aerial view the scene would resemble a rectangular bowl filled with minestrone. Harry stood on the other side of the ping-pong table, watching John watching Doris, her drink at the ready in his hand. Doris has kicked her shoes off, Harry notes this as he takes over from the last defeated player, the girl with the zither, who goes off hanging her head. Without a word he serves the ball. "Any sign of either of your old roommates?" she asks.

"What roommates?"

She won the first serve. "Found anybody to rape for the evening yet?"

"Johnny tells me Miriam took off early from work," he reported. "To contemplate." Her game stopped; she let a perfectly mild lob of his bounce and fall on the grass. Johnny picked up the ball. But it was as if she'd only paused to switch on her afterburners—she began to play with fantastic energy. The violence of her game made Harry feel a bit less unreal. A nice glow from the drinks appeared at his center, a star of warmth about which the ping-pong playing parts of him began to swoop in elliptical orbs. Snap, sweep, swirl, swish—why did seeing Doris stirred up about Arthur and Miriam make *him* feel less destroyed? He

didn't know, it seemed to be organized that way, she was playing mad-dog ping-pong, taking every point, the score was already 8-love. But he felt invincibly cool. She lacked his reach, his
sense of irony, look how she was *working* at it, biting her lip,
englishing the ball, slamming: in the long run she didn't stand a
chance. Smiling, he returned as many of her serves as he could;
pretty soon her antiperspirant would be in trouble, she'd start
wondering if she were losing her charm, and then *he'd* begin
taking points, moving in for the kill. But God, was she ever angry, it was lucky she had a ping-pong paddle to work her frus-
trations off with. She was murdering the little white ball, in the
absence of Arthur it would have to do. Harry moved like a
dancer, fell back, plunged forward, Ray Bolgered a high one,
Fred Astaired on the return. He felt sorry for her, but she was a
tough cookie, all right, she could take care of herself. Why did
she so much want to do him in at ping-pong? Because he was
male, obviously. When she took the tenth point she gave him her
swift girl-scout grin. If it was making her feel better to slaughter
him, by all means; but the strain was terrible: through her grin-
ning facade he sensed total hysteria welling up. "Isn't it funny
about *games*," she said, serving. "I mean, the way you get so involved?" Each time she took a point, Johnny applauded, but
when Harry snatched one, there was general booing. He could
feel the sweat on his brow. Across the ping-pong table, tiny
freckles at the bridge of her nose, Doris went in and out of focus,
so pretty in her yellow dress, her hair veering from side to side,
playing for blood, poor thing, trying like crazy, beating the hell
out of him and it was only a stupid game. Toward the end he
began to feel predatory, he could see himself throwing her back
over the net with a groan, humping her right there on the slanting ping-pong table with Arthur and Miriam (where the hell
were they?) leading the applause. In the automatic effort to
sweep his mind after this burst of libido, he summoned up his all-
purpose spiritualizer, the thought that she was not so much a
woman as his fellow mortal, his blood-sister, his former roommate's wife. The lewdness left him at once, he liked her more

than he ever had before, and he found that he'd lost the last three points in a row and the game was nearly over. Seventeen to four. He served. The ball beeped back and forth. "I notice you hardly ever slam," said Doris, smacking a back-hand corner shot smartly, as if with her elbow. She played with a set of small, swift gestures, seldom reaching far out with her paddle, shifting from side to side like a little buzzing machine on tracks.

"I've never been much on slams," Harry said, putting a maximum of spin on his returns.

"Easygoing type."

"Right."

"Gentle. Mildly suicidal. Noncompetitive. *Eighteen* to four!"

"Hold it," said Johnny. They had quite a little audience by now. "This girl has earned a sip of her vodka." John took her by the elbow and held the tall glass to her lips and Harry felt sick to his stomach once again. What was she doing flirting with Johnny of all people, letting him stroke her hair, smiling at him? Had she gone entirely out of her mind? The rate of play became even more rapid. This volley was going on too long, back and forth with the speed of light, and from stroke to stroke he was sure he would knock the ball right off the table, because he kept catching Johnny's lewd eye. He tried to slow Doris down but then he became afraid he wouldn't make it over the net. *Try,* his voice was telling him. *Don't lose gracefully. Play to win!* At which point he lobbed the ball too far, Doris drawing back slightly as if she had only to pull in her breath to let it pass and drop to the lawn. Johnny stooped at her legs to retrieve the ball, her drink held carefully in his other hand. This time the spectators applauded at length. She bounced the ball to Harry. "Ready?" she said. "Nineteen to four." He made a preliminary gesture with the paddle, as if clearing gnats out of the air, then served, and they were off again.

"Why do you do that?" Doris said, "that sort of clearing the air before you serve?"

"To clear the air," said Harry, keeping them low and fast over the net. They were under a floodlight, but a tree shadow covered part of his side of the table, she had an advantage, at least she could see, the sweat was in his eyes but his voice growled *excuses, excuses, you're just a born loser,* and with a growl in response he hit a lucky one that tipped off the far edge of the table; she picked it up somehow, drove it spang against the tight net-top and it fell sliding down the net on his side and he lunged for it and came down with his free hand and his whole side of the table rose like a drawbridge, toppling off the supporting chairs, banging his knees. He jumped up and down for a bit.

"Nice try," she said.

He was winded. She seemed as cool and smiling as ever. They readjusted the table, reclamped the net; as he shifted the two sides of the table their fingers touched momentarily.

"What's the score?" He had totally forgotten everything about the game.

"Four-twenty," she said. "Give up? Maybe Johnny wants to play?"

"Let's go," he said. The volley went faster than ever, he couldn't see, he spun all the way around on one shot and the next came at him high and to the right and he lunged into it like a knight in armor, coming down hard on the table again, both halves rising this time and the slammed ball flying high and strong across the shadows as the two halves of the table slid down, revealing the grimy bottom of the birdbath that served as central support, into which the ball popped, rattling twice around the edge as if in a roulette wheel, then rocking slowly to a stop at the bottom.

"Touché," said Harry softly.

"You'd probably do better at tiddly-winks," Doris told him as they readjusted the table. Again their fingers made contact. He was aware of her scent—could it be Arpège? "Let's go," said Johnny, handing Harry Doris's drink. "I'll take her on!"

Harry set Doris's drink on the lawn and moved away from the slaughter. Before he reached the terrace he realized she was coming along behind him, threading her way, the garden and the terrace crowded now, with people arriving in droves through the kitchen door. He made for the kitchen, keeping ahead of Doris. He wanted to get off somewhere and think, he didn't understand his mood, everything was going haywire, how did he wind up with Doris and Arthur with Miriam? In the kitchen Marjorie still fixed platters of canapés, pushing back her hair and throwing an hysterical smile of greeting at new guests passing by, most of them without a word, Marjorie looking up expectantly each time, hoping to spot someone she knew; big men with cigars were ushering silver-blondes in sequined dresses right through her kitchen and out onto the lawn. Maybe she'd have more fun as a blonde, like they said in the ads? Her fingers kept moving busily. All around her women were standing in clouds of Arpège, chattering to cigar-smoking men. Kempis from the shop reached right over her shoulder and popped an anchovy-and-egg-yolk-on-rye-round into her round red mouth without so much as saying "Hi." Men came in from the garden, came up to her, said "Where's the latrine?" It seemed as if they were all having a very nice time.

Harry lost Doris by finding an empty bathroom and bolting himself in. Suddenly it was very quiet.

What am I feeling? he asked his voice, sitting on the little cork-topped bench across from the gilt-framed wall-size mirror. *Despair and lust.*

Am I? Lust for Doris?

The voice nodded. *You're completely hopeless,* it said.

Harry looked at the oversized tub, at the golden dophin that served as its waterspout. He looked in the mirror at his figure hunched over on the bench, lost against the whiteness of the tiled wall behind. And he thought about killing himself. He really thought about it. For the first time in his life he allowed the idea to take particular shape in his mind and his voice seemed to stand off from him then in respectful awe. Slowly he took off his clothes and hung them on the brass clothestree. It was as nice a place for the occasion as he could ever hope to find. He turned the golden handle to TUB, clicked home the drain device, and started the water running.

They say it's physically impossible to drown by self-immersion in a bathtub, said the voice respectfully.

I know, he said, climbing into the tub. What I have in mind is drawing water up through the nose. Internal drowning, see?

Very clever, said the voice. *I'm full of admiration.*

Harry sat in the tub with the water climbing slowly up his hairy thighs.

"Poor corpus," he said. "Poor old delictus."

The water mounted. He studied the toiletries on the shelf above the sink. A bottle of Arpège. A tin of talcum powder: Lily of the Valley. A box of Band-Aids.

The water covered his navel.

Miriam would be impressed.

Are you sure, now? the voice asked him. *I thought you were feeling a little better?*

Oh, one time's as good as another, Harry said, if you're going to do a thing, you've got to start when the impulse hits you, otherwise you forget all about it.

But no note? said the voice. *No explanation? Aren't you missing a once-in-a-lifetime literary opportunity?*

My whole life has been an explanation, Harry said. What more can I say?

He turned off the taps and looked at the tiny cup of his navel shimmering just under the lip of the water, and tried to imagine the nurse, whoever she was, who'd washed him off and neatened him up some twenty-three years before in the Cedars of Lebanon Hospital in the Bronx, covering up his hairless private parts with a nice diaper and putting one of those bead bracelets on his wrist reading ZISSEL—his mother still probably had it in her dresser drawer—and thinking all the while, no doubt, the nurse, of the young intern who'd done the delivery, did she have a chance with him? how far should she let him go? in certain letters she'd read as a girl on the Woman's Page of the newspaper it always said to watch out for the erogenous zones, no monkey-business from the shoulders down—had the intern read the same paper? Harry imagined he was making noise then, and with a day or so off here and there he'd continued to do so ever since, though few had paid attention and in any case the noise was now about to stop. Definitively.

But in fact, as he closed his eyes, tilted forward, dunked his head, ready to sniff up a lung-full of water, not knowing whether he intended to go through with it but ready to give anything a try, at the very moment when he thought the sound of Zissel might stop forever, a new sound began. Someone was knocking at the bathroom door. "Hey, you asleep in there?" A male voice. At least it wasn't his mother and his Aunt Flora, thank God. He'd just ignore the knocking—the door was bolted, after all; whoever it was could find another bathroom, there were about six of them in the house. But the knocking continued. It made him nervous, he couldn't concentrate on his suicide attempt. "What do you want?" he shouted. "This bath is occupied, for God's sakes. Go away."

"Who is that in there? Is that Harry Zissel? Say, hurry up, will you, I got to take a leak. The odds are eight to five I won't hold out another thirty seconds."

Roger Hulbert, the son of the owner. "Pee in your pants," Harry told him. The knocking ceased. All was quiet. He leaned his head against the tiled wall, trying to recapture his mood. And then Roger knocked again. "Jesus, Harry, what are you doing in here? You going to take all night?"

"I'm going to take the rest of my life, Roger, if you've got to know. There are other bathrooms. Find your own."

"Look, Harry, this here is an emergency."

"Screw you," said Harry. "I'm committing suicide, and you talk about emergencies. Can't a man have a little privacy for once?"

"Just let me use the john for five seconds, okay? then you can commit anything you want, I'm about to have a bursted bladder out here."

"God forbid!" said Harry, beginning, despite himself, to enjoy the situation. He splashed out of the tub, raced across the tiled floor to unbolt the door, and popped back in as Roger entered and proceeded to create a truly monumental effect in the toilet bowl.

"It sounds like you're setting a new intercollegiate record," Harry said.

"I can outpiss anybody on the east coast," said Roger. "Thanks for letting me in. Sorry I bothered you, Harry. How come you're committing suicide? Don't you like the party?"

"Oh, the party's okay," Harry said.

"I see," said Roger. "Well, you'll sure have a nice clean corpse, won't you, taking a bath first. Don't forget to wash behind your ears."

"Right, Roger. I'll do that. Tell everybody out there so long for me, will you?"

"Sure, Harry." Roger turned again at the door. "I hope you're not serious?"

"Of course not. If I was ever serious, would I need to commit suicide?"

"I don't understand."

"That's all right, Roger. There's no need for you to understand. Just get the hell out of here, will you? You're lousing up my mood."

Harry took a washcloth off the shelf behind him and dunked it in the water and squeezed it out over his head, contemplating. He began to soap himself and had finished the left armpit when the crowd arrived. Now that the door was unbolted they banged in without even knocking, Roger in the lead, N. C. Nardiman right behind, then Billy Rupp and the other abstract-expressionists. There were additional people out in the hall.

"Close the door, for God's sakes," Harry shouted. "What is this, a public swimming pool?"

"Roger said you were going to kill yourself," Nardiman announced breathlessly. "I just got here, I thought we'd better—"

"Is Arthur Thompson out there in the hall?" Harry called.

187

No one answered.

"Listen, Harry, what are you doing in the bathtub?"

"Taking a bath, what do you think?"

"Well, Roger said—"

"That was a joke," said Harry. "Who but you, Nardiman, would believe a man would drown himself in soapy water?"

"It's a criminal offense, anyway," said one of the painters, sitting down with his drink in his hand on the cork-topped bench. "Suicide," he added. "It's a criminal offense." The others stood around watching Harry soak his feet.

"This is the biggest audience I've ever had," Harry told them. "How do you like my technique?"

"You use too much soap," said Billy Rupp, "but you're pretty clever getting in there between the toes."

Harry rose in the tub like a geyser and demanded a towel. He was feeling great again. Nothing like a nice quiet bath to improve the mental health. "How you been, Nardiman? I haven't seen you for days." Nardiman was a junior, he lived a floor below Harry on Beachum Street and owned the building's copy of *The Kama Sutra*. "Aah," he said, "don't ask. And as far as suicides are concerned . . . say, tell me, what was your gimmick, a book-length suicide note? Posthumous fame?"

Harry told him, slipping into his underwear shorts, that he'd planned to sniff water up through his nose and drown. "Been done," said Nardiman. "Old hat. Wouldn't have gotten you a half-inch in the papers."

It was pretty crowded in the bathroom, even for one of Johnny's bathrooms. Harry put on his clothes and pushed his way to the door. "I'm okay," he told them. "The suicide party's over, I've been rehabilitated by a calming bath."

He did feel refreshed when he rejoined the company; he wanted to tell Doris all about it, but where was she? He couldn't spot her anywhere and went wandering through the house looking, now and then calling her name.

As it happened, Doris had made a considerable mistake. When Harry slipped away from her after their ping-pong game her feelings had been hurt one time too often. She knew he'd seen her trying to catch up with him, and behind her, moving at the same rate through the crowd, Johnny had been coming along bringing her drink, and she'd turned to Johnny with a smile. So now, as Harry stands on the terrace wondering where she could be, she is in fact in Johnny's den, listening to some Dizzy Gillespie on the elaborate stereo and tape-recorder set up. Johnny had decided he was going to manage a successful heterosexual contact if it killed him. He'd locked the door while she was looking at the books on the shelves and the fossils and erotic sculptures on the library table. He locked the door quietly, made her a fresh drink, and then instead of more music put on a record which Doris found incomprehensible. She'd known hi-fi fanatics before, she'd heard her fill of the sound of jet planes breaking the sound barrier and the Queen Mary tooting before it left harbor and horses' hooves pounding around the outside turn at Hialeah. But this record seemed to consist exclusively of grunts and groans and laughter. Johnny perched on the desk behind the console. He asked her if she knew what she was hearing. "That's love," he said. "I got it on my trip to Algeria last fall. Four sides. They just go on and on, English tourists. Wait till you hear the second couple on this side—they talk all the way through, it's terrific. The Algerians recorded it, like with that hidden camera technique."

She said she thought she wouldn't wait for the couple who talked all the way through. In fact, she told him she wanted to leave before he came up with any new entertainments. And that's when she discovered that the door was locked and that they were in a padded, soundproofed room.

Harry meanwhile is out on the lawn again, listening in at the outskirts of conversations, looking for her, keeping an eye on the kitchen door for the possible appearance of Arthur and Miriam. One of Johnny's kids had come out to mingle with the guests, and Harry absentmindedly patted him on the head. The kid was in pajamas and barefoot; he held what looked like a glass of water, but it might have been straight Vodka, who could tell?

Harry ruffled his hair, distracted, and the kid tried to knee him in the groin. "Thank you," said Harry, holding him off, "that was very considerate." "It's nothing," said the kid, "be my guest." Harry went back into the house. The three girls from the shop, surrounded in the kitchen by seven portly business men each with a bald spot at the very center of the back of his head, turned in unison to see Harry push his way through, and giggled. From somewhere he heard what sounded like a rhythmic series of thumps. No Arthur. No Miriam or Doris. And no Johnny, for that matter. "Hi," said the girl in the angora sweater who had been talking earlier with Roger Hulbert. She was standing in the deserted living room. "I gather they argued you out of committing suicide?" "I was just practicing," Harry said. "What are Roger's latest odds on the foam-rubber or silicone question?" She giggled—"We'll never know, will we?"—and tottered against him, which made him realize that she was dead drunk. When he had her straightened up again he asked her if she were sure she really wanted the rest of her drink. "Hell *no,*" she said and dumped the contents on the rug with a lovely flourish, making him jump back so his pants wouldn't get wet. "Tell me," he said, "are you happy in your work?" The girl gave him a sour look. "It's sure hard as hell to impress anybody around here," she complained. "You've got to be more original," Harry told her, moving off. "Foam rubber, angora sweaters, aluminum-foil skirts, drinks on the rug—it's been done, it's been done!"

No Doris. No Arthur or Miriam. No Johnny.

Doris had taken to thumping on the padded walls as Johnny came after her again like a leering insomniac. "It won't do any good, the room's soundproofed for my hi-fi. Want to hear some hi-fi? There's a speaker in the shower, come on. I just want us to take a shower together. It's one of my mannerisms."

"You're drunk," she said. "I'm strong, I'll hurt you if you don't let me out of here."

"Swell," said Johnny. "Hurt me." Doris thumped on the wall and John Jr. thumped against Miss Muffet on his crib and Harry clumped around the house looking for somebody to talk to, investigating Johnny's collection of beds. Miriam had told him about the one that had the refrigerator built in and about the waterproof one in the shower stall in Johnny's den, but he'd never known about the alarm-clock bed, he tested it out, it rang and then gradually eased up electrically to a standing position so you'd have to get the hell out of there even if you held on by the teeth and nails. He wanted to see the rest of the beds, but some of the bedrooms were occupied, through the doors coming certain familiar squeaking and thumping sounds that stirred his imagination. The whole house seemed to be thumping, one way or another. It really was a perfect setting for a suicide party, he just hadn't had the presence of mind to bring it off.

Out on the lawn the girl with the zither was playing, various conversational groups were grinding cigarettes into the grass, false eyelashes were fluttering, bubbles were breaking at the brim, hearts beating under real and padded breasts. "Have you noticed our host recently?" Kempis asked Betty and Marcia in the powder room. "I bet somebody has volunteered to be a den-mother."

"Or a den-father," said Marcia.

"It makes no difference to John," said Betty, "give or take a few miscellaneous organs."

Harry wandered from room to room, inspecting; in the den Johnny and Doris circled one another with the stance of wrestlers about to come to grips. In his crib John Jr. thumped, and in the kitchen Marjorie prepared chicken sandwiches and coffee for the midnight exodus. People always seemed to leave Johnny's parties in shifts, some two-by-two and others in mass migrations at certain predictable hours. At one o'clock Marjorie would get rid of the bulk of them, and at two she'd go to sleep herself, leaving the serious party-goers, the three A.M. to six A.M. crowd, in her husband's care. Her wifely devotion wasn't one hundred percent absolute—she drew the line at getting a little sleep. But meanwhile, where are Arthur and Miriam? They did in fact return to Beachum Street, they found Harry's note tacked to the door, they actually set out to drive to the party. But now they are parked on a deserted lane off a minor highway partway to Hartford. They are in the back seat together and Arthur is saying in her ear: "We must be out of our minds!" and Miriam is thinking, "Oh God, another talker. You either get raped or lectured." The situation everywhere is complex, one might feel the need for a pause, a time to take stock, a contemplative moment on a lonely beach where the gulls are sailing through the twilight and the waves keep coming sanely in. What will happen in the den? Will Johnny succeed in washing Doris before she's rescued? Will Arthur and Miriam find joy as lovers if Arthur ever stops talking? Will Harry get a chance to tell somebody about his suicide party before he forgets all the details? *It's a question,* as the voice would say. Though not a sound has emerged from behind the locked door of the den, within all is frenzy—Doris is throwing every liftable piece of electronic equipment at Johnny, plus all available books, fossils, statuary, records, while Johnny writhes on the floor, laughing hysterically. Doris is more or less screaming as Harry wanders past the den, tries the door in the silence, finds it locked, moves on. Deserted, he thinks, feeling glum. Abandoned. Nobody to talk to. Typical. Even if he killed himself no one would notice.

Killing yourself—it's been done, said the voice.

And on Monday he'd have to decide what to major in. That is, if he stayed at school. Or stayed alive. He'd have to find a job, and now the Plato vs. Aristotle paper was *five* weeks overdue. But maybe he should make the effort. He could see now there was no future in *not* making efforts, so what was the alternative?

It follows, said the voice. *But how can you give up the suicide idea after just one try? You've got to work at it. Think of the noble Romans, falling on their swords. Think of the disgraced Samurai, the Wall Street bankrupts, the Buddhists soaking themselves in gasoline. And what about all the disappointed literary men, the classic self-immolators, the bridge-leapers, the shotgun addicts, the sleeping-pills chewers? Not to mention the*

*melancholy Viennese and all the common people doing away
with themselves every day of the week? So aren't you ashamed?
How can you hold up your head? Can't you take anything seriously?*

It was at just this point that Doris discovered what it was she
had in her hand about to be thrown at Johnny: a curious square
microphone with buttons at its base. She pressed the green button
marked HOUSE WIDE, and everyone's evening was suddenly
cheered by a blast of electronic sound followed by a 20 decibel
female voice shouting "Harry!"—the name reverberated from
eleven separate speakers in as many rooms—"Come help! He
wants to consort with me in his stall shower!"

TWELVE

Muse: patient friend: dear heart: we are moving toward the
end of our narrative and a certain amount of order must shortly
be restored, we can't just leave everything in a mess, Arthur and
Miriam off God knows where and Johnny with a swollen eye being administered to by Marjorie and Harry's career in such a
shambles that it must have been what Heraclitus had in mind
when he said *all is flux*. At least, thank God, the apartment on
Beachum Street has already been straightened a bit by Doris's
fine domestic hand, and it is toward Beachum Street that Harry
and Doris are being driven via taxicab at this very moment, after
the dramatic rescue from the den. Doris leans her head against
the half-opened cab window, her beautiful hair feathering in the
breeze. Is she still in a state of shock? Her eyes are closed. As they
drive along Harry studies her: a curious smile seems to indicate
that she is running off a sophisticated movie comedy behind her
closed eyelids, a private showing of something starring Cary
Grant and the Mediterranean Sea, an elegant, fluffy thing, strong
on love interest and magnificent scenery. They stop at a red
light; her face is partly in shadow. What was she smiling about?
Work and Women, that was man's lot, and so far both parts,

Harry knew, had been consistently too much for him. What was he doing taking care of Doris, when that was Arthur's job? For that matter, why was Arthur taking care of Miriam? The Organization. Very funny, he thought. Some organization.

He kept his eyes on Doris; her head was thrown back against the seat now, he observed the mild curve of her underlip, the struts of her jaw, the smoothness of her neck changing colors from mercurochrome to amber to moon-white as the traffic signals went through their paces, a flickering of light and shade taking her hair, her cheek, her nosetip as they drove on again. She seemed very still and large on the seat beside him, as if he were riding with a great female statue. Why were women so beautiful? And if they had to be that way, why weren't they organized more like men, so it all wouldn't turn out so damn frustrating? It was true that Doris was beautiful. If she could stay there collapsed on the car seat without opening her eyes or her mouth, he'd be glad to study her as they rode along in a taxicab forever. She looked so absolutely solid, so finished in herself, so smooth and cool. It hadn't been easy to get her out of the den; only when he'd gathered the same squad of commandoes who'd interrupted him in the bath and broadcast back to Johnny on the intercom a demand for unconditional surrender with the threat that the door would otherwise be battered down, had Johnny given up and unlocked the place. It was in no way certain that he could have carried out his threat to batter down the door, discipline would have been hard to maintain in his small assault force, because like the other guests still at the party they all really wanted to leave things as they were and listen to the rest of Doris's broadcast from the shower. But he really shouldn't have slugged Johnny so hard—why had he done that, when the man clearly couldn't help himself? Poor Johnny. A blow to the stomach and another to the eye, just like on the late-late show. Harry's knuckles still felt like cracked walnuts from the unaccustomed experience.

"I think I'm going to be sick," said Doris without opening her eyes or losing her slow smile. Her face looked like the death mask of an Irish queen. "Arthur," she said, "you'd better stop the car so I can open the door."

"I'm Harry," he reminded her, telling the cabbie to stop.

She was still pale and weak as he led her up the dark stairway to the apartment. The place looked strange in its neatened condition—for a moment he thought they were on the wrong floor. No Arthur, much less any Miriam. His note had been untacked from the door. Maybe they were gone for good and he was left with Doris? At least she'd keep the apartment clean, that was something. But in fact Arthur and Miriam were about five miles off, driving rapidly in Arthur's Chevy in a darkness lit only by the dashboard and the glow of their two cigarettes. "I feel just awful," Miriam said. "How do you feel?"

"Like Harry Zissel."

"What kind of a feeling is that?"

"Stomach-turning. I'm sorry," he said after a time. "At least we might have gotten a little . . . pleasure out of it. I just couldn't—"

"It was my fault," Miriam said. That, she knew, was what a woman was expected to say.

They had gone at last to the cabin out by the lake. Without turning on a light they had settled side by side on the bed where she had slept with Harry just a month before, the bed where she had awakened happily on a Sunday morning from a dream of her father to hear Harry's pen scratching in the other room. Arthur shivered, but didn't speak. He made a sound like a sob, he touched her and they had rolled together in a kiss, hips and shoulders pressing, hands beginning their journies . . . and then a raccoon, something, a sound, if there had been no sound would he have had to invent it? Did he need it that badly, the interrupting sound?

"I'll go see." She'd left him there to straighten his clothes, straighten back into his rumpled self. There was nothing at the door. It was nothing, but they didn't return to bed. Sitting on the floor before a fire of kindling he had made, they talked. Arthur seemed suddenly cheerful, relieved. They would write a play, he said, a play with no dialogue at all, a play about a man and a woman who came out to this cabin and gradually brought all their home furniture in.

"And that would be the end," Miriam said. "They'd just bring the last things in, like a grand piano or something, and stand there looking pleased."

"It would be called 'The Vacation,'" said Arthur, smiling ruefully. At least he could still laugh at himself, he was thankful for that. He remembered with distaste all the preaching he'd done that day, that evening—how he'd somehow gotten started with Miriam on the subject of marriage, speaking of the firm center, of the release to move humanly outward from a tended, central fire—and all the while his heart, crude hammer, had been beating at his lips to let out his desire, his desire for Miriam. All evening he'd given her advice. He was her new friend, her teacher, her father: a trembling moralist whistling as he passed through the graveyard of his flesh. Oh, he could have wisdomed the whole world into a cheerful orthodoxy if it weren't that his body kept laughing back, his sex standing up in the middle of the sermon to tell him to go to hell.

"You know what I am?" he said to Miriam before the fire, watching her affectionately as she gazed at the small flames. "I'm the philosopher whose pants keep falling down."

"Why did you stop?" she asked casually. "Lost the impulse?"

He brushed her hair back from her smooth brow, still desiring her.

"We're too different," he said, "and we're stuck with ourselves, aren't we? It takes a lifetime to change what you started out with."

He knew that if they had come together, either they wouldn't have risked true feeling and it would have been lousy, an elaborate masturbation, shaming . . . or else it would have been deep, good, and then? Then what? Simply leave her? Or leave Doris? It was unthinkable.

197

In the car, exhausted finally, she told him she was glad they'd stopped. She rested her head against his shoulder as they drove toward town.

"I'm such a mess," she said. "I'm so tired of myself."

Arthur drove at full speed, conscious of Doris waiting for him somewhere. Or not waiting for him. He had never felt so old in his life. The girl by his side, she might have been a member of another species. She was a child. He felt for her, but she had nothing to do with his life, his problems, nothing at all. *It isn't that easy,* Doris had said.

"It all happened because you reminded me of my father," Miriam told him yawningly. "Because you're . . . older, maybe I just need somebody older."

A silence fell between them.

"Maybe I'd better see an analyst."

"All you need is a strong man to love you." She still leaned against him, half asleep.

"Strong?"

"Very strong. One who doesn't hear noises in the night. And also just a little bit crazy."

"Where do you find them?"

"God knows," said Arthur. "I'm not sure they're producing that model anymore in your generation."

"It wouldn't make any sense for me to go back to Harry, would it?"

"Not unless you're in love with him."

"I'm not in love with anybody," she said. "Not even with myself."

"Poor Miriam."

But his mind was now focused exclusively on Doris. He imagined her sitting sternly in Harry's apartment, a shotgun across her lap, waiting for him.

Harry settled Doris full-length on the couch, and flicked on the table lamp. On the Wildroot Calendar above the plush chair the shadow-drawings of a troop of women came to light behind the profiles of Roman Nights, Commuter, Young Master. Harry checked the date, April 16th. Just three days ago he was a different man, reading to Miriam out of *The Kama Sutra* when his Aunt and Mother had knocked on the door. Doris shook her head. She rubbed her eyes with the heels of her hands. "Harry," she said. "I had too much to drink." He nodded, collapsed across from her in the chair. "Where's Arthur?" she asked. *He* couldn't tell her. "I've got to brush my teeth," she said, and walked unsteadily out of the room. "Nobody ever tried to rape me before." As she entered the hallway she kicked off her shoes, and when she came back she stretched out again on the couch. She told him she was feeling much better. "Why don't you read me some more of your play?" He'd read her one sequence that afternoon. "Or your novel—I forget which it is?" He told her they were all the same. "I guess you can stand anything now, eh? You've thrown up already." "No, I want to hear. Boy, am I thirsty!" He brought her a glass of water, and when she'd drained it, her head straining up, she fell back and giggled, said "More." He brought her another and she drank it down. "Are you sure this is water? It's making me dizzy all over again."

"That damn Johnny," said Harry, nursing his knuckles, waiting for Doris to give back the glass. "He's nothing but a maniac, he'll wind up in the electric chair."

"I thought that was only if they transported you across state lines? I don't blame him, Harry, he's just not my type, I tried to tell him that, but he was full of drink."

"He was full of libido," said Harry. "Unreconstructed Id. Some people in this world try to create a little decency around them, try to lead a mature—"

"Yes," said Doris, "you do have to admire him, don't you? At least he tries to get what he's after." She closed her eyes again, then popped them. "Wow," she said, "water and vodka just don't mix. I'm going around and around—"

"I'm going to put you to bed."

"Are you really? Around and around," she sang, "it's been a strange day. Arthur? I'm leaving you on the two o'clock bus. I think I'm pregnant, sweetheart, we'll have to get divorced."

"This is Harry," he told her. "You'd better get some sleep."

"Carry me," she said. "Please?"

All is silent in Arthur's car, parked in the lot beside the University Arms Hotel. Miriam sighs. "I guess I'd better go in. Why are we sitting here in the dark?"

"I don't know," said Arthur. "It's been a strange evening. I feel very clearheaded, but in a way I'm sort of afraid to go back to Harry's."

"Then don't."

"You mean stay with you?"

"If you want to. Back at the cabin."

"No," he said. And then: "Thank you, Miriam."

"Just a thought," she said. "Don't mention it."

He hardly seemed to hear her. "I guess I'm just the type who goes back and faces things. If Doris doesn't kill me, Harry will."

"You sound like you're looking forward to it," Miriam said, and grinned. She opened the car door. "You know something? They never even noticed you were gone."

"What will *you* do now, Miriam?"

"Me?" She cocked her head toward her shoulder like a bird. "Sleep for about sixteen hours. Then I'm going to sit down and think. I'm going to think of every conceivable thing I might do with myself and then I'm going to pick out one and do that one, and then when it's finished I'll do the next. My ambition at the moment is to keep switching until I hit on some version of me that doesn't make me ill. I'm sorry, Arthur. You're all stirred up. You've been . . . very nice. Very sweet and all. The important thing is the sixteen hours sleep, so I'll be strong enough to fight off the rapists in the morning."

"Or to encourage them."

"Either way. You know, there's one thing about making it all up as you go along: you get a certain basic suspense about where your next breath is coming from. I guess I'd better wake up that nightclerk." She reached for Arthur's hand. "It was nice meeting you," she said.

"Wait," he told her, getting out of the car, "I'll come make sure you get in all right."

"This is the University Arms Hotel, Arthur. The one way to make absolutely certain I *don't* get a room is for you to walk in there with me at four o'clock in the morning. It's an old New England establishment, they haven't recognized the sexual revolution yet."

The two of them stood facing one another in the semi-blackness of the parking lot. Across the wide street, beyond the monumental entryway to the campus, a lamppost was glowing distantly through the young leaves of the maples. Arthur is still in a dazed state, but for some reason he is deeply happy. Through most of the evening he'd worn an astounded expression, as if the normal, sober set of his features had somehow gotten lost in all the confusion. He and Miriam had told one another the stories of their lives. They had almost made love. They had talked for hours, driven a total of fifty-three miles, smoked between them thirty-six cigarettes. And now, dreamily, as if they'd been briefly introduced at a college tea, she said it was nice meeting him.

He put a hand on her shoulder as she stood before him in the dimness. He thought he might understand the girls at Cordelia College just a bit better now. And he knew one thing about himself as well, that if he were really going to get more excitement into his life he'd have to start from the ground up. But maybe it would be worth the trouble afterall. He wanted to say something to Miriam, to really thank her. But nothing come out. "Miriam," he said at last, "it's been . . . nice meeting you."

Their laughter rang into the dimness of early morning.

And Doris meanwhile leans against Harry as he leads her to the bedroom. In the hall she slips halfway to the floor, saying "ooops" very softly, and he is holding her up under the arms. "Come on, Doris, quit it. What am I going to do with you?" She falls asleep the moment she hits the bed. Her yellow print dress has climbed high up her thighs. He reaches for the hem to pull it down, but changes his mind and covers her instead with a thin white blanket from the shelf above the closet in the main room. He shuts off the bedroom light and tiptoes out, breathing a sigh of relief and frustration. Then she calls to him "I can't."

"Can't what?"

"Sleep with my dress on." Pathetically: "It'll get—all mussed."

"But you slept in your dress last night, Doris."

"Who said?"

"Arthur."

"He did? He was afraid there'd be a fire. He's afraid of me. Of everything. Come help."

"Take off your dress? Can't *you* take it off?"

"I tried. When I raise my head everything starts being circles again. Don't be mean."

He helped her off with the dress. "Thank you," she breathed, flopping back on the bed like a rag doll. Her bra held up her breasts like sacrificial offerings. "Stockings," she whispered. "My last pair."

"Oh no. Oh no, Doris, there are limits. There are limits on what a man's expected—"

"Stockings," she said. "Come on, Arthur."

Was she really all that drunk? He felt suspicion stir. "I'm Harry," he told her, "can't you remember? Take off your own damn stockings!"

"Stockings," she said, with the death-mask on her face again. Was she going to be sick? He screwed his eyes shut and reached in under her crinoline slip to unlock the damn things.

"I love you," Doris said, "you're so—you're so good. Come be inside me. Come."

"I'm Harry," he said. *"Harry,* not Arthur."

"Are you? You sound like Arthur. *You* two should be married." And she was fast asleep. Or so it appeared. He tiptoed out and collapsed on the couch. From somewhere in the apartment he seemed to hear a persistent, tiny rhythmic thump. The radiators. They were sending the heat up again. He switched on the rotating fan.

It was just too much. Altogether. He didn't even have the persistence or character or the intelligence or whatever to commit suicide. What could he do, spend his life in a bathroom, with meals sent in?

Maybe he'd better really sign up at the monastery in the morning. But how would they feel at the monastery about an atheist monk? Well, that was their problem, let them try to get him out, he'd just settle in there in one of those cells and start illuminating manuscripts right and left and if they tried to give him the boot he'd fight like a saber-toothed tiger.

Was Arthur somewhere with Miriam? The hell with it, let him see if he was up to her. He knew why Miriam was so changeable, why she dabbled at so many things, why she pretended to be overdue or took up the banjo or read fifty books at once: it was simply a matter of trying to make confusion take over for a failure of the will. She was an avoider at heart, just like him. She could only get things cooking by arbitrarily stirring the pot. She was just an avoider, the touch-no-evil monkey. One monkey or another, it came to the same thing. Avoiders, that's what they all were. Avoiders.

Doris included? said his voice. *Is Doris an avoider?*

And as if in answer, Doris entered the room smiling like a sleepwalker, barefoot, in her bra and crinoline slip. She settled down on the floor by the couch. His eyes fell into the sweet valley of her cupped breasts "For heaven's sake, Doris, put something on, will you?" He jumped up and fetched his terrycloth robe and tossed it at her. "Have some respect for the monks, can't you?"

Maybe she *was* asleep. Her eyes were open, but that didn't prove anything. The terrycloth robe lay in her lap. She looked up at Harry sadly. "You forgot to read me your play." Why was she staring at him with that strange smile?

"Read," she said.

"There isn't anything to read, Doris. Don't you want to put on some pajamas or something? Or get dressed if you're not going to sleep? What will Arthur think?"

"Arthur?"

"Look, it's awfully late, Doris. Isn't it time for you to be in bed?"

"Are you proposing?" She spoke a line he'd read her earlier from the beginning of his poor, mangled play. " 'If everybody's *dead* down here in hell, how come they talk so much?' "

"It's late, Doris. If you're not tired, I am. I've got to get up in the morning and do my Plato-and-Aristotle paper."

"Why?"

"Because I've decided, that's why. I don't have the brains or the character or whatever it is to do anything else, so I might as well get a college degree like all the rest."

"Arthur's left me."

"You think so? It is getting kind of late. Look out the window, it's almost morning, I'm starting to get a little worried about him myself, the irresponsible son-of-a-bitch."

"Maybe I'll put your robe on after all. You're not being very friendly." She rose with a scowl, put on the robe, and huddling into herself sat on the couch at his feet.

"Now you hate me too," he said, sitting up.

"Oh Harry, who could hate you?" He saw an exactly balanced mixture of tenderness and contempt in her face.

"You know something?" he said, as if quoting a memorized speech, "I bet I'm about to become respectable and trustworthy and so on. I wonder if I'm going to be able to live with myself if I get like that?"

"Poor Harry," she said. "Poor misshapen thing."

"What do you mean?"

For answer she went to the bedroom and returned with the half dozen manuscript pages of Harry's play. She found what she was looking for and read to him:

"VIRGIL: See those crippled fellows pushing boulders at each other over there? Why do you suppose they want to do that?

DANTE: (tugging at his laurel wreath) God knows. Nothing would surprise me in this crazy place. But how come all those big boulders don't make a lot of noise so normally I wouldn't be able to hear a word you're saying, or vice versa?

VIRGIL: They make the boulders out of cardboard, to cut down on production costs."

"I'm not sure I see what you mean," Harry said.

"You don't even believe in the boulders. Even hell is a fake."

"Where they worry about production costs."

"And whether their material is original."

"Been done, been done."

Pause.

"Is it my fault?" he said. "That nothing's real? Am I just supposed to pretend that everything's great, that I'm taking it seriously, that it's all *there,* for God's sake? I can't even commit suicide. I can't just *decide*—"

"Sure you can. You *can* just decide, that's all. What else can you do? So just *decide*."

"What?"

"To be alive," said Doris, "that would do for a starter. Just to be alive."

"You seem awfully sober all of a sudden, Doris."

"Do I? Then I'd better have another glass of that water."

He came closer to her. She must have put on some perfume at some point—the scent made him heady. "Doris," he said, reaching for her. And tripped over the bust of Leopardi on the floor, stumbled into the construction, which swayed, creaking, the face of Strindberg looming horrified above him, the automobile fender bounding loose, the whole thing lurching crazily, hanging together like a rearing wave, tumbling piece after piece like a

205

raining junkyard, the skull with the black buttons and the zipper bouncing off his shoulder, the automobile valves scattering like flak, the print of Strindberg smacking face down on the floor like a closed lid. When the clatter stopped he realized that someone was knocking at the door. "Oh God," he said, "they've come back!"

"Who?"

"My mother! My Aunt Flora!"

Doris dashed for the closet in the terrycloth robe, the knocking continued, Harry shrugged, picked up the alarm clock, and pitched it full tilt at the door, which stopped the knocking. To be alive, he thought. What he should do was join her in the closet, lay her richly and properly, standing up among the stored winter coats, and let the Muse and the critics and bloody Dickens and Kafka knock till their fists were raw, and his voice said *Amen, amen.* The knocking came again. Arthur's voice: "What's going on in there? I'm back. Can I come in?" Harry knocked furiously at the door from the inside. "Nobody's home," he shouted. "Nobody's home!" And then he opened up. The door wasn't even locked. "Make love to your wife, will you, for *God's* sake?" he spat at Arthur, shoving him into the place, slamming the door behind him. But Arthur was out again with Doris beside him, they were both calling down the stairs. Harry could hear doors opening on the other floors. A woman in hair curlers appeared on the landing below, waving a tack hammer. "I call poleeze! I call poleeze!" Harry snatched the hammer from her, gripped it in his teeth like a dog, and continued slowly down. "Harry," Arthur called, "where are you going?"

Harry's voice floated eerily back up the stairwell. *"Make love to your wife."*

And the front door closed.

To be alive. Maybe there was something to it, after all. Maybe it was worth a try, he thought, wandering the campus contemplatively as the sky lightens and the first cheeping of birdsound is heard. In Cordelia, New Jersey, waves lap the inlet. In China in the dark of night a new Chinese is being born every several seconds. On the small quad where a light is burning, a typewriter makes its way across the white parade ground of a freshman theme. And Harry passes through, swings along the campus paths whacking the trees with his tack hammer. Suddenly he realizes that he's feeling great, simply great, as if he could press down hard and fly. To be alive, he repeats to himself. It's a good place to start. To be alive.

He stops and pees against the rear tire of an Oldsmobile parked in the lot below the art center. He tosses the tack hammer over his shoulder. He's already decided that he'll surprise Arthur and Doris with lox and cream cheese for breakfast, but not for a while, he'll leave them in peace for a good long while. A frightened squirrel darts out of his path and he thinks: maybe I should major in animal husbandry? He asks the voice what it has to say about that, but the voice is nowhere to be found. Harry touches every second rung of the wrought-iron fence around the Administration Building, walking sidewise like someone playing an endless zither. "You just wait," he shouts up at the mindless administrative windows, emblazoned by the first light. "Wait till the *junior* year! Wait till I get on that radio station again, by God!"

And what *will* come of him, after the euphoria wears off, when the darkness settles again? At least, he thinks, it's a question in which I seem to have a certain interest.

One thing for sure: he'd finish that goddamned play for his creative writing course. And the short stories. And the poems and constructions. And if he ever saw Miriam again he was going to learn to ride her unicycle. And he was going to practice, practice, and beat *hell* out of Doris Thompson the next time they played ping-pong.

We will leave him now, sitting on a campus bench listening to the birds. He takes out his notebook, and beyond the wheelchair prices, under *telephone girls* and *United Fruits* and *love is cheap*, he writes in a looping hand, "To be alive."

And in San Mateo, California, a tugboat sounds its hooter.